WORD *of* MOUTH

WORD *of* MOUTH

150 Short-Short Stories
by 90 Women Writers

Edited by
Irene Zahava

The Crossing Press
Freedom, California 95109

Grateful acknowledgement is made to the following authors for permission to reprint previously published material:

Ginger Bingham — *Home* originally appeared in *Sonora Review*.
Jane Coleman — *Sketching the Island* originally appeared in *SPLASH: The Magazine of Art and Fashion*, July 1988.
Maxine Combs — *Esperanto* originally appeared in *Oread*, Summer 1987.
Sue Gambill — *In Motion* originally appeared in *Common Lives/Lesbian Lives #30*, Spring 1989.
Ellen Gruber Garvey — *Collected Speeches* originally appeared in *Sojourner*, October 1984. *Compound Fracture* originally appeared in *Conditions Four*, 1979.
Lisa Harris — *Sandra* originally appeared on the cassette "U.S. Choice Bloodtongue," produced by Slipstream Audio Cassettes (as part of a longer work entitled *Poems for Retired Cheerleaders*).
Rhona Klein — *Leap of Faith* originally appeared in *Berkeley Fiction Review*, I, no. 1.
Marilyn Krysl — *Jacks* originally appeared in *IKON*, #8, 1988. *Soaring* originally appeared in *High Plains Literary Review*, Volume III, #3, 1988/ 89.
Lesléa Newman — *My Father's Lap* originally appeared in her book *Love Me Like You Mean It*, published by HerBooks.
Linda Peavy — *A Common Language* originally appeared in *Bristlecone*, Winter 1989. *The Kill Floor* originally appeared in *Athena*, July 1989.
Lore Segal —*Lucinella Apologizes to the World for Using It* originally appeared in *Lucinella*, published by Farrar, Straus and Giroux.
Ruth Knafo Setton — *Embroidered Hands* originally appeared in *Response: A Contemporary Jewish Review*.
Amber Coverdale Sumrall — *Siesta* originally appeared in *Touching Fire: Erotic Writings by Women*, published by Carroll and Graf.

Cover design by Pacific Digital Company
Book design and production by Martha Waters

Printed in the U.S.A.

Library of Congress Cataloging-in-Publication Data

Word of mouth : short-short writings by women / edited by Irene
Zahava.
    p.   cm.
  ISBN 0-89594-396-4 — ISBN 0-89594-395-6 (pbk.)
  1. Short stories, American—Women authors. 2. Women—Fiction.
I. Zahava, Irene.
PS647.W6W67 1990
813'.01089287—dc20
                                     89-77902
                                       CIP

Contents

Preface

A great many adjectives are being used in front of the word "fiction" these days: short-short, sudden, quick, micro, mini, postcard, urgent, instant. . . . Any one of those words accurately describes the contents of this unique anthology of stories by ninety contemporary American women writers.

These are the kinds of stories you tell your friends over a quick cup of coffee, because you don't have time to linger over lunch. They're the snippets of conversation you overhear when you're waiting for the bus, and you hope the storyteller gets on your bus so you can hear the end of her tale. They're the calls you make from a phone booth, talking fast because you don't have any more change in your pockets — or the letters you write when you're far from home and have a lot to say, but only a postcard to say it on.

There is an energy and immediacy to these pieces that demands attention — secrets to be shared, memories to be uncovered and obsessions to be revealed. The contributors to this collection offer glimpses into the mundane as well as the marvelous. These women are talking in their mother-tongue and the language is called word-of-mouth.

Irene Zahava
January, 1990

Koré Archer

The Curse

Earth, wakening, releases the scent of lilac and manure toward the thin sun. Boot tracks disappearing in barnyard mud, the stablehand strides through bright, vaporous morning into yawning dark, aroma of linseed oil, horses and haydust. The gray, due any day now, blows and weaves as the apprentice heads for the empty stall at the far corner, disappears in shadow. Slips out of suspenders, steps out of britches, smells blood, touches, sees. It's coming from her girl place, the birthing place.

So this is it, The Curse. Well, it's not going to stop her now! It can't!

Stamping and rolling their eyes, the horses witness her resolution. Tonight she will rinse out the stained crotch, rip her winter blanket into strips. For now she reaches for the tack towel, blots red from her britches, takes a woolen stable bandage, folds it in three, wedges it between her legs, steps back into the damp trousers, hitches up suspenders, adjusts her hose, rinses the bloody towel in the waterbucket, wrings it, hangs it flat, stands, sighs, alone with this new complication.

"Charley! Breakfast ready!"

"Yes, Ma'am! Coming!" On the way out she snatches another bandage, tucks it into her pocket.

This summer when Ebenezer Balch's likeable young apprentice chooses to keep his shirt on no matter how oppressive the heat, no one makes a joke of it. She's that clever.

In Solitude She Appears

During the early twilight before supper, behind a canvas partition, calico curtains drawn for warmth and privacy, the stagedriver would step out of that well-worn costume: the wide-brimmed hat, the embroidered gauntlet gloves, the double-breasted coat, mildewed boots, pleated shirt, denim trousers and good pants underneath. The stiff mass of garments heaped on the pine floor would give off a rank essence of tobacco juice, 40-rod whiskey, horses, road dust and the days and maybe weeks of sweltering inside the rough, bulky layers of immunity.

In the moment before stepping into the zinc washtub she would stand: herself, naked, inviolate. Against her weathered face, forehead showing the diagonal slash-white where the eyepatch usually sits; against the leathery survivor's hands, fingernails broken and grimy; against this her pale, disarmored female body.

She'd lower herself gingerly into the steaming tub, wincing at the heat, feeling the river-grit through the towel under her. She would slouch deep into the soothing water before leaning for the bar of lye soap and beginning to scrub.

During such intermissions these features of her womanhood — her middle-aged breasts, her woman's belly, the unmistakable curve of her thighs, the tangle of dark hair and the seashell curves within — would appear, reassert themselves.

Sally Bellerose

MEME

Meme said that each person gets allotted so many foolish words at birth and after they're all used up the person dies. Meme lived next door, alone, in the house where she raised five sons and one daughter. Mama let me spend most of my time in Meme's old house. Mama had a new baby and my older brother and sister to take care of at home.

Meme married at sixteen and lived with Pepe until he passed away, sixty years later. When Pepe died I was very young, four or five. I remember him yelling my Grandmother's name. "Cora I'm cold" and Meme would cover him with the muslin quilt she was forever mending. He was bedridden at the end.

Meme tried to warn him, "You'll kill yourself with all that racket."

He persisted, focusing every want and need in her name.

"Cora!" We could hear him yell as we jumped rope in the next yard.

I sang and danced at his funeral. Meme clapped her hands, to break up sorrow. We sang,

> Jimmy Crackcorn and I don't care
> Jimmy Crackcorn and I don't care
> Jimmy Crackcorn and I don't care
> My master's gone away.

Then, long hours of silence. Meme all to myself.

If I spoke too much, "Ferme la bouche," she would say gently. Shut your mouth, from Meme it was a soothing remark.

After saying it she would always kiss my mouth. She would rock, humming prayers on her rosary beads. I rarely spoke. I sang. In Meme's house you could sing anything, anything sad, or funny, or foolish, as long as you didn't sing too loud. My favorites were her French songs. Memorized phrases, syllables strung together with no need for specific meaning. I sang. Meme rocked.

Some nights I slept with Meme in her big feather bed. The bed Pepe lived in. The bed he died in. Every morning Meme would sweep up a dustpan full of feathers. I took care not to bounce too hard on Meme's bed.

On weekends we played Nurse. She gave me a box of bandaids, all my own. I cried when they were all used up. Then Meme cut the *Daily News* into little rectangles and stuffed them into the empty tin bandaid box. She tore up an old slip for more serious injuries. Meme was a good patient. She would lie still, to be nursed with tap water potion from an old Coke bottle. Once Mama walked in while Meme was dying. Mama called me an unnatural child. Meme laughed. She knew I would always revive her.

Meme's eyesight was starting to go. She burned things, food, and her hands. Mama let me eat supper with her, almost every night, just Meme and me. After supper Mama would ask, "What did you eat?" Meme would smile and I would make something up. Something with a vegetable in it. Really we ate English muffins.

Meme would say "I want blueberry pie tonight" and I would spread the thick blue jam on the muffins. She would say "Shall we have tortiere. I feel like a holiday" and I would fry two hamburgers to stack between the muffins.

One night Meme didn't want supper. She hadn't hummed "Alouette" for days.

"Come. Rock," she said. I was as tall as Meme by then. She was much wider. I didn't see how I could sit on her without sliding off, so I sat on the floor and put my head in her lap.

"I'm ready to die," she said.

"I know, Meme." I did know. I had been trying not to get too big. I knew Meme would be gone before I got old.

"It's not so bad," she said. "My good little Indian, soon you'll sing and dance for me. You don't have to cry when the others do."

She left me then and began talking to all her dead relatives, foolish talk, to her husband, sisters, friends, her Mama and Papa, her own Meme. On and on, sing song, rocking, she used up all her words.

Ginger Bingham

WHEN THE ANALYST SAYS "FATHER" AND THE PATIENT REPLIES, "WAX"

It was too dark to play "Solo" and too quiet for "Happy Families." You would have thought we had the big house to ourselves. Of course, we knew different, Cal, Louise and I. We also knew that it was not exactly a game we wanted to play. More like an imitation of the hypnotist we had seen at a friend's birthday party. "Arise, awake, choose a partner and dance," he would command his motionless, silent subject. How we laughed when each thing came to pass. We needed a candle. (It was felt, strongly felt, by all of us that we needed a candle.) I suppose we could have asked Dutchie, but she was busy with the extra company and what was then called a cold buffet. Mama was of no use whatsoever. You have to understand that in those days no room used for such a purpose would have been locked. People came and went at all hours, paying their respects. You have to see that we knew about Papa. And that we had cried for a while. And then stopped crying. We knew that there were lots of candles there. Long, elegant tapers that had not been used since Louise's christening. Some hastily hired workmen had built the wooden trestle, laid on the greenery and set up the silver candelabra. I remember they smoked black cigars and sang strange, gutteral songs. It seems obvious that they also must have placed the candelabra far too close to the coffin itself. Even today I believe I can clearly, truthfully recall that it was not only my accidental jostling of the candles which caused the hot wax to fall. Or drip, I suppose one ought to say, onto my hand first and then Papa's. We all three of us let out a great shriek. Then Louise began to say very softly but very clearly (because I now held the candle, you see), "Arise, awake . . ." And we began to laugh. We went on laughing. We laughed until it hurt.

HOME

One father stepped out on his porch to whistle his children home. His whistle consisted of short bursts of sound with pauses in between. It reminded another father two houses away to come out to the edge of his lawn and begin whistling also. This second kind of whistling was long and sustained. Though he could not have kept one whistle going indefinitely, each separate whistle did trail off faintly rather than stop distinctly before the next began. Passersby remarked, "Those two are whistling to beat the band." Had the fathers heard it, they would have questioned the competitive sentiment. The fathers were very literal minded, and they whistled for one purpose only. Along the block several other fathers appeared. Whistles with particular patterns could now be heard. One long blast, for instance, followed by two shorter ones. A woman just opening her door wondered if any of the fathers owned one of those plastic dime store whistles which have a shrill but carrying sound or if any father had a silver whistle like the kind used to start races or referee games. This was nonsense because none of the fathers ever used an artificial whistling apparatus. Every father on the street was whistling now. No one could say it was one great whistle. The timing was not consistent, and the tones and styles were too varied. But the sound was loud. It had been going on for some time. A man who was trying to sleep, a man who had no children, cried out, "You're whistling to wake the dead!" All the fathers heard this. They were determined men, but practical, too. Each thought over the proposition, and each considered the odds.

Lucy Jane Bledsoe

ALIVE

Three weeks ago I slept with this medical student dude in exchange for an option on death, a small white pill which he promised would kill me within two hours. There would be vomiting, he said, a lot of abdominal pain. Dying is never easy, he said.

Life became a lot easier, though, knowing that I *could* die if I wanted. I measured everything up against that white pill: there's *this,* my life, or there's *that,* my death. A real choice for once. Just carrying that pill in my back pocket was like being on drugs. Everything shimmered and pulsated in its light. The halls at school throbbed with living flesh, rain fell on my face wet and crisp as chilled tears, my own skin felt as furry and meaty as a ripe peach. That pill was the blaring music that directed my life, an entire jazz band be-bopping in my back pocket. The world became so sweet it was painful. Eventually, it became more than I could bear. I felt like an alcoholic who quit drinking and the world became sharp-edged, clear and so focussed it was like maneuvering through a zillion slicing knives.

I cut school with my best friend Josh, and we went to the ocean because I needed something very big, something that could contain me. We sat in a small cove, the waves washing up and then receding, and I imagined the primordial sea, where all life began, slosh up into my heart, filling me, and then slide back, taking my insides away with it. I thought about molecules of me mixing with the algae, sea anemones, octopuses, and whales. Me, a sea thing, a primordial blob of amino acids. Josh smoked cigarettes.

At dusk we gathered driftwood and ripped up one of my shirts to use as kindling. We got a good blaze going and leaned against a log to watch it. A wind came up, forcing the flames to dance. Finally, darkness swept away everything extraneous. It was me, Josh, and the fire, alone in the world. The first creatures, or maybe the last. Prehuman primates or maybe posthuman survivors. Alone, was the important part. The fire. Josh. Me.

Then I told Josh about my pill. We'd talked about this before, wishing for a way out, because his life was about as screwed up as mine. But Josh said the pill was a fake and that I had never been that big a fool before. When I offered him half, though, he sobered right up. Josh reminded me of a cherub just then. Blond curls, blue eyes, no trace of a beard yet and a lot of baby fat on his hands and face. I bit the pill with my teeth and swallowed half. Josh ate the other half and lay down in the sand. I watched the firelight haunt his face for a few minutes. Soon, I slipped into what I thought was going to be a sweet, deep death.

Imagine my surprise when early the next morning a single ray of sunshine stung my behind, like a laser zapping me to life. Josh had been right after all. The pill was a fake. Funny, but the first thing I thought about was how the sun powered all life on earth. I sunk into Josh, burying my nose in his curls, his denim jacket dew-wet, as if he were soil, the only place on earth to sink my roots. Josh twitched and opened his eyes, wide and blue as the sea. The ray of sun splintered into billions of rays, shouting down on us. We're alive, I whispered to Josh. I'm a green shoot, and you're my earth.

Maureen Brady

SISTER, SISTER

"Get your little sister and get on out to the car. I'll take you both to the mall," Mom says in a gruff whisper.

"Okay, I'm ready," I say, leaning in to tell Holly in the next breath, "Come on, girl, in a hurry, Mom's taking us shopping."

Holly's hugging the mirror with her puss but she breaks back from it a little. "Be right with ya," she says, almost a whisper.

I sit on the day bed we use for a couch and bite my lip, waiting. Pop's right there behind a thin wall, sleeping it off. "Come on Holly, make tracks," I plead under my breath. The sun's coming in the window nice and I try to stretch my legs out in it but when I put my feet flat, my legs get jumpy. Nothing unusual, it happens all the time. Most often I wrap my legs up almost in a knot to keep them still.

I can't stand it anymore so I go back to prod Holly. "C'mon. We're gonna get outa here and have us a good time." It's the day after Thanksgiving. Mom usually works nights and has to sleep days but she caught up sleep because of the holiday. Holly's still at the mirror, dolling herself up with mascara. Her blond hair's combed to cover up one side of her face entirely. She's fourteen. I'm fifteen. She's thin and bony and looks kind of weak, but in a fight she springs up energy from somewhere you can't imagine and she can hold me down and wear the strength right out of me. I'm her same height but heavier. My hair's blond too but I put a red streak the color of raspberry sherbet right down the center of it. My father nearly croaked. He made me pay for it but he couldn't take it away.

I take Holly by the hand and tug her out of our room. Mom comes out of the kitchen and huddles us through the door like ducklings.

In the car, a '72 Chevy, rusting through the floorboards, I'm in the middle. Mom cranks several times to get her started. Maybe that woke him or maybe it was just because he felt us moving out the door the way a baby feels a pacifier go out of its mouth. We have to loop around in front of the trailer to get out to the road, and he's standing there in the doorway in a T-shirt and boxers and socks. Stubby. His belly wider than his hips and all propped on short legs. And up goes his hand to make us halt.

Mom brakes and we all three lurch forward in the seat like rubber dummies.

"Where you think you're going, Ma?" he calls.

"Going shopping. Won't be long." She tries to make it sound like nothing special.

I'm praying: Dear God, don't let him stop us.

But he says it anyway. "What you need both them girls for? Leave me one."

I'm praying again: Dear God, don't let it be me.

"I'll bring em both back soon enough," Mom says, "right soon."

"Naw, you don't *need* both them girls to do shopping. You leave me one now." He looks over the top of the car out to the field like as if we're nothing to him. He sucks his cheek in on one side of his face and makes an ugly sound. He's waiting for her to decide who to leave him and she doesn't say anything so he makes up his own mind. "You leave me Holly."

My gut turns. I look at her but I can't see much because it's the side covered by her hair I'm facing. I can't say nothing because there's nothing to say.

"You better go on, Holly," Mom says.

He stomps his foot to remind us he's waiting.

"Go on in," Mom says, and Holly, slow motion, gets out of the car.

When I look up, she's standing in the doorway, a blank look in that one eye that can be seen. He's behind her. She lifts her hand a little to wave. I look the other way. Oh, God, I think. I wish it had been me. I know what he'll do to her. It woulda been me if I'd a been left.

We're pulling out. Mom's shaking her head the way she does sometimes even when you don't know what's bothering her, like standing at the sink washing dishes. It looks like she'd got a twitch in her neck. Her head goes tick, tick, tick. I want to scream at her: *"Stop it."*

"Stop scowling," she tells me. "Your sister shoulda been a little swifter."

I wish it were me, I think again, breathing relief that it isn't.

Anne Cameron

JOAN OF ARC

How much of what we know or think we know is true? We all know Joan of Arc was burned to death: in those days the victim was brought from the cell and paraded to the stake, then tied in place, pleading or cursing, praying or trembling, depending on individual personality, then the fire was lit and the assembled citizens watched as the victim writhed and screeched, face contorted by unimaginable agony.

SHE was brought from the cell heavily veiled, supported on each side, her feet dragging. The Maid of Orleans? She who led an army? Unable to walk from her cell? She who cropped her hair and showed her face proudly went to her death heavily veiled?

SHE was tied to the stake, sagging against her bonds, unable to stand, and died without a sound. The one too terrified to show her face, too terrified to walk, died without screaming, or begging, or praying?

What if a dying prostitute was given painkilling drugs then veiled and taken, unconscious, in HER place? What if she burned without screaming after she was already mercifully dead of a drug overdose?

What if Joan, dressed in the clothes of a jailer, went out the back way and escaped? What if SHE took with her the infant daughter of the starveling whore who had expired of childbirth fever plus the painkilling effects of opium?

What if SHE took the child to Pouligny to raise as her own? Pouligny where Robert des Armors was under investigation or suspicion of being homosexual, a charge which brought, on conviction, a sentence of death by burning.

What if Joan, the woman who loved women, married Robert, the man who loved men?

What if the Church, on discovering Robert was the father of an infant daughter, cancelled the Inquisition and turned its attention to more important things, like quelling the rumor that JOAN of ARC was still alive?

What if the dyke and the faggot then dedicated their lives to finding children doomed to starvation and took them from the prisons and the festering alleys, from the hovels, the orphanages, the sewers, from filth and disease to Pouligny?

And fed them eggs and milk, cheese and meat, bread and fruit. What if the waifs and strays, unwanted and cursed, found fresh air, green grass, good food, and love?

What if M. et Mme. des Armors were known far and wide as decent, gentle, charitable souls? What if they lived long lives surrounded by their healthy, well-educated children, then died in the bosom of an enormous family, and were buried in the churchyard in Pouligny?

What then the truth they teach us in school?

EIGHT YEARS after she was supposed to have been burned at the stake, the City of Orleans granted 210 pounds of gold to Mme. Robert des Armors, nee Jeanne d'Arc, "for service to the city of Orleans and His Majesty the King."

What then the truth?

9

Anne Carson

STONEHENGE GIRL

"The left palm tells what you were born with," Paula explained, "and the right is what you've developed since—oops!"

The bus swerved, making her lurch against the arm of Alice's seat.

"Jesus, English drivers are worse than the Germans," observed Mark. "And I thought the Autobahn was bad!"

"On the Autobahn there's no speed limit," Alice remarked to anyone who was listening.

"There she goes again," muttered Debbie, intent on re-applying her eyeliner. "Miss Know-It-All."

In fact, Alice cared nothing for cars, or Germany. What was most important in her life right now, apart from the Beatles, of course, was that at the age of seventeen, after ten years of dreaming about it, she was really and truly touring her beloved England. She *was* in the company of a dozen other American teenagers, when she would have preferred some intense young Englishman dressed in black (a poet, named Colin or Nigel or something), but she was nonetheless Home. As far as she was concerned, today was the culmination of their tour before they settled down for the summer in Oxford, for today they were on the road to Stonehenge.

Perhaps she would find some interesting rocks to pocket as souvenirs. In her luggage rattled books from Edinburgh, a Donovan LP from Dublin, and Welsh rocks. Stones, records, and poetry — Alice's life was nigh complete.

She turned back to Paula — a kindred spirit, not like the other crass suburban youth. "Can you teach me palmistry when we get to Oxford?"

"Sure, if you'll teach me to read tea leaves."

When their bus pulled into the parking lot, the great stones were visible many yards off. Alice's heart quickened as she and the others filed outside with their cameras and guidebooks. In order to get to the site, you had to cross the road via an underground passageway lined with stalls, stocked with the usual pamphlets and tourist maps. They re-emerged into the sunlight, and there before them stood Stonehenge itself, tourists milling among the megaliths like curious ants.

Alice immediately left the group to explore on her own. The stones were huge, massive and impassive; she was struck by their silence. Like ancient trees they towered above the callow sightseers, having led their own lives for more than thirty centuries.

Alice looked behind her and saw the grey-and-yellow expanse that was Salisbury Plain. After the steep hills and closed-in coziness of Scotland, Wales, and the English West Country, this sudden spaciousness was exhilarating. The stone circle stood as a comforting haven against the extreme openness of the sky.

She walked around the perimeter of the site, counting each of the fifty-six whitened Aubrey holes, which formed a ring around the stones. The stones themselves she approached warily and in reverence. Elephantine grey they were, green with moss. She ran her hands over them, sniffed them, pictured Hardy's Tess of the d'Urbervilles stretched out on the fallen monolith called the Altar Stone. She took photographs, careful not to show any of the people swarming about. Sensing the weight of the massive capstones above, she stepped in between the lintels.

We can tell you nothing now, said the stones. Come again when you can be alone with us.

Outside on the grass, Alice began running back and forth with her arms outstretched, schoolgirl jumper and headscarf askew. She pulled up handfuls of the grass from the sacred ground, even ate some without knowing why. I must have been a Druid in a former life, she thought, unaware that the megaliths had been standing for a thousand years before the Celts with their Druidic priesthood arrived in Britain.

The stones remained oblivious to the Japanese families, the American teenagers, and one seventeen-year-old girl drinking in the sun, grass, sky, and ancient powers. They ignored everything, and spoke only to each other.

At last it was time to go. Alice wrapped up the rest of the grass in a tissue and placed it in the bottom of her purse. Invisibly, she waved goodbye. She would not have another chance to touch the stones, for in a few years the authorities would be forced to erect a fence around them to protect the site from the careless and the impious.

They filed back onto the bus.

"What comes next?" asked Debbie, flipping through her guidebook.

"Windsor Castle."

"The Queen's Dollhouse is four feet tall . . . " began Alice.

TWENTY YEARS ON

Ever since I saw an article in the *Village Voice* entitled "I Was the Dyke at My High School Reunion," I knew that whatever my sexuality, nothing

11

would keep me from going to mine.

The first question to be answered before going to a reunion is, of course, "What on earth will I wear?" We all want to impress our classmates, if only to make an anti-impression, but which impression to choose? Should I wear my best, most prosperous clothes and startle everyone with my sleekness? Should I come in '60s clothes, and I don't mean tie-dye and denim, but the tailored wool skirt I got in 1965, jewelry from eighth grade, and of course, vintage black fishnet stockings? Would anybody notice? Or should I come as Myself, which would mean men's slacks from the Army-Navy store, maroon jersey, tweed jacket, and Rockports? And which pendant to wear — the double battleaxe, emblem of matriarchal Crete and hence radical feminism, or a silver pentacle, the symbol of magic? In the end, my outfit was a blend of all three styles: blazer, lace blouse, flowered skirt, pentacle — and those fishnet stockings.

After I fretted about what to wear, I started doing sit-ups. Alas, my slimming regimen, which was only so I could fit into my twenty-four-year-old skirt, soon fell by the wayside. Very well, then, you can't expect that many years and motherhood to leave no traces. I would pass.

In high school I was not one of the "popular" crowd, but a long-haired girl known as Nancy who wrote novels and poetry, read voraciously, daydreamed romantically. I was almost never asked out on dates, but instead went around with groups of people, all girls when I was in my early teens and, later, mixed groups in platonic friendships, European-style. Looking at the list of people who were planning to attend, I was crestfallen to find that almost none of my closest friends would be there. Many of the names I couldn't even link with a face until I got out my yearbook.

My first real shock, as I joined the crowd picking up their name tags, came not from recognizing the men as this or that youthful crush, but from the way the women were dressed, which was dressed to kill: cocktail dresses, sequins, strapless bouffant things, clutch bags, and there were more blondes than I remembered. Too late, I thought of the glittery knit outfit hanging in my closet back home, the ludicrous silver evening bag I'd never gotten rid of — I was acceptable in my flowered skirt and tailored jacket, but I knew I could have done better. At least I hadn't committed one of those fashion disasters the junior high girls so thoughtfully used to bring to my attention. "The hell with it," I thought defiantly. "This is *me* when I get dressed up."

I was at the bar chatting to my old lab partner (whose name tag read "Rainbow" instead of "Susan"), when my best friend from childhood appeared. Liz (we'll call her) and I had first met in kindergarten when she shoved me down a hill. The next year we were best friends, or perhaps I should write "Best Friends," for this is not a description of our relationship but the social office that we filled in each other's lives. Throughout childhood we played kickball together, dressed our dolls together, learned about life together, while she bullied me, belittled me, and in general taught me that I was ugly and inept at everything, especially at social relationships with boys.

And like many a battered wife, I put up with it and learned passivity, because no one told me that it was permissible to reject your Best Friend in order to preserve your self-worth. During girlhood I felt very much married to my Best Friends, and when I did leave this girl for another at the age of eleven, a girl who cared more for me but continued the criticism, the two of them fought over me as fiercely as if a divorce were in progress. Ironically, they became best friends themselves, and after we all found new Best Friends in junior high, they grew quite tolerable.

But here she was, over thirty years of my history bearing down on me. I suppose I had hoped she would exclaim (there was a lot of exclaiming going on that night), "Nancy! I'm so glad you're here! You look fabulous/just the same!"

"This is my oldest friend," I tried to tell Rainbow, but Liz was planting a large, lipsticked kiss on my cheek and seemed either about to devour me, so close was she standing, or to pat me on the head ("Little Nancy! How you've grown!").

She was heavily made-up and wearing some sort of light-green cocktail suit that reminded me of the early sixties. She had developed a New York accent and a brassy New York style to go with it. The word "harridan" drifted through my mind. We caught up, and for a few minutes Liz became a serious, real person as she described her work as a nurse. Skittishly, she joked about not having married yet.

There was so much noise, so many bodies. So little to really say. She was off in a whoosh, descending upon some other crony from the popular crowd. I was overwhelmed, disappointed, relieved. She no longer had any power over me.

Turning back to the bar, I found one of the two boys — now men — whom I had dated in senior year: Ted, in his day a wild-haired sixties radical and the first person I had smoked pot with, had become a patent lawyer who confessed, "The most important thing in my life isn't the multi-million dollar deals — martini, very dry, no twist — it's singing 'Itsy Bitsy Spider' to my daughter."

During dinner, awards were handed out, which consisted of large chocolate T's (for Tenafly High) in gift boxes. I was hoping to see Most Divorces, Still Hippie After All These Years, or at least an Out-of-the-Closet Award, for the most "out" lesbian or gay man — if my classmates had seen fit to bestow it, it would have gone to the other boy I dated in high school, who since graduation had lost about a hundred pounds but had kept his sense of humor. Instead, we were treated to Good Clean Fun: the Fertility Award — we were suposed to be the birth-control generation — went to two women who had had four children each and were still sane; the Guidance Counselor Award, to our lone Afro-American classmate who had been advised not to bother with college and was now a school principal; the Least Likely to Succeed Award went to Dottie Valiente, a tough girl from the wrong side of the tracks who admitted that her most important extra-curricular activity had been smoking in the girls' room. I remembered her as a smart cookie, though, and a good artist. She had battled her dragons, graduated from college, become a mother and a successful businesswoman.

Our former senior class president continued, "Some of you who went to Mackay Elementary School [applause] remember Nancy Carson, who in high school never said a word. She now speaks eight languages, and we're giving her an award for it, which she will accept by thanking us in each language."

They could have warned me! As I blushingly made my way to the podium, all I could think of was, "What's the Latin for thank you?" The challenge hadn't really been serious, but I thought I could do it. I began, "Merci, gracias, obrigada . . ." My voice trailed off. It was oral report time, show-and-tell: faces expectant, bored, smirking, encouraging. ". . . and thank you." If I had impressed my classmates, it was with my inarticulateness. I accepted my chocolate T and fled. When the festivities were over I swiftly downed two gin-and-tonics.

At eleven-thirty the bar shut down, so the drinkers headed for the hotel lounge and I decided it was time to leave Oz and get back to Kansas. As I made my way down the hotel corridor to my room, Liz and a couple of the other "popular" girls floated by, all teeth and hair and sparkle. Liz stopped.

"What was it that you said up there? I couldn't understand a word."

I set my jaw, looked her right in the eyebrow, and replied:

"*Merci, gracias, obrigada, danke schön, spacibo, arigato, efcharisto,* and *gratias et vale,* which is Latin for thank you and goodbye."

Nona M. Caspers

MARIA LEARNS ABOUT LIFE

Buried under heaps of stinging snow are the large front and back yards of Maria's neighborhood. Eight houses filled with children, built with wood and painted every five summers. Her own grey house, the fifth house with the flat roof, shivers, but inside lies warmth and Maria's mother and Maria's mother's books and Maria's mother's words.

In the tiled kitchen that smells of milk Maria's mother and Maria, in matching reindeer sweaters, page through the books. From her high stool chair at the table Maria sees pictures of bubble gum colored fallopian tubes, pearl fish egg ovaries and blue vaginas that remind her of the tunnels her brothers and she dig into snowbanks to get to the fat part where they carve out an igloo. It's too cold to go out today. Maria watches the creases around her mother's lips squint, watches the pictures. Her mother traces the colors, turns the pages and tells Maria that when she is older, she will fall in love and her husband will build her a house and plant a seed in the igloo part where a baby will grow. Her mother points out a full page spongy blue violet womb.

"That's where the baby lives," she says.

Maria tucks her chin, round head jutting back from her shoulders. Then she straddles the page with her elbows and pushes her eyes close.

"Doesn't the baby get cold?" she asks.

"No," her mother tells her. "It's very dark and warm in there. It's the safest place for a baby to be."

Outside, the angels the girl made in the snow are sanded flat by icy wind. Her plastic slide and sandbox have vanished.

"Can I go in there?" Maria asks.

Her mother laughs and fits the girl's loose black hair behind her ear. "Not anymore, antsy pants, you're too big."

Maria thinks about this. She thinks about size and houses and husbands and igloos and icy winds. "What if I got small again?"

Maria's mother's smile turns upside down and she shakes her head. "Oh, Maria." She whispers. "You'll never fit in there again."

It makes Maria cry.

Her mother holds her in her spongy arms. She rocks her to the rhythm of her heart while the blizzard blows over.

BRIDGE

From where Tanya lay in shadow under the couch she could see her mother setting up the card table. The white legs snapped out one at a time like a turtle's — snap, snap, snap, snap. Then her mother made it stand in the middle of their living room, in front of the couch. The sun spread itself across the floor, but didn't reach Tanya, in her secret spot.

Tanya liked the shadows, and the carpet on her cheek. She liked pressing her ear into it and pretending that half of her was under water. Clack, clack went the shiny beige metal things her mother turned into chairs. Her mother could do magic.

The wooden bottom of their couch hung above her. The dark grain lines reminded Tanya of the marble cake mix she'd helped her mother bake that day. She pretended to stir the lines quietly with her fingers. The doorbell rang like a bird and she heard her mother's responding chirp, "Hello, hello, hello . . ." The other mothers chirped back: Tanya's best friend Mara's mother, who they all called Mrs. Mayor, and Lori's mother, and icky Jimmy yuk-y-o's mother. Tanya thought their voices sounded different from under the couch, their words were muffled and they bubbled up their throats like the trilling of her cat. They didn't sound like mothers anymore, Tanya thought, they sounded like little girls. Then all the shoes got quiet under the table, and the legs turned into trees that grew dresses the colors of leaves and acorns. Tanya wanted to run her hands over the scratchy cinnamon bark that wrinkled under their knees and ankles. Once, just for play, she had worn that kind of skin, but her legs started to choke so she peeled it off. When she was older it wouldn't feel like that, her mother told her.

"2 clubs," Jimmy's mother bid.

"3 hearts," her mother countered.

"4 hearts," Mrs. Mayor said quickly, "I'm no dummy."

The cards fluttered in their hands like the fan in her room, their voices purred, the shadows deepened and Tanya felt herself drift. Through her long eyelashes she watched the far away tree-legs twitch and shift.

Then one foot broke out of its shoe and slid deliberately across the carpet. Tanya followed it, lids drooping. There was a dark seam across the top of the toes, like a smile. The foot slid until it rested near another, then it rubbed up and down, like her cat rubbed against her face when she was sleeping. Up and down and up and down it slid. Tanya heard her mother and Mrs. Mayor laugh. They sounded so happy from under the couch, she thought. The second foot pushed off its shoe and the two sets of toes curled together. Tanya moved her head to the edge of the shadows and looked up sleepily at her mother's face.

"Trump you," her mother called out, and laid her card down on the table. Mrs. Mayor laughed and folded her hand. Tanya noticed the smile across Mrs. Mayor's toes pinch her mother's ankle playfully. Then Tanya settled back into her warm shadows as the cards and her lids fluttered shut. The two wrinkled ankles twined over the soft rug like the roots of trees, and Tanya wondered when she would be old enough to play bridge.

ANOTHER MEAN MINDED CHILD

You were born in Minnesota, you can't help it.

You took piano lessons for one year then broke your finger pushing a boy you didn't like down a hill. He broke his arm. Your mother grounded you for two months in your room so you wrote bad poetry all over the walls in irremovable permanent black magic marker.

You never liked Mr. Rogers or Big Bird. Your favorite cartoon is the Road Runner.

You used to spit up a lot on your father's designer shirts. They do not ever let you forget it.

Now they make you eat granola. You want bisquick pancakes and sausage links. You scream when your mother refuses to make this.

Your father doesn't really like you and you don't like him. Your mother is flaccid in the presence of black labs. You have no respect for her. Your three older sisters are vain and vapid and vociferous. They don't know how to cook. They wear long silk scarves wrapped around their necks like Isadora Duncan. You hope your parents give them a convertible for their birthdays.

You had a pet frog once. When it died in the Planter's peanut jar that was its home you did your own autopsy. There was nothing inside.

You vowed never to love again.

You joined the neighborhood club and became
Another Mean Minded Child.

ESTA BIEN

I met Jesus once, in Guatemala. He was traveling light — a robe, sandals, and a backpack. It was in a little village on Lago de Atitlan. A village without roads. I was hiking around the lake, and there he was, helping the

17

villagers make rope out of a type of plant I forget the name of. All day they pounded and twisted and wove the fibers together to make the strongest, smoothest rope I'd ever seen. I knew the man was Jesus right away because of the pictures I'd seen, and he had that same passive look on his face. There were, of course, holes in his feet and palms.

I asked him, What is your name? "Como se llama?" And he made no ceremony over answering, I am Jesus. Of course he said this in Spanish, "Yo soy Jesus." I nodded my dusty gringa traveler's head and sat on my own backpack to watch them weave rope into the night. Then I asked about a place to string up my hammock, and Jesus invited me to share the hut they had made for him.

I played my recorder while he meditated. Then we talked about the weather and about my travels and his much longer ones, and then I asked him some questions, since I figured this may be the only time in my life to get uncensored answers. First I asked him about some contradictions in the Bible, which he'd never read. I'm not much for reading, he said, of course in Spanish, "No leo mucho." And I nodded, though I am much for reading, and at the time was reading the sixth book in the "Chronicles of Narnia." I asked him if he wanted me to read a chapter to him, but he said, No thanks. "No, gracias. Tengo dormir. Much trabajo mañana." Much work tomorrow. And, of course, I understood, but before we went to sleep, I did take the opportunity to mention that I was lesbian, just to see his reaction. I was at the stage of coming out to everyone. I don't know what I expected, but Jesus only nodded with his eyes half shut and said, That's nice. "Esta bien." And went to sleep.

Now I was only 19 at the time, with my intestines full of bugs and my ears full of dust, so I could have misunderstood the whole situation; but I swear he said, "Esta bien."

The next morning Jesus got up before the sky to make rope while me and my bugs slept in. When I woke and packed my bag, the whole village was out of sight, working in a different part of the forest. I trudged on to the next village where the people fed me boiled green weeds. "Coma. Coma."

I have always remembered the words of Jesus. Especially the last ones.

Naomi Feigelson Chase

WHAT'S SO GOOD ABOUT THE END?

I.

You're an artist, you'll use it, I tell myself. At first, this is not a comfort. Then I take out my sketch pad and do Zack in Picasso's African Cubist style, half front, half back, half white, half black. I call it "Ambivalent Zack."

That takes care of him, I tell myself, but I'm looking at him, not me.

I go to my studio and spread drawing paper over the floor. Then I sit down on it and outline the lower half of my body. I lie down, and as best I can, reaching and squirming, outline the rest of me. From my collection of studio junk, from odds and ends, whatever I can find, I start filling in my paper self. I glue old beads and discarded jewelry on the arms and legs, adding layers of paint, and as that dries, odd cloth and paper scraps. An old bird's nest I found last year becomes my heart. I add a bit of cracked eggshell. I spend the day building myself up with paper and paint, leaves and feathers. Finally, I sprinkle gold and silver sequins on my crotch. I'm finished. I title my variegated self APHRODITE FROM OLD PATCHES. I feel better.

II.

"Oh, Mom. I hate that bastard. He should drop dead," my daughter Rebecca says when I tell her Zack and I are through. How can you feel absolutely dreadful about life with a daughter like that?

I do feel dreadful, but I try not to talk about it. Here's this hurt, I want to say, I can't get rid of it. Looking at the sky, I can't see what kind of day it is. A big black cloud marked PAIN is lodged between two others marked REJECTION, LOSS. They turn into road signs. Everywhere I go I'm trapped between them. At night in bed they are presences on either side of me. I hate him. I shut my eyes and think this is the worst way to be alone.

III.

"Hey, I miss you. Let's have dinner. Let's be friends."

This is Zack's message on my machine tonight, a month after we broke up. I'm furious. There's no phone in my studio, so when I came home at night, I'd look expectantly for that flashing green light. I was just getting used to it not being Zack when he called today and left that message.

His tape answers when I call him back. He's got new music. Last month it was something funky by The Five Blind Boys. Now it's Vivaldi. "Fall" from "The Seasons." A rare tape with original instruments.

"Screw you," I want to tell his machine. "I gave you that tape. Give it back. Along with *The Love Poems of William Butler Yeats* and *The Architecture of the Italian Renaissance*. Give back the button that says, "Nixon Cares," the yellow plastic solar fan you clip on your lapel, the holy medal of St. Sebastian pierced by 100 arrows, and the humidifier I hoped would seem like me blowing in your ear at night.

I am working myself up into a fine rage. I would like to take those gifts, pile them in the middle of Zack's studio, jump on them, douse them with kerosene and set them on fire.

I try to think of something clever and nasty to say about dinner, about friendship. Vivaldi's "Fall" is over, and so is Zack's tape. I hang up.

POLITICS

Rebecca is always protesting something, starting when she was ten right there in our living room, between the Danish sofa and the giant avocado plant.

"I refuse on principle," she told the census taker.

"I don't get it," her brother said later. "What are you against?"

She told him, "Counting."

In high school, she was against hierarchy and faculty domination. At college, she demonstrated against South Africa, studied Navaho and spent two summers on an Indian reservation looking for female shamans. I supported her all the way.

"What kind of job will I get with elementary Spanish, advanced Navaho, and a record of getting arrested at every student demonstration?" she asked when she graduated.

Not many, she discovered.

It stunned me when Rebecca told me she wanted to be a doctor. I thought she was an artist. She writes music and poetry. She's an accomplished weaver. I never thought of her as a scientist. I do know Rebecca wants to bind up the world's wounds. Whatever is wrong, she wants to make it right.

When I asked her, "But why be a doctor?" she said, "Doctors have power. If I'm going to do it, I'm going to do it right."

It scares me how little I know about my children.

Cathy Cockrell

MUFFIE'S MIDNIGHT LOUNGE

A dark, unventilated room the size of a giant
olive stuffed with, oh, a hundred women.
Cologne and clutch purses, T-shirts worn
backwards, double-breasted jackets, grey banks
of smoke, scared sweat, so-sweet perfume.
'lectricity and nerves. A lightbulb over the
entrance blinks red, blinks off, to announce
or warn of each and every newcomer: vice sex,
vice horse, vice squad. A pair of legs
dangling from a barstool twist around each
other, tight, like pretzels. An arm stretches
out along the leatherette back of a chair, so
near the next woman's neck, where the small
hairs prickle with interest, at the edge of
the pearl choke. A quarrel breaks out at the
back over the fate of a femme. They press so
close on the miniature dance floor they could
be grinding corn, while a trio in DAs coax the
newest hits from the juke: Hello Stranger; I
(Who Have Nothing); Da Doo Ron Ron. "Mint
Frappe!" "7&7!" "Comrade Kelly!" the bartender
calls the drinks out as she sets them down. A
kiki thing in soft sweater and Peter Pan
collar (tense, scared-looking) poses with her
Chesterfield King, whose spirals of smoke
hover, run surveillance from the stamped tin
ceiling. Wall flowers and sunglass mystery
ladies, fancy dancers in furs and silk. Now
Lou Christie, now The Orlons, now Randy and
the Rainbows, now Ivory Joe Hunter: The way
the woman walk/she set my little soul on
fire!/The way she talk/She's my heart's
desire/And oh if she leaved me/I think that I
would die!/Sometime I call in the midnight
hour:/"Yeah Yeah Oooooooo!/Don't leave me
baby!"

Strange Loves

The Glands
of Destiny

Psychoanalysis As
A Potent Remedy

Can Inverts Be
Reformed by
Marriage

Transmutation
of Sex Energy

Menstrual
Disturbances
in Urnings

Lesbian's Defense

Are Astrological
Factors in Any
Way Responsible
for Perversion?

The Bearded Lady

Tribadism in
Many Cases a
Protest Against
Existing
Conditions

Hardly a
Race Exempt

21

Monday, Barnacle Bank International, Corporate Lending Division, Tetra Tower, Suite 900

"You're from the agency?" Elbows tucked, fingertips touching the candy wrapper deep in the pocket of my dress coat, I say "yes." Grace Finz auto-introduces. I follow close behind as she does the tour — coat closet, coffee room, women's room, conference room, reception desk, overnight mail pouches, horizontal and hanging files, phone books, supplies. Long, swinging black hair, like pissed-off surf. Into a tiny airless room, warm and buzzing with electromagnetic energy, we go. The Heavy-Picker LizardJet printer, the Saline 9350 copier, and the Piety Bowles FAX machine.

It's a fat white document she's got in her hands now. The copy machine reaches as high as my nipples. "Like this," she instructs me. Her fingers flutter at the speed of hummingbirds over the Saline's single sided/double sided, collate/no collate, number of copies, light or dark original, percentage enlargement/reduction options.

I nod, distracted, meditating on Grace's thin forearms and minuscule waist. My x-ray eyes see the laminated calorie chart in the wallet on her desk; I know she munched lettuce like a rabbit last night for dinner. Grace thrusts the documents into my hands and leaves me to it. There's trouble in her life, I'm sure.

Real Estate Group report on proposed loan for the New Native Project, a three-tower L.A. office/retail complex. Occasional double-sided pages with charts and diagrams on the reverse. Other pages with UHU Stick glued-on aerial snapshots of the proposed site, a pedestrian's-eye-view of the corner of Mandible Boulevard and Echobrittle Street, where Tower II will go. Photos must be laid on the glass, not fed through the automatic loader. Three copies, collated. Original to be returned to VP Willy Scatter. Copies to REG Chicago, New York, and L.A. via overnight pouch. Bow-tied bankers and quick-motion secretaries mix, converse, at the FAX machine altar: successive conversations about herpes, then foreign exchange rates.

A man in a white shirt and askew blue bow tie enters, asks to make one copy. "Urgent!" An All-American with a caved in nose. Bob, Bent Nose Bob, Recreational Drug Addict, rushes from the room, leaves his original on the glass. A bill from a daycare center. Make that Father, too. The machines' fuzzy heat prickles at my skin. I resume my task. But which page were we on? How many copies completed? Four piles on the floor. Which the original? Organization! Panic! A project gone askew. Grace Finz, eyes rolling, to the rescue.

Later. After lunch break. After lemon croissant at "C'est No More!" Bob delivers another REG report section, marked with hieroglyphic arrows, inserts and deletions, to be typed. "Urgent!" He leaves. Grace inhales. "Just do what you can," she confides. "I've got a meeting, but I'll be back. You can use my work station."

Yours truly logs on. Password: Rosie. The name of the little girl with feral eyes in the photo pinned to the modular wall over Grace Finz' IBM Selectric II. I am welcomed by the VAX/VMS System, Node 0002. I feel a strange, low-grade excitement. I ENTER. I select WP from the

WP	Word Processing
SEL	Select
SC	Spell Check
EM	Electronic Mail

menu. I ENTER. I'm in. I'm pushing around and processing words — words about land and value, words about venture partners and new commitments, words about a great guy (a real estate advisor) and his senior management team, words defining words:

Borrowers	Fees
Purpose	Fees to Barnacles
Barnacle's Share	Term
Total Loan	Prepayment
Interest Rate	Borrower's Equity
Amortization	Security
Pricing to Barnacles	Value
Conditions to Loan Commitment	Loan Value

And more: A peck of words. A pack of words. An extravagant bonepile of words. By late afternoon I've processed all the words. I save and exit. I send file NNATIVE.REP to the printer. While the LizardJet is spewing out the sheets, I steal a fistful of paper clips and a box of staples, make a personal phone call. I fill out my time sheet for Grace to sign.

Before I leave I take a moment to study the picture of the little girl — wide-open, scared eyes — and wonder what it was she saw.

Jane Coleman

SKETCHING THE ISLAND

I.
This is a prison island for first offenders. Gorgona, Elba, Monte Cristo, fortified for more serious criminals or political exiles, float like pale moths

where the horizon dips, flows around the world. Here the prisoners, lightly guarded, dig at rocks in the road, in the uncompromising soil of the villa's garden. They lean on their shovels and look out over the water, and they shrug and smile to themselves. "People pay thousands of lire to come here," one says to another. "We're here for nothing."

Despite their efforts, all that grows is prickly pear, wild thyme, a bush of rosemary laden with bees, and, in a terra cotta urn, Rosa's geraniums whose petals drift and scatter.

Local legend says that lilies grow in the crater of the extinct volcano that forms the island's heart; that there is a lake, tongues of purple fire. I walk there along the vertebrae of rock. I hold to myself in the dry wind, narrow my eyes against the glitter of sun. The lake is dry, the flowers blown away.

II.

Carlo the goat boy watches me from behind rocks, follows me up the mountain and down the twisted streets. He does not speak, or cannot; the sounds he makes are like seeds rattling in the gourd of his throat. Sometimes he capers on the cliff edge a hundred feet above the sea, a dust devil dancing. His choreography, the starkness of what strives to be song, derives from some lost source, are unintelligible except in the blood, the spiral of memory.

III.

When I go to town in search of conversation, the widow in the window waves to me. Her face is a web of lines; her eyes shout madness or the terror of old age. On the sill at her elbow is a baroque gilt cage wrapped around a bird that sits ruffling its feathers. At mail time the woman lowers a basket on a rope, hauls it up again eager for letters. What does she wait for, I wonder, watching the quickness of her hands.

IV.

This morning there was a bird in my room — a large, dark, swift-winged thing that dashed against walls, battered itself on ceiling and bedposts while I hid beneath the sheet. When it lay spent on the floor, I called for Rosa who, seeing it, trembled and crossed herself, made the sign of the horns with her other hand. "Bad luck," she said, and fled.

When I went out I saw that a goat had hanged itself from its tether, that its small hooves flailed in the emptiness of air, and that on the rocks below the spear fisherman from Firenze, he who poses in his wetsuit for us each afternoon like a slim and gleaming Neptune, had caught an octopus and was beating it upon a stone. Thunk! Thunk! I felt it like my heart.

V.

The wind rises; the hot wind from Africa that rattles windows, parches my mouth, turns the sea to silver, the hollows of waves to opals. Restless, I walk down past the black walls of the prison, past the woman in the window, past bougainvillea trembling against white walls. Always behind me the goat boy's feet, quick and sly.

In the harbor the ferry drops anchor and waits for the tender that sets out from shore. Island women disembark. They cover their heads with dark shawls, clutch the fringed ends as if to steady themselves. Behind them, crates of chickens, a goat, feet hobbled and bleating like a child, are handed down into the shell of the boat. The procession passes me, steady, silent, a frieze set in motion. At its end, Rosa's husband, his face ashen, his knuckles white around the handle of a tattered carpet bag. "Che brutta mare," he says as he goes, shaking a fist at the sea. "Che brutta mare." The ugly sea, its waves gnawing the rock upon which we stand.

VI.

I think we are all prisoners here; that we are fastened to this place by force or fate, each of us separate, each of us alone with the taste of our bones in our mouths, and that no matter the dance, despite the reaching out, what we grasp will be no more than the wind. What we speak will be lost like geranium petals swept away, hovering for one scarlet moment over the brilliant sea.

Maxine Combs

FROZEN VEGETABLES

When my father, a vegetarian, developed an incurable disease, he joined a Cryonics society that promised to freeze his body at death. The initial payment of fifty thousand dollars and the monthly installments to assure "perpetual care" promised to eat up the rest of his fortune.

As soon as he died — he was only fifty-four — they wrapped him in aluminum foil and encased him in a capsule that resembled a thermos bottle. The capsule, filled with liquid nitrogen, was supposed to preserve the body at an extremely low temperature.

He hoped at some future date to be revived, cured, and

25

rejuvenated.

Cryonics, in Father's opinion, lay halfway between a fad and a science. He considered it common sense; he considered it his best alternative.

So there he lies frozen. The moment caught forever. Like a work of art or an image in memory.

My early memories are faint, but I still remember 1) always being cold and 2) Father in a smock — he was an artist — the color of the inside of a swimming pool.

Once he painted a mud-colored portrait of me, but my cabbage-like head had been removed. In another study I appeared as a Bloody Mary with half-gnawed celery stalks for arms. In another I was portrayed as a roast stuffed squash with grease-spot eyes, surrounded by baby carrots and peas.

He exhibited these works in a gallery that stayed open only between midnight and two a.m.

Current scientific opinion holds that Father's chance of cheating death isn't good. In the process of freezing or thawing, some brain cells and other delicate tissue may suffer damage. It's probable that should he be resuscitated centuries hence, essential personality traits — such as memory or a sense of identity — would be missing.

I relate to this. Already, I remember very little, nor am I certain what I look like. Sometimes in the mirror I see a face divided into numbered squares. It's necessary to paint the squares according to directions, but I have lost the directions.

Nor am I a painter.

Sometimes, wrapped in sweaters, I stare in the mirror, but I see only a moldy vegetable shape which has remained in the refrigerator's blue-green lettuce bin too long.

Another danger pointed out by critics of Cryonics is that resuscitated persons might be revived into a totally alien and hostile environment.

Such a contingency shouldn't bother Father. He could be as hostile as the next person. Once he boasted: In this lifetime I have eaten soup, nuts, vegetables, my mother, my father, one sister, three university professors, and a daughter.

ESPERANTO

My mother once kept angel fish; I stay up all night listening to my parakeet.

I cover his cage with a blue bath towel which doesn't help, so I

26

remove it, turn on the light and stare at him — at his bone structure delicate as calligraphy, feathers the color of faded willow-pattern plates, the shadows of his wings fluttering like memory.

I am familiar with the myth that the original language was the language of the birds, and that this language expressed (metaphorically, mathematically, or some more subtle way) the exact nature of each thing. Utterances in this language were said to reveal every dimension, aspect, and implication of the original.

I don't exactly believe this. Still I sit up and listen, imagining I understand his peepings and chirps, his sounds like a seabird, his chicken cackles. This takes more than one night. It takes every night for a month. Or, maybe it takes a year.

In my insomniac state I hear the bird's notes. They float in the air as if an accomplished flutist had dropped them there, they sound like what you hear in the forest when trees grow or shrink, they remind me of the cries of spirits lost in the cane brakes.

The angel fish that glided in my mother's tank had whitish bodies and big floppy delicate grey fins. Their eyes always remained open, and when she sprinkled food in the water, they rushed to the surface to gulp it down. A tiny statue of a mermaid with silver hair and a green tail sat near a half opened treasure chest on the bottom of the tank. Her eyes also stayed open all the time.

I pick up a book. In the first paragraph I discover the heroine is 34 years old, a feminist, her parents live in Florida, she wears bedroom slippers she owned in high school, she once studied piano and still keeps the music, she has always been a good student.

I make my list: my mother didn't like artificial flowers but she liked fancy evening shoes . . . satin, beaded, some decorated with brocade flowers. She once played the violin. She kept three angel fish swimming in a tank.

Disconnected bits. Dead stars. No heat. No music. I know more about the heroine of my book than I know about my mother. I believe that if I could understand the language of the birds I would be able to retrieve what I no longer remember. If I had a new (truer) name for my mother, she would remain the same, but my vision of her would expand.

I work at it night after night. Sometimes I pick a modifier at random and try it out. Ill-got mother, I say. Does this expand her meaning? Red hot mother. Red hat mother. (Did she ever have a red hat? No.) After-thought mother. (What will it take to unglue the world?) Forget-me-not mother. Red Medoc mother. (I think I see her face in the winestains in the carpet.)

The bird keeps chirping. Polyglot mother. She rises from the bottom speaking several languages. In all of them she contradicts herself.

She is the Lady of the Lake. She is a fish in the mud. She is singing along with the radio. She is waiting to be photographed.

Theresa Corrigan

MEMORIES AND MOLES

Memories, like moles, travel dank muddy corridors. I know they're there. I see mounds and scurry over, knowing full well that by the time you spot the mound the mole knows you are there, has sensed the plodding above and nosed away. Yet I jam in the shovel, hoping to bar memory's escape. Dig it up fast, faster. Beat the elusive creature's retreat. Piles of earth, mole scat sometimes even, but mole is not trusting, will not appear to one intent on digging with such crude instruments.

Or like the invisible burrowing sand crab. You see the bubbles, bubbles, bubbles. Aquatic smoke signals arising from the fragments of rock decay. I surround the tiny bursts with my hands, scooping deep, hopefully deep enough, and lay out the sand on my palms. Sift and sort, sand and more sand, but the crab has already scuttled deeper, has avoided my grasp in her subterranean world where my ancestors are a part of her.

The surface of the earth and of life is so solid, smooth with the appearance of immutability. Yet just below, just a tiny crack below, moles and memories and earthworms and crabs live and die, build homes and memories of their own. A kind of earthy Tommy Tippy cup — the bear on the cup holding a cup with a bear with a cup with . . .

My father is with them now. I don't go to see the mound, yet I still approach with my shovel in hand. It's been a year and by now I'm sure the worms have figured out how to reside in him, nosing tunnels into the very heart of him. An accomplishment undoubtedly they are much better at than I ever was. Does he welcome them? Relieved, perhaps at last, to have someone, anyone, find the true heart of him.

My memories burrow through him as well, turning the muddy soil of his flesh and our past over and over, creating endless passageways, a maze of discovering and uncovering and recovering. They have built interior villages, makeshift camps until they can find their way out.

I thought when he reached his underground bed, my memories could finally rest sleepily and comfortably on his pillow, could snuggle up next to his scraggly old face and doze. But no. I hadn't counted on his body becoming a world of eternal excavation. I hadn't counted on my memories finding kinship with worms and moles.

I am learning, however slowly like digesting mud, that if I truly want to commune with moles or dance with sand crabs, I must either sit as quietly as possible near the latest sighting and concentrate intently on being as molish or as crabbish as patience can be taught, hoping the creatures will grant me shared essence; or dig, not with shovel or pickax, but as the creature does herself, nose first, pushing her whole body through all earthly resistance.

DeeAnne Davis

NESBITT CRUSH

Remember please for the soda out the soda pop machine window. I could taste the Nesbitt strawberry and the solid one good pull from the cold to get out that thawing icicle. It's in the strength you got stored in your biceps, I'd heard my daddy splain to my brother. And I got biceps. Yes I do. Never got to drink soda pop in the grocery store before. But I got stitches in my upper lip and a nice cold Nesbitt would sure feel good, kinda like medicine when you're sick.

So I'm trying the best I can to drink that soda like I got some sense and manners, even though respectable children would never ever drink soda pop in the Eagle's grocery store — cascading through the aisles like she's too good to wait til she gets home. Dropped it. The bottle with stubble going round its base like my daddy's face on a Saturday when he ain't shaving for nobody. And I couldn't go and find my mama for knowing she was gon give me one a those looks cause I was being a little show-off. Bad bad girl.

That bag boy with all the legs and the bangs hanging like weeping willow branches in his eye came to me where I was standing all pitiful and sorry. He bagged the glass and mopped up the sizzling strawberry liquid real easy like. I wouldn't've moved, cept he kinda pushed me aside, patted me on my arm, and asked could he see my stitches. I was scared my mama was gonna snatch me away if I was to act proud of those stitches, so I lowered my head like I was one of those mute children in the Hallmark

After School Special last week and pretended I didn't hear him or know how to say a mumbling word.

Mama came from the other aisle, cart all out in front. And I saw that look in her eye. She was working up to bein mad. I could see it coming. Maybe raise her hand real scary-like to give me something to cry about. Then she came round. Asked did I bust a stitch. Took a look like medicine when you're sick. And kissed me on my forehead. She said maybe we both need to think through our actions a little bit better next time. Asked me did I agree. I agreed. And took her hand.

In My Daddy's Arms

He rocked me. My legs hung over the edge. Silly drunk. He rocked me, rocked me, held me against his chest. My legs over the edge of the rocker. Silly drunk with my daddy.

Mad at my mama. Scarin me with her puffed up chest and mighty roar. Pushin, draggin, blowin four kids into the blue Chevy station wagon. And me in the front, my legs danglin over the car seat, cryin the more she be tellin us how we some rotten little hyperactive brats that need to go and bother their dad some. See how he like fightin, screechin, bad-mouthed, second-rate-no-good thiefin kids.

He rocked me. My legs hung over the edge, silly drunk with my daddy. He rocked me, held me against his chest, legs hangin over the edge of the rocker. I was silly drunk with my daddy hush hushin my snottin, gaggin, sniffin and carryin on. He rocked me. Rocked me. Kissed me on my cheek. Rubbed my head flat, frizz shootin up out of the braids. He rocked me til my breathin was easy. Legs hanging over the edge of the rocker's arm. No more gulpin and flyin eyebrows frantic for a fresh breath of air layin against *my* daddy's belly.

I started playin in the wool of his red sweater and that yellow cake, warm in the oven, got under my nose. I was thinkin bout gettin down. Not too fast, though, cause I was silly drunk. In my daddy's arms.

Margaret Davis

PEAS

"Wait!" cried the last two peas in the can. My hand stopped its arc to the garbage.

"What do you want?" I asked them, the two peas that clung in the silvery cylinder.

"We want out."

"What do you care? You're peas."

"That's right. We're peas. What is there for us but the fork and the plate? How can you deny us our place on the plate? We've lived on the vine, huddled in our pod on cold nights, striving only for greenness and roundness. It's all been in vain if you throw us away."

"I didn't know peas had feelings," I said.

"We do," they replied, "and this is our moment. We have nothing higher, no krishna, no green goddess, no madonna of the vegetable garden. This is our calling, no other, the climax of sun and rain and humus, green energy pushing through vines, this is us, this is what we are. We are the peas."

"How can I help?" I asked them.

"Give us butter and salt," they said, "and maybe pearl onions."

"You know you'll be eaten." I said.

"Yes."

"Does it hurt?"

"No one knows," they answered.

Terri de la Peña

LABRYS

She stands behind the desk, high heels planted apart. She is a bulky yet stylish woman who favors eye-catching jewelry. "What's that you're wearing around your neck — some kind of charm?"

My heart quickens at her question, but I casually hand her the stack of typed forms. "It's a labrys."

31

"A what?" Her brown eyes seem magnified through her designer glasses while she stares at my silver amulet.

A bit uneasy, I grin. I wonder how much to tell this heterosexual woman about the symbol I wear proudly. "A labrys — a double-bladed ax."

Her raised brows emphasize her bewilderment. She gulps. "Looks kind of lethal."

I roll my eyes and step nearer to allow her a better inspection. "You've heard the term 'battle-ax,' right?"

She nods.

"It's a derogatory word for 'uppity' women, but if some guy ever calls you that, don't be insulted." I finger my labrys and hold it out to her. "This is a battle-ax — the legendary weapon used by Amazons. For me, it's a symbol of empowerment."

"Oh, gosh." She laughs. Does she sound nervous, or is that only my imagination?

Turning, I prepare to leave. Better to cut out while the going is good.

But she will not let me off so easy. "Wait."

I glance over my shoulder, wondering what else is in store.

She gestures with the stack of forms. "Did you ever see the film *Black Widow*?"

I try not to smile, still remembering the glimmer of lesbian attraction between the characters portrayed by Theresa Russell and Debra Winger. That film sits securely in one of my VCR storage boxes. "Yeah. I've seen it."

She sidles up to me. "Some of the movie theaters sold black widow pins during the film's run. They were big and silver — very striking. I bought one and used to wear it on my shoulder all the time. Just loved that movie."

I blink at her. What is she trying to communicate? Am I dealing with a flirting straight woman, or what?

"What'd you think of the film?" She presses.

I get a little daring. "There's a lot of chemistry between those two actresses."

"Oh, yeah. It's so mesmerizing."

Though I become fidgety, I cannot resist a question. "Why did you want to wear a black widow pin?"

She laughs. "It's like you said — empowering. I dared anybody to make a comment." She points to my labrys. "Where can I get one of those?"

It is my turn to gulp. "Well, I bought mine up north."

"San Francisco?"

Does my face look as hot as it feels? "No. At the West Coast Women's Music Festival." Will she grasp that hint?

Her eyes register no recognition. "Oh. Do you think I can get one somewhere around here?"

"Sisterhood Bookstore carries them," I hear myself answer.

"Great. That's near the campus. Maybe I'll stop by soon. Are they always this plain?"

At that, I grin, remembering her taste in jewelry. "No. Some have gems — usually amethysts — embedded either on the handle or on the blades."

Will she ever realize the significance of the purple stones? I am amazed how ignorant heterosexuals are of our culture while we know everything about theirs. Noting her blank look, I recall how none of my white co-workers ever question the tiny Mexican flags which adorn my office calendar. Until today, no one has ever wondered about my labrys either. My cultural symbols — clues to my identity — are ignored. No wonder I often feel invisible.

I try to maintain a stoic expression. I have to get back to my office, but do not want to rush out.

She puts down the stack and watches me. "Well, gee — thanks for telling me about — what's it called again?"

With a smile, I meet her gaze once more. "A labrys. Good luck finding one."

I walk away without turning back.

Mary Russo Demetrick

BONES

She told me of paleontologists who removed them from the ground delicately with brushes and small fine dental instruments. Each bone lifted from its place, hidden from time and living human eyes. Some of the paleontologists were women, I guessed. The article, she told me, elaborates in detail — brave and savage men kept the tribes alive, stalking animals whose paws shook the earth when they fled in the chase. Men who risked everything, even the lives of their women and children for the hunt. Men who were our ancestors. Men.

Where were the women? I wondered if women never hunted, simply kept fires burning for other's needs. If women never hunted, why then Diana, goddess of the hunt? But the article mentions no women. Later, as an afterthought, written as a postscript for the reader's benefit: "Most of the bones were female."

I grieve for my sisters. We are lost even when we are found. We are overlooked even when we are visible. We are ignored even if we saved our children from annihilation. We are invisible even when ancient cultures are unearthed. How many of us have been lost through oversight?

We who tend keep tribes and families alive, we who carry babies on our backs into rice fields, we who journey on ships vomiting and pregnant to give freedom to our children, we who deliver our sisters of those babies and help to abort them because of hunger, we who pick cotton, tend others' babies, raped and treated like cattle, we who are called whore and slut or worse because we refuse to believe what they tell us, we who try to maintain order while the powerful plot our demise, we who refuse whatever we refuse and are lost because of it.

What of the women who helped to unearth their sisters' bones? Did they feel connection, certainty that the earth holds the key to our past? Were they able to feel oneness with each fragment, a wholeness from the simplest scrap, reconstruct lives and vision, faces of hope, of strength, of possibility?

All of my bones are female. And I keep no fire burning or food simmering for returning men with hungers. Will I be lost among the bones like my sisters? Will I be found by men, and tossed aside into the pile marked "unidentified," "marginal," or "unknown"?

All of my bones are female as are all of the bones of those I love.

Kathryn Eberly

WHAT HAPPENED

Was that my friend Esperanza got pulled over for speeding and she was driving her little blue Honda with the dent in the left fender seventy miles per hour on a steep hill and over the bump and she got caught. I was scared shitless as she kept on yelling, prick, prick, prick in that accent of hers, prick, as the cop approached and she rolled down her window saying hello officer and not very polite either. Well, she got a fifty dollar ticket and the cop ran a check on her and he found eight hundred dollars worth of unpaid fines so he impounded the car and we took the number 24 bus home. She was pissed off but it all ended up OK meaning she got the car back. Of course she had to appear in court and came out of it with 200 hours of community service and a stern talking to. She kept right on parking in those red zones. Also, Esperanza had a handicapped parking sticker and she used that sometimes. I was so embarrassed but I went along with it. She could make me laugh so hard I'd practically bust a gut but she scared me too with her outbursts or when we did those U-turns or a sudden screech to a stop. Much later when I found out I couldn't possibly imagine it, her death, I mean. No, it wasn't a car crash, she took the pills and it wasn't by accident. Everyone was so shocked because Esie was so funny all the time but she was illegal too. You know, no one ever mentioned how terrified she must have been about getting deported especially her being a dyke and all.

Carol Edelstein

BREAKFAST

I am sitting in my usual spot in *Petronella's* across from a blue-haired lady who must be new in this town. We have both ordered raisin toast. I can see Dickie putting down the four slices of bread with a little flourish. A few weeks ago Dickie bucked up his courage and said he wanted to take me out. I knew that meant out of *Petronella's* and into some other eating joint where we could both sit down. But I said, "Dickie, it's an offer I'll consider, but I'm not going to give you false hopes." In school, Dickie was kept back, twice. Each time, it shocked him, but not the rest of us.

Thank God I stalled and Dickie got the message. I've already had enough love trouble. The last one a married man who kept trying to fix things around my house until I got the real idea. He was nice enough but I don't want that on my conscience, and even now, you wouldn't believe how many near-useless appliances he left me with . . . it's one of the reasons I like to eat my toast out.

I never actually had to say anything, Dickie got the idea. Now I'm watching him work and I must say we are lucky to have our work. It is better this way. Simpler. He does his work and I do mine. I have a home knitting machine and I do a steady business. I like to design fancy sweaters for the outdoor types — with reindeer, snowflakes, whatever they pick from my swatchbook. But it's the plain baby stuff that always sells. Winter and summer, you can depend on booties.

My two boys had lime-green booties — not ones I made myself. I was busy accompanying Petronella's dance classes back then — she had the world's most rotten piano, but with the soft pedal you could do alright. That was, of course, before Petronella had opened *Petronella's*. It was good — her moving from ballet and tap into flapjacks and eggs — even though naturally I lost my job. But those classes — her girls were getting filled with false hopes — it was breaking my heart.

There's more to it than the tu-tu and the toe-shoes, but before I caught onto it I myself wanted to be a ballerina. My gram had given me for my ninth birthday a black lacquered jewel box lined with red velvet. Inside was the dancing girl who sprung up and twirled the instant you lifted the lid. She was so fast — I tried to catch her lying down, but never did.

Funny how a thing like that can get you on the wrong track. There was the city, that good-for-nothing Edwin Currie . . . well, he wasn't all bad . . . he gave me the babies. I came back when Daniel, my youngest, was three months. The boys turned out 50-50 — that's another story.

I'll say one thing for Petronella — she runs a tight ship. The salt-shakers are always full, the ashtrays are always empty. The brass unicorn which gallops across the register, she herself shines it with a special rag.

Dickie is bringing over our toast on heavy, beige platters. He knows I like marmalade and has given me a double dose. He knows I like to lay it on thick.

"Dickie," I say, "aren't you going to introduce me to your friend over here?" I give Miss Blue a wink. Dickie looks puzzled and sets down the plates with two clicks. Miss Blue is turning red. She's shy, maybe. But I'll find out about her.

"Not my friend," says Dickie, and turns about. I notice he's got mustard on his back pocket. That's another good reason for putting off romance — he's not a classy guy.

"Well," I say, calling him back over, "let *me* introduce *you*, then." I make Miss Blue tell me her name (Stella) and do it all proper. Then I eat my toast, and tell her the previous story, and a few other things you ought to know about this town if you're new. Dickie has gone back to the grill and that is that for three-way conversation.

What I did not mention yet as my Gram always said hold back on the important parts until you are sure the party is listening and now I think I have you, is — I've changed my mind about living. That is, yes, I think I'll go on doing it. Sometimes just the taste of marmalade can keep me here.

36

Jyl Lynn Felman

WAITING

As I knock on their door, I know with sudden clarity, that I am not prepared for what is on the other side. I want to run back to the elevator, have breakfast alone with myself. My own good health, my abundant relationship with the world terrifies me as I hear my father walk towards the door.

She is lying down, propped up on three pillows with the blankets pulled all the way to her chin; she has no neck. My mother's eyes are closed; her face is tight with the Parkinson's mask, and her arms — without motion — are buried somewhere inside the covers. "I am so cold," she says, in a voice that is not hers, and that I barely hear above the news.

This morning my father is handsome; dressed in a suit, clean, fresh shaven, rugged full of color the red of life. He stands in front of the TV, listening to the morning news. "Here's something for you." He hands me the paper.

I sit down to read the headlines. I sit down, open the paper then realize what I have just done. Closed them both out.

"I am so cold, can you get me another blanket?" I think she is dying. I put the paper down, fold it back as though it was never opened and wait. Then I remember — the medicine has not yet begun to take. It is only 9:10, and it takes at least twenty minutes to work.

"When did you take the pill?"

"9:00."

I stand up to turn the volume down; I can't stand the noise and feel sure it is blocking the medication from taking. I am enraged that he has the TV on. Why can't he sit with her, hold her in his arms until the pill takes? But he can't, not this morning. I remind myself that I started to read the paper. It's almost twenty past. Soon, she'll sit up, we'll be alone; she will be the mother and I, the daughter.

"Yesterday, I had to send the food back, the medicine didn't take, and I couldn't even answer the door," she says in a whisper.

We don't answer her; we don't even look at each other. We act like she is not talking to us; who is she talking to? He's ready to leave for his meeting; I hug him.

Does he kiss her goodbye? I feel sure I would remember, if he bent his head to her face on top of three pillows, kissing her while she waits for the medicine to work. As though his single kiss to her heart could start the medicine running life through her blood. Today he does not kiss her goodbye.

37

I wait.

It is 9:30, the food arrives, she begins to sit up. How will she get to the table that has just been rolled into the room; how she will eat; what will she drink? I can't remember if I called back room service to order decaffeinated coffee. There are two pots on the table. One of them has a red ribbon on the handle. "The ribbon is the decaf," the waiter says, closing the door. I look for the milk.

Then she starts to move for the first time since I knocked on the door, thirty minutes ago. In her movement, I am exhausted. There is no room for illness and health to coexist; there is only illness.

---

from a longer work entitled "Private Rituals: A Prose Meditation in Five Stories"

Thaisa Frank

POLAND

Her husband died suddenly of a heart-attack right in the middle of writing a poem. He was only thirty-eight, at the height of his powers — and people felt he had a great deal more to give, not just through his poetry but through the way he lived his life. His second wife, who was nearly ten years younger, found the poem half-finished, moments after he died, and put it in her pocket for safe-keeping. She'd never liked his poetry, nor did she like the poem, but she read it again and again, as if it would explain something. The poem was about Poland. It was about how he kept seeing Poland in the rearview mirror of his car, and how the country kept following him wherever he went. It was about fugitives hiding in barns, people eating ice for bread. Her husband had never been to Poland. His parents had come from Germany, just before World War II, and she had no sense that Poland meant anything to him. This made the poem more elusive, and its elusiveness made her sure that it contained something important.

Whenever she read the poem, she breathed Poland's air, walked through its fields, worried about people hiding in barns. And whenever she read it she felt remorse — the kind you feel when someone has died and you realize that you've never paid them enough attention. She thought of the times she'd listened to her husband with half an ear and of the times he

38

asked where he put his glasses and car keys and she hadn't helped him look. After awhile, she began to have similar feelings about Poland — a country she'd never paid attention to. She studied its maps, went to Polish movies. The country was on her mind, like a small, subliminal itch.

One day when she was driving on a backcountry road, she looked in her rearview mirror and saw Poland in back of her. It was snowy and dark, the Poland of her husband's poem. She made turns, went down other roads, and still it was there, a country she could walk to. It was all she could do to keep from going there, and when she came home she mailed the poem to her husband's first wife, explaining it was the last thing he'd ever written and maybe she'd like to have it. It was a risky thing to do — neither liked the other — and in a matter of days she got a call from the woman who said: *Why are you doing this to me? Why in God's name don't you let me leave him behind?* There was static on the line, a great subterranean undertow, and soon both women were pulled there, walking in the country of Poland. He was there, too, always in the distance, and the first wife, sensing this, said, "Well I think he can just go to hell." She said this almost pleasantly, not as a sentiment of malice, and the second wife, understanding completely, answered: "I agree. It's the only way."

Judy Freespirit

THREE MEMORIES OF A JEWISH GIRLHOOD

I.

I am four years old and we are living behind my parent's used furniture store in Detroit. It is Halloween and my mother has bought me a costume. It is an Irish girl costume, a green and white dress with green shamrocks on the white part. She puts make-up on me, rouge and lipstick. She combs and curls my hair so it looks like Shirley Temple's and puts a big green bow in it. I'm not sure I like the dress. It is one of those shiny dime store dresses with stiff material and it scratches. My mother takes me around to all the shops in the neighborhood and the store owners give me candy and gum and pennies. Each man and woman at each store tells me how pretty I look, and what a beautiful red headed Irish girl I am. I decide I want to be Irish all the time.

II.

I am nine years old and at summer camp. Each Sunday there are church services for the Catholic and Protestant children. The Jewish children have a choice to either go to one or the other service or to stay in the cabin till services are over. Usually I stay in the cabin, but I am feeling lonely and don't want to be left out. Besides I am curious so I decided to go with my friend to the Protestant service.

The minister has brought a felt board and felt cut-out pictures which he uses to illustrate the story he is telling. It is the story of The Good Samaritan. I am sitting on the bench with the other girls, pretending I belong there, trying to look like I understand what is happening. He tells the story about the man, a Jew, who is on the highway and gets robbed by a group of thieves. The man is injured and penniless and needs help. Other Jews come by and he asks for their help, but none of them will help him.

Each time the minister says the word "Jew" he emphasizes it as if it were a swear word. "The 'Jews' would not help the poor man," he tells us. "The 'Jews' just left him on the road. Then a Samaritan came along and although he was a poor man and didn't have much he did not hesitate to help the poor injured man."

When the story is over it is clear to all the children in the camp lodge that Jews are selfish and do not help someone in need. I try very hard not to show my embarrassment. When we get back to the cabin I give away all my candy and gum to the other girls.

III.

I am ten years old and at summer camp. On the first day I am in a line with my cabinmates. We are waiting to eat lunch in the mess hall. The girl next to me asks me which church services I go to and I tell her I don't go to any because I'm Jewish. Suddenly she is enraged. "A Jew!" she shouts at me, "you dirty Jew."

I don't understand what is happening.

"The priest told me all about you," she screams at me, "you killed Christ!"

"No, I didn't kill anybody," I say, in tears. "Honest, I didn't kill him."

"Yes you did," she shouts, "priests don't lie."

I am horrified. I'm not prepared for this. Nobody ever accused me of killing Christ or anyone else before.

That afternoon, during rest period, I write a letter to my parents telling them I changed my mind and I don't want to stay at camp. I hate it and I want to come home. I want them to pick me up as soon as possible.

A week later my parents show up at the camp and the head counselor calls me to her office. "Your parents are here to take you home," she tells me.

"But I don't want to go home," I say, "I'm having a good time."

My mother is angry. "We rushed right up here for you as soon as we got your letter," she says.

"What letter?" I ask.

"The one saying you want to come home," she says.

Then I remember. "Oh," I say, "I remember now. I wrote it when Kathy O'Shea told me I had killed Christ and I felt bad. But she never said it again and everything's OK. I want to stay."

My parents return home without me. I no longer want to be an Irish girl.

FELINE FABLE

She would never have known that it was going to happen except that KitKat was acting very strangely. KitKat had a history of unusual behavior for several days before some natural disaster was about to happen. Her striped cat fur would stand up on end, especially the hairs behind her head. And her tail would arch and wiggle more often than usual. She had a kind of wild look in her eyes as she skittishly raced back and forth through the apartment, jumping first onto the armchair, then to the floor then up onto the couch, back down to the floor and quickly out of the livingroom. She dashed down the hall and into the bedroom where at another time she would have curled up just below the pillows at the head of the bed. This time she just kept moving, jumping down as quickly as she had jumped up.

So the woman knew something was going to happen. But what? And what could she do about it anyway? She was too busy trying to get her new fall wardrobe together. Her job was draining her. Her friends were needing much more of her time and attention than she wanted to give and she was tired. She was worried, too, about how she was going to make it through till next payday.

While the woman noted KitKat's behavior, she quickly pushed it out of her mind. Whatever was bothering KitKat would work itself out eventually. So when it finally happened, the woman wasn't really surprised.

"I knew something was up," she said as the building began to rock.

"What a smart cat," she grinned as the dishes and knicknacks began hitting the floor.

"I should pay more attention," she mused as the house slipped off

41

its foundation.

"What a mess," she grumbled, as plaster fell all around and covered her clothing with fine white dust.

"I wonder where that KitKat is," she thought just as the ceiling beams came crashing down.

But of course KitKat had left long ago. That cat's no fool.

Sophie Freud

THE RESCUE

I am a well known lady professor which means that I am forever traveling to different places to share whatever wisdom I may have. So far I have not been too nervous about the wisdom part, although the day on which I shall not have a single new idea is fast approaching. Yet these constant travels are not without stress because mishaps frequently occur. Each time I decide to be for all future times on guard about a particular matter but then a new misadventure arises which I had not yet foreseen. There was the occasion I mailed a big pile of letters at the last minute, before a long trip to Europe, and the airplane tickets also got into the mailbox. I never did that again. Then once I accidentally put my tickets in my suitcase, instead of my purse, and could not find them when checking in at the airport. This incident happened right after I had fallen down on an electric staircase, in the huge Frankfurt airport, and was only rescued after the stairs had eaten up my very best skirt and slip and mangled one shoe. After that I never again pushed a cart up electric stairs. I should not even mention the time I realized in the airplane on the way to an important conference that I had forgotten my glasses at home, because, luckily, they had just started to sell magnifying glasses in drugstores. Once I left the paper I was to deliver at home, but was able to reach my husband and there was time enough for him to read the entire paper to me over the telephone. It cost us $67.76 on daytime long distance rates.

I was determined not to let anything happen on my last trip. It was a two-week travel through Germany to promote my new book. I was scheduled to leave on Thursday afternoon, right after teaching my last class of the week, and was due to arrive in Berlin early the next afternoon, with just enough time for a brief rest before participating in a TV panel discussion which had received much advance publicity.

The evening before had been very busy. My daughter and I had one of our big telephone fights. The timing couldn't have been worse and while we talked, I tried to water the plants and wash the kitchen floor. I try to clean my house and get everything in good order before I leave, since I don't like to come back to a messy or dirty house. Then I called my friend who is my packing consultant, for help with those endless decisions that need to be made. As usual, we discussed possible weather conditions and the formal and informal dressing occasions that I would be facing. Someday I would like to leave for a trip without a late last night, but that never seems to happen. This time I stayed up very late to prepare my next day's classes. Still, things were going well. A friendly colleague took me to the airport about an hour early and I had the kind of itch on my shoulders I get when I am ready to grow wings of self-satisfaction.

As I stood in line to check my baggage, I heard the word passport being mentioned and . . . I realized that I had forgotten my passport at home, located in a suburb that was a forty-five minute drive from the airport. My mouth became completely dry. I explained my predicament to the ticket officer who suggested casually that I would need to postpone my departure until the next day.

I called a neighbor and told her where the passport was, and begged her to bring it to the airport. She agreed with a reluctant voice. When I called her back fifteen minutes later to make sure that she was on her way, I was aghast to find her still at home. She explained that my ex-husband had been at my home, in the process of moving out the last of his things. He had insisted on bringing me the passport himself. For the last forty years this man had obviously had many opportunities to rescue me. I think it was what he enjoyed most about our marriage. Eventually it may even have been the only thing he enjoyed. I would have preferred not to be rescued one more, presumably last, time. I waited for him to come. It seemed like an endless wait. Meanwhile, I missed my plane to New York, but there was, after all, hope of a later plane that would still arrive in time to connect with the plane to Berlin. Then he arrived with the passport, and I said: "It took you so long" which I should never have said. "It took me only thirty-five minutes," he replied. As soon as I got to Berlin, because I did get there, I wrote him a card of apology. When I got back to Boston, I heard that my ex-husband had told my angry daughter that I had said something awful, even though he had only taken thirty-five minutes to get to the airport. I wrote him a second letter of apology, acknowledging the record time in which he had made the trip. Then I went for a walk with that same neighbor and she told me that my husband had repeated to her what I had said. She reported saying to him that he should have thrown the passport at me, and he agreed. After that conversation I wrote him a third letter of apology. At least I shall never again forget my passport. But perhaps it is high time that I start to slay my own dragons.

Carolyn Gage

THE RED SHOES

I can't write fast enough or hot enough to tell you what I saw when I picked up this woman . . . no, *not* woman, girl, Girl. She was hitchhiking in the rain, on a bridge, in a pair of red high heel shoes. And she got in my car, and told me to take her to Grand Avenue, where she was going to wait by the Sears building for some man to pick her up and screw her, or ask for a blow job, or a hand job, or whatever else he could think of and pay for. And I didn't know what the hell else to do, but give her a ride where she could go to work, to get the money, to pay for the baby she had, which she might not have had at all, but told me to make me think kindly, which was *so* unnecessary, because I thought she was lovely. She was maybe sixteen, bad skin, ashamed of it, asked if I had any make-up . . . No. I don't. Don't wear much. You see, I don't give a damn what men think of me. And even when I did, they didn't anyway, as you will grow to see, if you don't already, but try to believe anyway. I mean, I just can't write fast or hot enough to tell you about this . . . this *girl* in my car, who I am taking to a nice convenient spot where some man can buy her. I mean, those shoes are the part I want to write about. They were not just red. They glowed in the dark. They were radioactive. She was contaminated. And my car was hot. Her heart must have been a nuclear reactor, where some reaction had gone out of control.

Sue Gambill

IN MOTION

There was this gradual distance which appeared between the lovers. First there wasn't as much kissing. Then the casual touching that had graced their conversations disappeared. They began to fall into sleep without making love. And sometime later they always fell into sleep in separate beds in separate homes. This probably happened over a period of months though they really can't quite remember.

At this stage in their relating the telephone serves the only satisfying means of communication because it is not visible. In this way the one lover is being like people who do not like their photographs taken because they believe the image will capture and carry off their souls. This lover says, I don't like that you showed my photograph and told people we are lovers. The other one says, you are an important person in my life and that is what I tell them.

Both lovers have always spoken often about non-monogamy. Both lovers have successfully lived quite independently of each other. Most people would probably not even call them lovers.

The one lover says often, I will always live alone. I will never have much time for any one person. My work is my priority. She says these things often. She is the one who says, I am pulling back. The other lover says, deep love is possible without possession.

Both lovers are very passionate about freedom. If they could paint the feeling it would be the shifting blue of a twilight sky with grey gulls floating between land and sea; it would be the hot and sensual sound of Miles Davis blasting in a fast moving car, cruising across the continent with no particular destination.

One of the lovers had lived for a period of time in a very small town where the people live passionately and intensely, and, at the same time, you could die in your room and no one would look for you. It was the ultimate in self-responsibility. She says, it was here I learned that love has wings.

The one who is pulling away says, I don't know if I can trust this language. She says, I don't know what is beyond this point. She begins sometimes to say nothing.

The lovers always had said they would love like Lillian and Dash, years without possession. And always they had said, if opportunity came to one of them, in a motion independent of the other, that freedom would fly like a single black bird fast against the sky. They could not plan their lives in unison, it was foreign to their nature.

And so it happened. One day one of them moved away to another state and one of them did not. It was a new thing. The lovers now were not lovers because they had stopped sleeping together and now they never made love and even now they lived in two different states. But sometimes love filled a chest with yearning, sometimes it crept in shadows of unresolved anger, sometimes it tore a heart against the tremendous night sky, sometimes it rushed in with sudden pleasant memory. Always love was in motion.

And so the lovers began to learn that love was expansive and multifarious and, of course, did not have to look like the images from a TV

45

screen. Finally they did not have to say lovers, like a possession. Instead they said love, like a verb.

If The Sky Could Tell Stories and the Ocean Could Sing

Slowly Alexandra unbuttons her blue denim shirt, her eyes like a magnet holding me. She pulls back the sides of the denim and for the first time I see the small rise of her breasts, the nipples deep brown and large. She smiles her wide, familiar grin and lets the shirt drop back off of her shoulders. I want to reach across the space between us, to cup my palms around her smoothness. I want to lean forward and place my tongue lightly along her skin, to take her nipple full into my mouth and suck between us. But I wait because timing between us has always been crucial.

Alexandra reaches for her shorts and pulls them down the length of her legs. Stepping out she tosses them to the side, and then reaches for the elastic band of her bright red underpants and pulls them down. Her pubic hair is jet black, like the thick hair under her arms. She smiles and steps under the shower, the water glistening her skin satin. I join her, still not quite ready to bridge this final distance.

Then she leans, oh so slightly, back against my chest, and lightly I wrap my arms around her, placing my open palms onto her thin brown stomach. She lays her head back against me and we both breathe out deep sighs, like we'd been holding our breath for sometime.

Alexandra turns, her deep black eyes seeking my own, and here is the sensation sharp and sweet in my stomach, of falling, falling into her eyes. They say, falling in love. They probably mean how it feels when the eyes are open like this, the spirit cast free of closure.

Then our lips touch, like the feel of mango, and my stomach builds hot fire in every direction. For months now I've wanted to touch these lips that are touching me. These teeth against my skin. This tongue that circles and enters and tastes hungrily along my cheek.

But, really, that is not how it happened.

We are swimming in the Gulf, Alexandra and I and some friends. I am very happy with these people who have invited me into the long history of their friendships. Pleasure rides in my stomach and chest like the warm water that swells about us with the incoming tide.

The friends swim off in search of the sandbar now covered with

46

water. Alexandra and I continue floating, revealing new intimacies with stories of our lives. Our hands touch briefly under the water, our legs momentarily brush in the silky smoothness of the Gulf, like fish darting past our skin.

Alexandra tells me she doesn't believe in naming someone gay or straight. She says maybe relationships never last forever. She explains how her male lover is moving out soon because she needs space for her own inner self.

I want to kiss her. But I'm not really sure how she feels. Later, when she steps out of the shower dripping wet, my breath leaps inside my chest. Is her smile in pleasure of my pleasure? I don't know. We haven't spoken of these things.

She seems to feel the way I do. But maybe for her the stories are not even intimacies. Maybe she tells the same stories to everyone. Maybe she makes them up, only for what I wish to hear. Maybe she floated beside me only because she was too tired to swim off with our friends. I won't know these things unless I ask her. And, yet, I do know.

Over dinner we all talk easily and laugh readily, eating for hours as the tables around us empty out and fill up again. It's nearly midnight when the waitress finally says they're ready to close up. I look across the table and see Alexandra looking at me, her eyes steady and sure.

When we say goodnight she places her lips on my cheek, very, very close to my lips, and kisses me. Then, with arms still wrapped about, we look into each other's eyes and let silence be our guide. I want to kiss her lips. But I wait, because timing is everything.

Maybe we never will. I know we will. But maybe we won't.

Or maybe we will.

Ellen Gruber Garvey

COLLECTED SPEECHES

I.
From the stone balcony overlooking the park skating rink, where anyone might stand to call to a friend, she mutters and watches skaters swing

around or cling to the guardrail. Pigeons poke along the stones as she calls down what she has to say: "I know I'm no saint, but it takes two to break up a friendship." No one looks up. "I'll meet you at three o'clock then." She stubs out her cigarette and walks on.

II.

The coffee shop is named "Amity." The straws are wrapped in white paper stamped "Sweetheart." I've come alone. Another woman alone is leaving her table as I get there. Her plate has the remainders of the meatloaf special, the cheapest meal on the menu. I push her plate away and order the same.

The customer at the counter has draped her furs over her shoulders and holds a poised, witty conversation with her reflection in the pie case. Her hand, extended part way across the counter, intimately brushes a phantom arm. She orders more coffee, lifts her eyes, and murmurs over the rim of the cup. In ambience borrowed from the Muzak, she talks quietly over drinks in a smoky nightclub, luxuriating in regret. Her cigarette smoke drifts past the napkin dispenser.

III.

Lunchtime is a time of transformation. Two pieces of bread with tuna inside them suddenly become worth $3.50 and a ten-minute wait. A spot sitting in the sun on the pavement is worth running to be the first to get to it. Office elevators reverse their early morning direction and send the employed down to walk the streets.

Tables have been set out for lunch and civic improvement at the plaza near my office. A woman is talking animatedly at one of them. Only her portion of the table is visible from my pavement seat; the other is hidden by a pillar. I like her smile — its warmth, the pleasant wrinkles it makes around her eyes as she speaks or tilts her head, listening. I twist the stem of my apple for a wish: Let there be someone on the other side of her table, holding half of the conversation.

COMPOUND FRACTURE

I work for the city. You know what it means to work for the city. We all know what it means. I do something vague during the day. I shuffle papers. I pass them along to someone at the next desk, who sorts them, and then to the supervisor, who shuffles them and deals them out again.

"What do you do for a living?" my prospective landlady asked me. I told her I work for the city. "Ah," she nodded, and I turned into a gray spot in her eye, doing vague things all day with a good pension plan. I pass her candy store on a Wednesday afternoon and she remembers city workers get a lot of sick leave.

"No. That sick leave isn't covered, and you're not entitled to unemployment. You weren't employed as of June, so you aren't covered in the contract." Frieda Gilgul in personnel blinks behind her records. But I was just working, I put in the same work time as everyone else, don't I get the same benefits? "No," the chorus of the personnel department has memos and files in front of them. "She thinks she's entitled? No. She's not entitled. No. That's what it says. It's in the contract." But I was told — "No one ever said that to you. No. We never said that. Who told you? No. She didn't say that. She couldn't have said that, because you're not entitled. It's not one of your benefits." They crowd around the table. They reconstruct theory from the bare bones of the contract. The voices of my relatives, my aunts and cousins in city offices across the city, fly through the door and settle at the table. They must uphold the principles of working for the city. They must hold onto the scraps, take them home in their handbags, in their bellies.

Words rumbling along rocky paths. Words emerge in rock slides, grating rock on rock, speaking in gravelly voices. Nail on slate, words crack from the rocky bottom. Cracking and breaking, voices are mined, bones are excavated.

"No," says payroll. "It wasn't in the contract. There's nothing I can do about it. Do you want to speak with personnel?"

No I don't have to speak with personnel. I know what they sound like already. They have the voices of my dead aunts, buried under stones in Brooklyn, Long Island, and Zublutza. Their bones rise from under headstones, their heads rise in full voice, bones rattling, humming in their throats, teeth still in their heads. Their bones rise from the graveyard. They reconstitute themselves.

She stands, bones sway, the bones of her forefinger snap together: a miracle without cartilage. She wags her finger at me, shakes it in my face but the bones do not fall off: "Not entitled," she shakes her finger. "She's not entitled," says personnel as always, forever. "She thinks she's entitled. No, she's not entitled." That voice pours into me and chills me. It pushes outward; my clothes fray and tear, money drops through holes in my pockets. That voice is in my bones, shaking without the expected money, without my money. That voice is in me already, it speaks in my bones already. Now I hear it: it shakes my eardrums, rattling inside, hammering at me. External hammers play pattycake with internal hammers. Her bones merge with my bones.

I bought spareribs at the butcher shop. I drink your blood I chew your bones. "Do you want them whole or cracked?" said the butcher. "Crack them," I said. I wanted them cracked along the bone, splitting from slab to pieces — individual bones to be scattered, thrown, clattered, gnawed; flattened, sucked; chattered, clawed; grunted, broken hard against stones and teeth; demolished to reincarnate as rage transformed.

I have no money. I will have to become someone who remembers to put beans up to soak in time not to have to buy canned beans. Someone who washes out old plastic bags and hangs them inside out on a line in the kitchen. Someone who remembers to take them along to the store to get them filled with more dry beans.

I will learn to boil bones for soup.

DEMONSTRATION

Lynette and Pam bring their baby along to the demonstration. Everyone gathers to tweak toes, run a large finger along Sophia's tiny hands. The couple has told and retold the story of her engendering through artificial insemination. Many have heard it by now, but curiosity returns in waves of new acquaintances: where do babies come from? At last, a new answer: turkey baster or tea cup; charts, calendars, and vinegar douches. She's cut a couple of teeth now, and gurgles. "She says Dada," her mother's lover shrugs, apologetic. "All over the world men think babies are saying Dada for them. It's just what they say."

THEORY AND INACTION

The subway is full of noisy radios, dirt, a smoker in each car. My friends have all gone off to live in theories. I've gotten a seat; I read a theoretical article. Next to me is a seat on which something bright pink and sticky and disgusting has dropped, congealed milkshake or melted bubblegum. Each time someone is about to sit down, I look up from my theoretical article and point out the guck on the seat. I feel apologetic about it. I wish I had something with me to clean it up. I'm no help. A woman is about to take the seat; I'm almost too late to put my arm out to bar her from sitting back. I point. She opens her purse, pulls out tissues, spreads them on the mess. It's not enough. She perches on the edge of the seat; I go back to the article. I don't notice when she leaves. Soon, a couple, a woman and her boyfriend, rush for the empty seat from the other direction; I look up too late to warn them. She sits on top of the tissues, on whatever it is that's oozing through them, and settles in to spend the ride kissing her boyfriend. What would be the point of telling her now, interrupting her enjoyment before she gets up and finds those tissues sticking to her? I mark my place in the theoretical article on responsibility, and get off at the next stop.

Sally Miller Gearhart

DOWN IN THE VALLEY

"Deborah! God, I'm glad to get you! I called you right away. Ronnie's been shrieking ever since we got back from Canada. Can you hear her?" Linda held out the phone, then recradled it against her shoulder as she pulled off her Reeboks. "Ed's worn to a frazzle trying to get her to stop. Nothing will do."

"It's the trees."

"It's what?"

"The trees. Didn't you see the three-mile strip by the highway? All the oak trees uprooted and the stumps burning. Cal-Trans. Widening the road."

"We saw it. Pretty awful, even in twilight. But what's that —"

"Every kid in the valley is shrieking, Linda. Every one not yet two years old, that is. Some as old as twenty-eight months. Won't stop crying. Won't say why. They just bawl. They've been doing it all week, making themselves sick with screaming. Ever since the bulldozers started. All the mothers I know with infants have taken them out of the area. Down to the City. Or to the coast. That apparently calms them."

"You mean they're affected —"

"Velma Hartman's baby died. Just after they got her to Children's in the City. The little thing had finally stopped crying but it was too late. She had literally exhausted all her physical strength. The whole valley's up in arms. There've been meetings."

Linda looked up as a haggard figure lurched through the door, bouncing a yowling bundle. She put her hand on the receiver. "Ed, take her back down. I'm finding out from Deborah." Ed rolled his eyes and obediently disappeared again.

"Deborah? Are you there? Let me get this straight. Well first, how do you know it's the trees?"

"Just get Ronnie away from here. See for yourself. If you both take her, you can bring Stan and Jeannie over here to stay with me. Just get out of this valley with Ronnie. At least for the rest of this week."

"Yes." Linda was dazed. "Good. Yes. I'll call you back." She hung up.

There was a light summer breeze nudging the curtains. It brought with it the smell of burning wood.

"More fire for the judgment." The thought rose out of nowhere and raced by the edge of her consciousness. For no reason at all that she could determine, she shuddered. Then she focused on the wailing below.

"Ed," she called, pushing her feet back into her Reeboks. "Get the kids back in the car. We're going to Marysville!"

Celia Gilbert

LONG DISTANCE

She's always calling. The trunk line extends like a tap root to my voice. Just a hello and her pulse rate slows. Griefs well up. Small victories told bead by bead. She did this even before speech. She rollicked on the billows of her sound, her tiny fist clutched round my finger. Feet waving, she punctuated important mysterious bulletins with waves of an arm. Little prisoner of the horizontal, how cheerfully she bore it then. Now, vertical, she strives to keep from falling back. She can't sleep. She calls round the country, wherever lights are on.

A HABITATION AND A NAME

When the doctor told her she had high blood pressure and explained how it eroded the walls of the veins and arteries she understood for the first time the architecture of the body, the rhythm of activity, the strength that passes into weakness. Somewhere a white marker of despair. The body moved into the mind. House is a heaven that falls like her house where the gutters, although repaired, still leaked and the paint peeled. Thought of bees and their hives, the tentative measurements of wasps, the dazzling strangeness of a bird's nest made from its own feathers, tiny hairs, stalks, fibres of hedgerows, mud and saliva that holds together long after the occupants have perished. These thoughts distracted her but gave no comfort.

VISITING DAY

The warden rules on time and space, on anti-worlds where I become alarmed, become my anti-self, sister to you and your confusions. I'm concealing a judgement on my person afraid it will go off. You point out the stories around us. You weigh me and I'm wanting. I'll never have your admiration. The territory's yours. You're a black hole growing denser in your cell with its snapshots and banners. Eros keep out! Lovers walk through keyholes anyway, you whisper. Lies form continually, crusting over fires, but when a child comes to visit tears scald. You've fucked a woman, fucked a man, hate everybody. How a guard's breasts differ from an inmate's despite their reaching out. Locks force words that settle into blows. There's no comfort like the comfort of kin though I've no pardon for you. Negative negative liberty. And barbed wire inches its *via dolorosa* along the walls.

Maria Noell Goldberg

SITTING IN THE DARK

My mother makes the Christmas fruitcakes in July. She doesn't let me help but I hang around, stealing bites of this and that when she's not looking. The counter is spread with things we never have at other times — bags of walnuts and chocolate chips, tiny glass jars filled with green and red candied cherries, real butter instead of margarine. There's even a jug of whiskey, towering like a giant over the stumpy bottles of beer.

It's funny to see my mother in shorts, with her gardening gloves sticking out of her back pocket, and be thinking about Christmas. I wonder if my father will come downstairs to open presents with us on Christmas morning, or if he'll stay in bed like he did last year. When dinner was ready, he lurched to the table in his underwear. His head dropped forward before my mother'd finished carving the turkey, then he fell asleep with his cheek resting on his plate.

My mother's halfway through the chopping and mixing when the last bit of sun shines through the window onto her face and neck. Her upper lip grows shiny and wet. She reaches for her beer and takes a sip, then holds the bottle against her forehead and rolls it back and forth above her eyebrows.

After the fruitcakes are baked, she'll wrap each one in cheese-cloth soaked in whiskey then line them up in the cupboard above the stove. They'll sit in the dark all summer. They'll still be there on the first day of school, on Halloween and even Thanksgiving. No one's allowed to open the door and look although my mother will sprinkle them with whiskey now and again, flicking her fingers like she does over clothes before ironing.

She pours the batter into loaf pans. There's a fruitcake for the mailman, one for the milkman, the Fuller brush man, and Father Bigliardi. My parents don't have any friends; I don't know why. Except for each other, there's no one else we give presents to. Nobody comes to our house at Christmas like they do next door at the Appleby's, climbing from their cars with presents piled high, then leaving with different boxes wrapped in the pink foil Mrs. Appleby says is her 'Christmas motif.' Gwennie Appleby is in my class at school but my mother says: stay clear of her. "A nosy Parker just like her mother," she whispers if Gwennie comes over to play, or stops by in the morning to walk with me to the bus.

My mother puts the fruitcakes in the oven. She leaves the empty jars and eggshells on the counter and takes a new bottle of beer into the living room. The sun has disappeared but she doesn't turn on the light. She sits on the couch and hands me a comic. She chews hard on her cuticle and holds a murder mystery close to her face. Together we turn the pages of our books and wait for Christmas.

LIFE IN TIBET

In the blackness of a subway train stalled under the East River, a woman tells a story. Her talk leaks into the dark out of secrets she's been keeping.

"I will tell you my life which is nothing much although I'm living it backwards." Her voice slices through the darkness, the sound as bright and welcome as a light.

"Some parents want a boy, others a girl, but all mine wanted was an adult. My parents were immigrants made peevish by a language they could borrow but never possess. 'In America,' they warned me, afraid I would shame them, 'you had better watch your foot.'

"To students selling magazine subscriptions, the climb to our apartment was worth the trip. My parents ordered everything—*Newsweek, Life, Farmers Today*. They poured over magazines targeted for Boy Scouts, movie fans, the owners of cars and pedigreed poodles. Memorized the table of contents and articles on carburetors and canine diseases. If they had enough words, they thought, people would understand them. They would feel safe, at home. They would be happy. 'Language is like money,' my parents cautioned. 'Without the right words, a person could go hungry.'

"For twenty years, I travelled around the world to places where English was an afterthought. I was happiest listening to words I couldn't understand. Early on, I discovered that's where the heart is hiding — on the other side of language. People reach toward each other with words and never meet. They lose hope. In foreign lands, I had no words and refused to get any. I made many friends.

"In the east, I collected prayer wheels and Thanka paintings, having a particular fondness for the persecuted beauty of Tibet. I rescued a wooden statue of the Dorje-Shakpa from a Chinese pawnshop and when I returned to America, found I was well known among Tibetan refugees.

"One stopped me on the street outside the laundromat and unrolled a painting on rice paper. A bald headed saint, majestic on the back of a purple dragon, was sailing high over the clouds and grinning. The refugee tucked the painting into my coat and held out his arms for my laundry.

"I took him to my apartment where I gave him tea, which he understood, and Oreos, which he rolled across the floor for the cat. His hair stood up like the bristles on a shoe brush and his skin was sooty, as if he had leaned too long over the smoke of a yak butter lamp.

"For some time now, we have had a life, although he speaks no English and I will not learn Tibetan. I have learned he loves noodles and will not travel, not even to the bodega, on a Tuesday or a Saturday. He knows the Christmas tree is for looking beautiful and should not be chopped to pieces and piled in a corner for the chickens and sheep we do not have."

In the darkness, a small bell rings. The echo hums up and down the subway car. The Tibetan, perhaps.

"Sometimes we sing together," she continues, "our rhymes

55

tumbling over each other like lovers in the night. We do not speak. It is like early childhood. There are no words, only life."

Susan Ruth Goldberg

HILDA AT FORTY-FIVE

Hilda found herself perennially surprised by the seeming rapidity of events — other people's events, anyhow. She secretly referred to the phenomenon as "other people's time," and laughed to herself with pleasure at how aptly she had turned the tired old verbal formula to her personal use. She felt a bit uneasy at following its implications too far — who (one might be led to wonder, for instance), should be allowed to use such an inherently xenophobic kind of phrase: the in-groupers, mocking themselves, or the outsiders, looking critically in? — and she veered off before she became mired in the question of where she stood, and, therefore, who she was. Who she was was the problem anyway; it always seems to end up there, she thought uncomfortably; when I wasn't thinking about that at all, she added angrily, still thinking about it, as she banged through the screen door and closed in on the stove. She poked a large spoon into the pot that sat on it. The cabbage soup she'd been cooking for hours had almost boiled out, beginning to burn the pot and having just now alerted her on a gust of breeze that had reached her in the garden where she was struggling with her recalcitrant lawn. The soup was a mess, vegetables ragged beyond recognition at the bottom, a black, acrid smell lurking angrily beneath them. Hilda swore and grappled the pot into the sink with a charred potholder and shot cold water into it. It steamed and hissed balefully at her.

Other people's lives seemed to be set on a much faster timer than hers. Did that mean she would outlive them? She played with that notion sometimes (as now, picking futilely with a fork at the flakes and sludge hopelessly drowned at the bottom of her handsome Le Creuset soup kettle), imagining that her own, slower metabolism, clicking peacefully along, was bringing her, with grace, in mysterious ways and with no temporal limits, to that place where she would emerge, without effort, into wholeness at last. She was ageless in this vision, but obviously — a nod of concession to reality — she was older each time she had it, since it was always in the future. She would arrive there in full-blown maturity, like a

56

great ship berthing, making the earlier, youthful arrivals of her friends and peers look insubstantial, showy. And they would marvel at her achievement — whatever it was to be — saying that they had always known she had it in her, that she had allowed it all to happen in the only true, the only right way — to ripen, gestate, mature — at this point Hilda often found herself uncomfortably reminded of an old lover who, having left her, had said, "Oh, Hilda takes so long to make a move, she'll still be around in a few years if I want her back." Brought up short by this, a particularly painful memory, she retreated now a few steps, casting about for the exact spot where she had cut herself adrift from profitable speculation and tilted off into pointless fantasy. For there was a difference. In this way she named the subtle shifts of her reverie to herself, judging herself harshly for one, dignifying the other as the imaginative exercise of reason. Or perhaps it was the reasonable exercise of imagination. Nothing was really coming together very well yet, she thought; but I am measuring by other people's time, she said severely to herself; not by my own time. Still things were not looking promising. The soup would not simmer reassuringly on the stove every evening for the next week, steeping and improving with age. The grass was probably not going to green up much, either, despite the bursting, burgeoning season, despite the yearly bowing in on schedule of other people's lawns.

She made a pot of coffee. She lost count of how many scoops she'd measured out and had to keep tasting it as she added water; thus she was able to let her mind slip, like a dropped stitch from a flashing needle, to slide off and away, and she thought about slow, majestic ships on the vast, open sea, and about how there might still be a great deal of time for them to glide along, sedately and solemnly, making their dignified, considered, triumphal way to shore.

Miriam Goodman

WRITING TEACHER'S STORY: FIRED

I'd like to stay, but I have to grade exams. Life doesn't hand you a niche. My father threw me out before I finished high school. It was a literary household. I was having my first love affair with William Hoag. My father drank a lot of Black Label. One day, he confronted me. "If you bring that boy here again," he said, "I'll throw you out." "Why don't you get out, you old buzzard?" I said. He hit me across the face and threw me out.

Then I had to get a job. I decided I'd better learn typing so I began to teach myself. I thought you were supposed never to look at the keys. I went for an interview. They asked, "Do you type, Miss Clark?" "Oh yes," I said. "Fine," they said. "Fill out this application; then we'd like you to take a typing test." I didn't know typing was tested, but I said sure. Well, I typed their sample and was careful not to look at the keys. They looked at the test and said, "It seems, Miss Clark, you type around 10 words a minute with mistakes."

Finally an industrial designer hired me. I was supposed to type form letters. There were people around me all day long, typing along clickety-clack, much faster than I, so I picked up my pace. At the end of the first day I had quite a nice stack of letters, so I put them in my purse. At home I saw they were full of mistakes so I threw them out.

Eventually, the boss called me into the office. "Miss Clark," he said, "your work is not good enough." I straightened my spine, looked him in the eye and said, "Mr. Lowey, if my typing isn't satisfactory, you should just go ahead and fire me. Go on. It's your right. Fire me." He said, "Now Miss Clark. We're not going to fire you, but you must do better."

Eventually, of course, they fired me and I began taking college courses at night. I got a job as a receptionist with Dumont through my brother and taught myself to type on the job. After a year, Channel 5 bought them out and fired everyone. From my father, I got good bones, but how far did that take me? Now I teach five courses at three different colleges and keep myself in butter.

THE HOUSEMATE'S STORY: VOODOO

I'm weird about symbols. I take everything at face value. It never occurs to me an author manipulates a reader — that people do it to other people to get a certain effect. When it comes to me that a story is symbolic, I pretty much have to throw the whole thing out. I'm just learning there's more than one way to tell a story. I couldn't tell it differently unless I bit my lips.

I always thought symbols were dishonest. If I could get past that, I'd probably be an artist — well, anyway, more productive. You see, I'm thinking this way and I didn't even speak to my mother today.

I read a book about this rich guy who saved everything he produced — even his nail pairings and his shit — and kept it in mason jars in his basement. I don't have any mason jars, but I do have this jar of belly button lint that I collected from Tom. We don't have sex that often, either one of us, and there are all those places you forget to wash.

Tom's so wordy. He'll never say yes or no. I'll say, "Do you want salad for dinner?" He'll say, "You know, I always liked the way you made your string beans." When it comes to his novel, he'll rewrite the first 20 pages over and over, paring it down until it makes absolutely no sense. He loves to use jargon and technical terms. 15 to 20 pages didn't make the least bit of sense. All of it was technical terms. It didn't even have a human name — all the guys had code names. There was rain at the airport, that's all I understood. Now he's being clever in another way. He makes sly references that only people in the know would get. This guy, his hero, goes into a bar for a glass of beer. Two guys at the bar — they have nothing to do with the story — start a little discussion, a little business going, and the two guys he's describing are characters from another person's book. I recognized them.

I told him, "You come off it or I'll take the belly button lint and make a voodoo doll." He didn't believe me. "If it's necessary," I said. He knows what I mean.

Joan Joffe Hall

LOTTERY

That woman's face looks blissed out.
Well, she's just won almost eight million in the lottery.
Look at that! Her daughter is home on spring break, she went and bought a dress she passed up on Monday because it was too expensive.
Does it say? Were they regular players?
No, she wasn't, he was; she said this time she'd just pick one up if she had time.
Oh, yeah, I see: she bought the five dollar kind because it was easier.
Well, there's a real home town feel about all this; the paper's certainly playing that up. They look like nice people.
Yes, they didn't have to scrape to buy that ticket; they had the five dollars right in their pockets.
Hey, plenty of people who can't afford five dollar tickets buy them, too.

Are you pissed because a poor family didn't win or because you didn't?

Me? I didn't even play.

But you said you were going to. Imagine pulling in $350,000 every March for the next nineteen years.

What would you do with it? I mean after the regular stuff you've always wanted, the private swimming pool and massages morning and night.

I'd quit.

What? What do you mean?

I wouldn't teach another term.

What would happen with your writing?

I might not write another word, either.

So you'd rather have money than immortality.

Well, if I could be sure of immortality . . . No, you have to be a rock to be sure of that.

Still, "The Rockies may tumble, Gibraltar may crumble . . ."

The thing is to have immortality without getting old.

I know, we could have ourselves frozen. Listen, this is really exciting. For ten years or so we'd travel around the world, but meanwhile we'd stash some of our money in a trust. Then at sixty-five or so we'd have ourselves frozen and when we were thawed out we'd still have money.

How long should we chill out?

I dunno. We'd have to figure that part out pretty carefully.

Maybe we'd miss all the fun that way — grandchildren growing up, whatever, and Rip Van Who? When we woke up we wouldn't know how to use any household gadgets.

We'd be lucky if there were households. Then we could go back to writing, people would listen to us.

Maybe. But maybe we'd be like Ishi — freaks. The last people alive who remembered the Brooklyn Bridge.

Phillips head screwdrivers, Schmoos.

Maybe we'd better take the money now, heaven can wait. Just look at her face.

60

Lisa Harris

SANDRA

This girl was golden. Her strawberry blonde hair hung ass-length, ringletted, and she led Danny Kalinski around with it. One overnight at my house, we crowded into the pink bathroom and listened to Lou Christy wail "Lightning striking again . . ." As we lit the ceremonial Winston and passed it hand to hand, the gray smoke circled upward out the open window. She talked in a voice as soft as the padding in her maximizing bra about what she and Danny did before practices. In the meadow past the football field underneath the shedding maples, Sandra spread her narrow legs wide open to let Danny in a little. "Just so he'd know I'm not a cocktease," she said in her silky voice and she gave a giggle. "I didn't think he could get so hard or that I'd want him. I let him in the rest of the way and now I'm not a virgin. I guess I'll have to wear my circle pin in the middle."

VEGETARIAN LOVE

All my life, I've been a shopper. Wegman's in the northeast, Kroeger's in the south, and I don't remember the name of the big chain in the midwest. Even as a little girl, my mother'd send me to the IGA with a list. The clerk would walk ahead of me reading it while I put the items in the metal shopping cart.

It wasn't until my mid-twenties that the process changed and my orientation toward food became obsessive. I was often broke, and for the first time in my life, I understood what hunger was. I began to experience food anxiety. Where was my next meal coming from? And when I was presented with food, I'd eat as much as I could, hoping to stave off the next hunger attack. I think especially of the years I lived in Wichita. My lover at the time was a musician and he had gotten a job playing for one of the university's fraternities. One night while he made music, I scoured the kitchen, loading boxes from the van with eggs, bags of peanuts and loaves of Wonderbread. I had always hated yolks, but that night when we got back to our place, I ate four fried eggs, yolks and all. And I learned that sometimes you embrace with passion the thing you used to hate. After a couple of months, I left him and began living by myself in a run-down yellow brick apartment house on McArthur Avenue. I had enough money to pay the rent or eat, so I bought a large olive green overcoat from Hal's Army Navy. It provided ample space for me to sew in pockets with reinforced hems. For every one thing I put in the cart, I put three in my pockets. I'd watch the other fools sorting coupons, counting food stamps, and feel proud of myself for being above both forms of what I viewed as charity. I stole. In the two years I did this, I never got caught.

By the time I moved to Charleston I didn't need to steal and my ethics prevented me from doing it for fun. But I no longer could just shop, so I developed a new approach to shopping. My primary focus became the vegetable section. I'd spend ten or fifteen minutes on carrot selection, carefully choosing either the thickest short ones or the thinnest long ones. I'd rejected the notion of hotdogs since I'd always found the idea of "meat" applied to genitalia offensive. And cucumbers were too big.

A friend of mine had suggested candles, and I had tried them, but one day I scared myself. When I sat down on the toilet, and looked into the soft cotton crotch of my underpants I saw red. I didn't have my period, and I couldn't understand why I was bleeding. Then I remembered the heat of my solitary passion the night before, and the red candles I had used to satisfy myself. I touched the red patch, and the smooth wax relaxed me. Temporarily, I switched to white candles, but the insipidness of the color interfered with my arousal.

It was then that I became interest in carrots. I knew I couldn't melt them. Besides there was something almost healthy about them. I experimented. I'd leave some at room temperature and put others in the crisper for when I needed to cool down.

My friend, Sarah, shopped with me sometimes and had observed the care with which I selected my orange tubers. She assumed I was a carrot connoisseur, so for a treat she bought me gourmet infant carrots. She told me just how long to cook them and suggested adding honey and butter. Not a bad idea since all I could do with those little fellas was eat them.

Another girlfriend of mine suggested I get a vibrator. She was worried about me since I didn't have a man. I told her I didn't need a vibrator. She thought I was a prude, unable to meet my sexual needs. I didn't bother to explain it to her.

HELD TOGETHER BY STRINGS

Red crab apple blossoms littered the curb and sidewalk, looking like discarded pistachio shells. I stared at them. It was their number that convinced me they were petals. I was waiting for Rick, the other driver, to return with the van so I could begin my work day. First stop, the Sheraton. Driving the "limo" to the airport and back wasn't difficult work, just monotonous. Sometimes I'd arrive and realize I didn't remember any of the drive. My preoccupation with my own thoughts disqualified me as a conscientious chauffeur.

Since I couldn't smoke in the van, I chainsmoked while I waited for Rick. I alternated between Kool filters and Camels. I carried Kleenex mini-packs in my back pants pocket. Between the cigarettes and the air pollution from the paper mill, my sinuses ran constantly. My friend, Maxine, asked me if I thought that was normal. I said, "Yeah. It's normal for me."

At night I sang in country-western bars, usually sitting in, trying to get work so I could give up this day job. I wore dark blue mascara and metallic blue eye-shadow. I'd waited a year, spent observing the customers and pictures from Tammy Wynette albums, before I'd gone in for the "do" and had my hair peroxided and permed. I didn't look like myself when it was done, but I hadn't felt like myself in years. It was almost a relief to have my appearance match my emotions.

Last night, I had a gig at Bubba's Barn in Jessup, sort of a modified quanset hut. I sat in with "Looking at Country," hoping they'd want to hire me. I liked singing in the band because when I stood in front of the crowd, they ignored me, and only listened to my voice. When I sang, "Our D-I-V-O-R-C-E becomes final today," I let the pain float out with the notes. Half the people in the room were divorced, and the other half probably would be before too long. When I was on stage, I didn't think about anything else, just matching my voice to someone else's melody.

Bubba was smart, and didn't serve any beer in bottles, only cans. It was a recent decision. He'd changed his policy after Big Jim and C.J. had gone after each other over Maxine. They'd struck their empty Miller bottles on the table to make weapons. C.J. still had stitches in his cheek connecting two pieces of flesh. It made me feel all the more that he wasn't human, as though all of him was held together by strings.

Bubba made me laugh. He wore heavy leather biker boots and green Dickey workpants. His fly was always half-zipped. No matter what season, he wore flannel shirts and smelled like dried sweat. During the summer, he put on his "jewelry to please the ladies"; live salamanders dangling from his ear lobes. "They'll hang on here forever if I let 'em," he'd say. But I knew they could only hold on for about eight hours. My granddaddy had shown me the same trick when I was a little girl. But it really impressed the Yankees who came through on Route 17 and stopped at Bubba's for bar-b-que and a beer.

OUR EYES GLOW SILVER

The colonial blue clapboard wraps the house. Trees drape the windows; the porch holds wood and birds' nests. Trees and porch tighten shadows, keeping windows dark. Inside where I sit a fire burns. I wear a pale blue Victorian sweater; ruffles line the v-neck collar and trim the sleeves. Outside, a stone walk leads to the door. Two people appear who mean to harm me. I remember what I know about vampires: They cannot harm you, unless you invite them in.

Cast in a spell, I move to the door and let the man and woman come. It is the woman who will hurt me. She is me at seventeen: thin, with hair long enough to sit on. She hands me a cat, predictably black, that bites my neck. Five tiny raised spots appear like the marks left by a TB test. Five purple drops of blood squint from the holes. In numerology, five is the number of change.

I tell Jeff what's happening. He's fixing a hole in the ceiling. He doesn't believe what I tell him is possible. I cover my neck with my hand. Blood drips on my clothes. I take them off. I lie on the floor on a U-Haul blanket. I leave the room to pee, my bladder the size of a make-up kit, packed tight for vacation.

On the toilet, I release linguine-length mucus with well-defined reptile heads, and remember the girl in Savannah, small and thin and white, huddled on a toilet looking back between her legs at whitish worms swinging. I hear her scream as I scream for Jeff. He looks on calmly, suggests I get paper towels and clean up the mess. I watch the mucus spawn shrimp and flying insects.

I go to the red wall phone and dial Linda in Atlanta. I tell her about the vampires, my bite, the mucus. The phone explodes in my hand and burns me, leaves ridges like a charcoal grill on hamburger. I go to my mother's grave and collect her long white hair. I wrap the burn and it heals. A man from Bell is home fixing the phone. He knows I am a vampire, but likes me. I call Linda and she astral projects to come to me, leaves her body in Atlanta to take the plane. We go to drink beer. We eat the cans and our eyes glow silver. She uses the pop top to cut the bite bigger, then stuffs the hole with garlic. No cure, just pain.

Sarah-Ruth arrives with the black cat. She has pulled its fang-like teeth. And I remember before she was born, I dreamt I bore a black cat instead of a child. Before I could nurse it, Jeff pulled its teeth. From drinking my milk, the cat became a person.

Sarah-Ruth cuts five holes in the cat's neck, rubs its blood with mine. The blood turns from purple to red and I am free.

ELECTRICITY

Zoe's lanky bones clanked under her skin. The sinew of her muscles, tight from exercise, made her body a belltower, her walking its carillon. She didn't like the noise she heard when she walked. The pitches and vibrations of her body pleased her only when she ran. Five miles a day: rain, wind, or snow. Electrical storms cancelled her jog, the one thing that did, because she knew about electricity and metal. She saw her bones as copper and brass, so she feared the lightning, seeking her out to ground itself, and in doing so killing her.

She could draw and paint without anything ringing, so she did that in the evenings at her desk, the kind people use for mechanical drawing. The tilt allowed her to rest her elbow. The elbow's position in turn diminished the movement, so the bones in her hands and fingers thlunked slightly, like the top two keys on a piano touched by a cat's paw. The sound of the hammer louder than the notes themselves.

Her pictures always began the same way, a pencil sketch on watercolor paper; the lines dribbled across like drool.

During the thunderstorm season, Zoe spent time inside alone. She ate lettuces and broccoli. She sat with pillows behind her in her wooden chair at the table, her right arm in her lap, feeding herself with her left. As soon as she heard the thunder, she turned out all the lights and went from room to room unplugging the computer, the toaster, the TV, its antennae, the clocks, the microwave, her blow dryer, the phone. Stopping the clocks gave her power, locking herself and the world in that minute.

Once she had forgotten to unplug the phone and at the height of the storm, it rang. Her bones' memory vibrated to other bells. So she had to answer it to stop the ringing. It was Stephen checking to see if she had bought the tickets for their trip to England, the country of bells. She told him that she had, but she hadn't. He had been there several years before, studying John Stuart Mill's theories at Oxford. When he drank dark beer it reminded him of Bitter, and the Bitter reminded him of the bells. He described the multiple ringings by retelling an old "Twilight Zone" where a man was sane until the bells' chiming drove him to commit insane acts which finally drove him to assert his individual will and climb the tower where he confronted the big bell. From the way Stephen told the story, it was clear to Zoe that the character had no plan, no weapon, and as a result was killed by the metal bell beating him against the grey stone walls of the tower. She had her plan intact: she would run.

Zoe imagined herself in England with the bells ringing her apart. The vibrations setting up an earthquake in her body that not even tight sinew could withstand.

She told Stephen she didn't like to talk on the phone during electrical storms, but that she'd call him soon. When she hung up she realized that she was going to have to end this one, before he got inside her and weakened her control.

Margo Hittleman

THE CAGE

I will share a story with you, a story that came into existence yesterday, a dream, a story that has existed for generations, a history.

The predominant image is the cage, a cage with yellow bars, large enough to hold a wild animal, or a full-grown man. I found it in the basement of my house. I never knew it was there. I always knew it was there. My grandfather was in the cage. Or at least, a man that I was fairly sure was my grandfather. You see, I couldn't be certain. My grandfather was also upstairs, a robust, healthy man who carried on all the usual day-to-day affairs of robust healthy men. We knew, or we thought we knew, that this robust man was an impostor, that he had come into our lives from somewhere outside. To avoid the confusion of two people being one, we put my grandfather into the basement cage.

So that's how he got there. How long he had been held here, in the dark, in captivity, I don't know. He had the look of the shipwrecked survivor found decades later by a world that in finding him remembered that he had been lost, remembered that they had initiated a search but that somehow the search had gotten side-tracked, obscured by the pressing matters of the world — dinner breakfast the leaky faucet the economy. He had the look of the forgotten prisoner, beaten, tortured, then in boredom left to choose to live or die as he would while his assailants returned to their poker game.

Even in the dark, he recognized me as soon as I reached the bottom of the stairs, pulling himself up on shaking legs, coming as close as the yellow bars would allow, his fingers groping, reaching. It took me slightly longer to recognize him, though I had always known it was he. An old man, made even older by deprivation, unshaven, a grey grizzly stubble covering half his face, scrabby, half-starved, filthy. It is the filth that I remember, urine, excrement, sweat — filth that only a caged man could have, filth to which only man among the animals would allow himself to

66

submit, filth that moves one at once to revulsion and to pity.

I let him out. After all, he was my grandfather. No one was home; they need never know. I helped him to clean himself; gave him food, a meal. And convinced him that it was necessary to return to the cage as the others returned home. I told him it was for his sake; if I told you it was really for mine would I diminish myself in your eyes? As the impostor delighted to remind us, we could never be sure who was who. Our uncertainty was his power. We didn't believe him and yet he might be right. So we waited for a way to know, knowing that it would never come.

When the others returned, I confronted them with our crime, with the horror of knowing that they knew as I did that we had known all along, that we had abandoned him even as the world had — for dinner breakfast the leaky faucet.

Here the story becomes unclear. I raged at the betrayal, at the horror — not so much of the cage, but of the filth and the cage. I lie, I did nothing. I said that we must let him out, that if we didn't we must bear the responsibility for our complicity in this crime. I lie, I said nothing. I didn't know for sure that the caged man was my grandfather. I lie.

I want to defend myself, my actions. I will tell you that the fear of knowing was too great in the harsh light of the livingroom. How can I admit that knowing, I allow the betrayal to continue? How can I admit my complicity in his caging? The others tell me that if I will just quiet down and set the table for dinner, the conflict will ebb as it always has, we will go on.

The story fades further. I made up this ending. The story has an ending, but I have forgotten it. I lie.

Joy Holland

FISHCAKES

Because I was a girl, and because I came home from school earlier than my brother, I had a part in the making of the fishcakes my dad sold in the shop.

Go and get the taties, said my Mam, and I took the washing up bowl from the sink outside to what used to be the coal shed until we got a gas fire. I reached into the dusty jute sacks, or later the thick layered paper sacks, and felt down for the knobbly tubers. Later I came to know those sacks all too well when I picked them up off the assembly line at the paper works and stacked them; there my hands learned to be their own mistresses, as my mother's had in all her years at the shirt factory, the cigarette factory, the bomb factory. Sometimes a bad potato came up in a pungent soggy gob. I piled the good ones into the bowl, scraped off the worst of the mud with my fingers and hefted them back to the sink.

We peeled wet, under cold running water. In winter, in the unheated kitchen, our hands were quickly numb. But this we took stoically, peeling the skin round and round with our knives, gouging out eyes, slicing the rest into three and tossing the crisp yellow flesh into two pressure cookers. All the while, the fish was hissing and bubbling on the stove, filling the house with the smell of boiled coley or ling.

Those were the times when my mother would lift back layers from the past, if I asked her and if she was in the mood. She would tell me about cousin Clarence, for instance. "Well he fell off a tree and scraped all the skin off his legs. You wouldn't think that could be so bad, would you? His mother put ointment on and she always said it had healed up too fast, I don't think that can be right, anyway he died of it. Septicemia, is that what you call it? It wouldn't happen nowadays."

Then there was the Time My Mother Nearly Died. "I came in from my bedroom — I'd been dreaming of something ooh I think I dreamt I was burning up — and I went in to my Mam and Dad and said 'Mam I'm burning all over.' They told me to go back to my bed but then after a bit they moved over to let me in. I lay down beside my dad and the second he felt me he jumped up out of bed. 'My God!' he said. He put his trousers on and went right for the doctor. I had a temperature of a hundred and three, it was pneumonia. I don't remember after that, I was delirious for days."

But best of all were the little scraps she would throw out to me about my father's family. Never anything very much, just a mysterious hint about something scandalous or a sigh and a remark about somebody who had died. Making anything of it was like trying to build up a potato again from the skin you had just peeled off. The flesh of it must be somewhere, but for now you had to just imagine the feelings that had been gouged out and tossed away. "She was nice, Joan," she would say, with that falling away in her voice, and then a little silence that meant regret, waste, something unfulfilled. This was the talented aunt I never met who was a draftswoman for Hawker Siddelely in the war, and who died of TB at twenty-six. Or "Poor Bob. Grandma was never the same again after that." That was Joan's brother, my uncle, killed at eighteen in an accident on the building site where he was working.

Soon though my Dad would come home from work and the intermittent stream of water from the tap would dry up, and so would my mother's stories. We put the taties on the stove, the pressure cookers hissed and rattled. Mum made our teas, then, peering into a big bowl, she picked every single bone out of the boiled fish.

Then Dad was in the kitchen, and I could hear him from the living-room pounding the potato and fish mixture with the tatie posher. He mixed in the herbs, a handful from a box, a shower of salt straight from the cylinder, and then squelched the lot through his hands to make sure no lumps were left in the paste. With two deft pats of his big, red swollen hands, like a huge baby's, he formed the mixture into round cakes which he piled in pyramids on three big plates.

My mother, with her lighter, quicker hands, that knitted and rubbed pastry dough and when I was younger had dressed and patted me into a smart little cake myself, spun the fishcakes into a plate piled with orange breadcrumbs, twirled and shaped and imprinted on each the marks of her square fingers.

Mary S. Holley

SMALL TALK ON A BIG DAY

"Lyn . . . over here," the young man waved.

"I really didn't come to eat," Lyn said as she sat down opposite him at the secluded booth in the back of the restaurant.

Jack leaned across the table. "So what happened?" he whispered.

"Not much." Lyn shrugged "The test was positive."

"You're not . . . ? 'mmm . . . you are," Jack decided. "You should have taken precautions."

"*You* shouldn't have taken advantage." Lyn giggled. "Shall we get married?"

"That's not one of my short term goals."

"Okay." Lyn became serious. "What could you contribute towards this pregnancy? I figure you owe me at least 50% of expenses. You make more money than I do, and half the responsibility is yours . . ."

"My money's tied up in investments. You know that," Jack protested.

"Well, thank God for other solutions," Lyn murmured.

"Hey . . ." Jack frowned. "You wouldn't have an abortion. Would you? You wouldn't do that to my baby?"

"Our baby," Lyn reminded him. "And, yes, I would do it . . . this

69

very afternoon, in fact. Insurance will cover the cost. Don't worry."

Lyn stood up abruptly and extended her hand.

"It's been fun, Jack," she said. "Thanks for . . . lunch and everything. Now, I simply have to run. Can't keep that doctor waiting."

Lyn pulled hastily away from his lingering grasp.

Unmoving, Jack watched her push her solitary way through the now-crowded restaurant and run outside into the bright light of day.

Tryna Hope

WHERE THERE'S SMOKE

The most lovely thing happened to me the other day. I'm waiting on the corner for the bus, you know, the one with the ad on the back for smoking the right cigarette, if you smoke. I'm watching all that black smoke coming out from underneath the back of the bus like an exclamation point to what I'm thinking about. Which is, how the heck can they keep advertising that stuff when it's so darned dangerous.

So there I am, waiting for the bus and obviously the wrong one came or else I wouldn't know so much about the back of it. And I'm looking at this ad and at the model with the blond hair which looks like it was straightened. I'm thinking, I didn't know they did that any more, and the model, she's looking right into my eyes, when for goodness sakes, she winks. I'm not kidding. Right at me. So I smile and wink back.

She throws down the cigarette and climbs out of the ad. She's dressed in this flimsy black dress and I'm glad it's not cold out or she'd have frozen herself. Then she kind of wafts over to me. By now, all the people at the bus stop are looking at us. So I know it's real for them too, and not a hallucination.

She asks me for a ride, which is funny because if I had a car, why would I be waiting for a bus? But I think, what the heck, if this woman can walk out of an ad, maybe I've got a car. So I check my pockets and sure enough, a car key. I know it's a car key because it's got that black rubbery thing on it and it says "Subaru." The ad-woman points and there is the car, right behind me. It's green, not a color I'd have picked. But I don't complain. At least it's got a sun-roof. In we climb and off we go, just North and West. We laugh a lot and talk about Wisconsin and the Finger Lakes.

70

If they're not there, who cares. We'll find something just as nice so thank you very much.

Roberta B. Jacobson

COLLECTIONS

I collect owls. There, I've said it. Don't laugh. I have 318 of them. All female. Miniatures, statues, wickers, candles, postcards, clay figures, banks and wall posters. I find them at garage sales, curio shops and street vendors. And I receive quite a few as gifts ("It's her birthday again. Let's get her that dumb owl clock over there. She'll love it.") If it's got an owl on it, I'll cherish it.

My owl collection began some 18 years ago with a felt barn owl, a strange creature with an orange nose. My newest owl is a radio with the volume control button in her vaginal area. It fits right on my dash board.

But allow me to get on with the point of all this owl talk. I have a lover. We've been together for about four years, which is less than one-fourth of the time that I have been collecting owls.

My lover collects pigs. She started not quite a year ago, last summer in fact. She has 60, perhaps 65, piggies, primarily little stuffed ones or porcelain figurines.

Real pigs are sort of dull, rather on the grayish side. Uninteresting and no personality. But her stuffed porkers are always so adorable and pink and friendly looking. Pig posters feature curly-tailed creatures with winning smiles. These darling piggies are kept in the same place as my owls, our bedroom. Pigs on one side, owls on the other.

My owls are my prize collection. Of all the junk I've saved during my 36 years, my owl friends are the most important to me. Now, I'm not saying owls are particularly unnoticeable. But most of them are motionless and you'll see that in most photographs they have their eyes closed. Owls just sort of perch in trees and, well . . . hang around doing nothing much at all. They stare a lot. Mostly without opening their eyes.

So it has come to my attention that my owls are overshadowed by certain pigs. When women come to visit for the first time, we usually give them a quick tour of our little apartment. And the piggies are always a big hit. They have names like Prima Pig, Priscilla, Snout-Snout and Petunia

71

Piggy. On the other hand, my owls have practical, fitting names like Big Eyes, Sitter or Sleepy One. Let's face it. Owls just aren't known for their creative personalities. Come to think of it, they aren't known for much at all.

So next time you see a smirking pig on a postcard, don't get taken in by her cunning smile. Look to see if there are any owl cards displayed on the rack and give them a few moments of your time.

Rhona Klein

BABY LOVE

Ed came by around one this morning, again, pounding on my door.

I still have no intentions of letting him in. Why should I? He's a selfish little bastard. Besides, he did me wrong. Oh baby baby.

Ever notice how those rock 'n' roll lyrics seem to say — that is, just about anything worth saying — better than anyone could ever say it? I mean, maybe you know someone who could say it better than Aretha or Otis or Diana. But I don't. When I hear one of those songs about boy-girl problems I know just what they're talking about. And they get right to me.

Like yesterday, I was listening to the radio and I heard Otis reminding guys to treat their woman right. You gotta hold her, squeeze her (squeeze her?), anyway, he was telling other guys not to be such dumb shits when it comes to understanding their woman. Try a little tenderness. Yeah, Ed, you dumb shit, try a little tenderness.

If Ed thinks I'm gonna let him back in, oh baby baby, he's got it all wrong. Christ only knows what that jerk wants to do now. Besides, I just don't trust him anymore. He could say anything. I know, he's done it before. Says something sweet. Some line about missing me. Baby, can't live without you. My world is empty without you, babe. *Babe!* Oh, baby baby, please baby baby, and anything that big bag of lard wants, he gets. How the hell did I turn out to be such a pushover? Ed's such a liar. And I'm such a moron.

Sometimes I think that the whole world, with maybe just a few exceptions (though I've never met these exceptions. Maybe they're out there. I don't know. I *do* know for a fact *I've* never met them) is all the product of two liars making up bullshit stories to each other. They fight, they make up, they make love and then Bang! The product of those lies: babies. And those babies grow up, they fight with other grown up babies, they make up, they make love and then Bang! Here we go again.

And to think, that's been going on for billions of years. We're no better, certainly no smarter, than those cavemen. And that's how Ed got here and how I got here.

And he said he wants more of that. I say enough's enough. Right? But nooo, not for Eddie baby. Not enough jerks on this planet for him.

Like don't I and everybody else around here know that he's got this other tootsie. None of your damn business he says when I bring it up. I'm with you now, ain't I? You're where I wanna be, he says when I ask him about Debbie.

Look, buster, I know about Debbie. *Everyone* knows about Debbie. So don't lie to me.

And then he scoops his hand under my skirt and starts kissing me up and down my wazoo. And then, guess what? Bang! We're making love.

It's your baby, your baby I wanna make.

What? You crazy or something? You think I'm retarded? Huh? You got yourself two boys you couldn't even feed, and the court won't let you see them anymore. You got yourself these two ex-wives who want to string you up, cut off your balls and feed them to you. And you want more? How stupid do I look? Come on now, I can figure out a thing or two. Just cause Debbie knew enough to marry a rich guy and only play around with you, and I'm just stuck with you, doesn't mean I'm a complete idiot. I know what I'm doing, you know.

Oh, but baby baby, baby love, I want a little girl.

Christ! A little girl! What does he think these are? Toys? Mix 'n' match or something? And what if it's a boy? No good? Throw it back? No siree.

So, I just put my foot down and said, No way.

And he said, Oh yeah?

And I said, Yeah, buzz off.

And then, guess what? We made up, and then Bang! I got pregnant.

Only, *this* time he says, Uh oh, I didn't mean it.

Didn't mean it? Is he crazy or something? Didn't *mean* it?!! What the hell *did* he mean? Huh? You tell me. I told him to get lost. And for the first time ever, he listened to me.

Fine. So he just sorta disappeared. Good. So when he wasn't around I went out and got an abortion. And I bet, I just bet, one of my "friends" (probably Lydia, the bitch) told him I got the abortion. Cause now, sure enough, guess who's hanging out by my door, sniffing and panting like a dog in heat? Knocking like he's got a goddamn *gift* or something for me. Hah! I swear *this* time he's gonna knock till his knuckles fall off. Then we'll see. Oh baby baby, sweet baby baby. My baby love.

LEAP OF FAITH

Sarah was old. She lay down, to rest from the mystery. She had put three matzo balls into the soup. Of that there could be no doubt. But when she went to take them out of the pot she discovered not three swollen matzo balls, but one gigantic smooth ball. Oy! I better lie down, Sarah told herself. She did lie down and dreamt she was lying in bed.

Her mouth was open just a drop. Puffs of breath slowly pushed her enormous breasts up and down to the beating of her heart. A nudge at her side caused a sigh to escape her nostrils.

"Sarah?" a voice covered in a whisper poked her. "Sarah, are you sleeping? Don't get up, you don't have to get up," the voice continued. "Just listen to me. Have I good news for you! Listen, it's set. You can go to heaven. Everything's ready. No problem. And best of all, no more of the garbage from down there. You know, forget about those hoodlums. No more dirt. Sarah, you're gonna be in heaven."

"Hey, wait a minute, O.K.? Listen. For one thing, what happened to my matzo balls? And then, for another, what if I don't want to give up the hoodlums or the dirt? Huh? And you know what, whoever you are, there is no heaven. Hah! So there."

"Sarah, now you're talking stupid. You're not a stupid woman. Listen. I promise you can even have Strauss waltzes and Hershey chocolate bars every day in heaven. Now, what do you say to that?"

"That you sound like a jerk! What, you think I don't have a radio? Or that I can't buy chocolate? Huh? Besides, I can fly without you."

And just to prove that she could fly, Sarah lifted her arms, flapped them a couple of times, and rose from the bed. The cool night air, as sure of itself as youth, opened her bedroom window. Out the window Sarah flew. Higher and higher she flew.

Claudia Kraehe

THE WOMAN WHO LIVES IN THE ELEVATOR

The woman who lives in the elevator has lived there for over six years. Before moving in, she viewed numerous apartments, but the elevator was the most affordable, and since management offered to put in new lighting, polish the elevator button panel, and install carpeting (wall-to-wall), in she moved.

The woman who lives in the elevator has made some adjustments. She would prefer to take baths, but in the elevator there is room only for a shower. Also, when entertaining she can have just four people over at a time (that is, four if they stand — two if they sit).

There are advantages to living in the elevator. At night, if the cat on the first floor is screaming, the woman can move her apartment up to floor three and listen to the symphony; if she is on floor five on a Saturday evening, and does not wish to listen to the organisms in 503, she can escape in the elevator to the rooftop. And, if she is behind in her rent payments, or if an irate lover is looking for her, she is hard to find, for there are nine floors in the apartment building, and the woman who lives in the elevator could be on any one of them.

Of course, the other tenants continue to use the elevator for transportation between floors. So throughout the day and evening they come — the man in rational emotive therapy; a woman accompanied on skateboard by her orangutan; the man who brings home a fish and chips dinner every Monday, Wednesday, and Friday, and sausage with sauerkraut the other days; the drunk who urinates and retches — into the elevator they come while she is fixing dinner, watching television, or reading. But the woman who lives in the elevator rarely notices these intrusions anymore, and the tenants in turn ignore her, standing in the elevator with their backs to her, staring dumbly at the door as water from her drying laundry drips on their necks.

THE ACT

Every day they greeted her. Following Sword Lady and preceding Snake Boy, she would appear, taking her seat in the middle of the stage. She began by gnawing her nails, her hands, then the arms, and the crowd watched as she consumed them one by one. Then she swallowed her feet, her legs, her hair, her stomach, until only her mouth was left. That too, she devoured before an enthusiastic audience until all that remained was her very breath which spun in a vortex in the center of the stage. When time enough had passed for the crowd to appreciate the greatness of this, the drum would roll, and she would push through her breath, emerging one limb at a time. And the applause was wild and extended.

One day, she failed to reappear. The drummer kept rolling in an attempt to alert her, but her breath continued to spin and churn on stage.

The crowd waited. A few approached the breath and reported they heard yelling. Others of them heard singing. They were at first intrigued, but they grew weary, then angry because she would not reappear, and they demanded their money back.

There were other inconveniences. The police were at a loss — it wasn't murder (the act had been hers); it wasn't suicide (where was the body?); she wasn't missing — there was her breath.

Authorities attempted to impound the breath, but it whirled, swirled away. A disgruntled manager replaced the act with Galvanic Man.

Marilyn Krysl

JACKS

We played jacks in the hallway at the top of the steps at recess. Was it early spring? On balmy days the doors were propped open and a warm breeze wafted the smells of flowering up to us. The hallway floor was a checkerboard of green and white tile, smooth and polished. You sat cross legged or one leg crossed under you and the other straight out, a prop. The formula of play was one at a time first (the ones), then pairs and on up. When you finished you started over with ones again, eggs in the basket. You played until you missed. If you moved a jack other than the ones you picked up, it was the next girl's turn.

"That one moved!"

"What! Where?"

"That one, dope."

"Whaa-aaat! I didn't even touch it!"

"We all saw you, Chrissie."

"No I didn't! I didn't come *near* that one!"

"Chrissie, everybody *saw.*"

Chrissie slams both hands down across the field of play and sweeps up her jacks defiantly. "This is *not fair.*"

"You don't have to get so mad."

The little kids crowded around, watching. They could not quite believe we were that good. Sometimes two or three boys sauntering down the hall would stop to watch. Once in a while a wicked boy, needing disaster, would charge through us, through the field of flung jacks, on purpose, then run like hell away, powered by our screams. Usually though the boys just watched. Jacks was a girl's game and this was girls' territory. They were curious about girls' territory. This was a good time to look us over good without appearing to be interested.

When the boys watched, the ambience of the game changed. You couldn't play your best with boys watching. You got the jitters and the juicy flow of your play dried up. In fact you prayed to miss soon so as to get out from under the hard scrutiny of boys' eyes. The easy camaraderie around the circle of players tightened up. We became unusually quiet, and when we argued, unusually shrill.

Only if it was a boy you liked did you like being watched. Then you suddenly became very good. You became, in fact, spectacular. You rose above everything dim and known and went flying off on a winning streak. Your temperature rose, your face flushed, and you went right on climbing the sky, playing perfectly. The other girls fell back in awe. They were pleased for you and they were jealous too. Above all they hoped some of your glory would rub off on them.

But this too was unnatural. It wasn't the way the game, at its best, went. At its best it was a girls' game, requiring the presence and participation of girls and only girls. Your skill was what it was. And it was a game not of competition but of demonstrations of skill. You did not play against the other girls. Instead you were each other's witnesses.

Your skill was what it was and you were as good as you practiced. You practiced at home alone on the kitchen linoleum or the floor of your bedroom. When the weather was warm, you practiced on the sidewalk. And you sewed a little cloth bag with a drawstring to keep your jacks and ball in and carried the bag with you everywhere. You kept it with you while you washed the dishes, in your pocket or hanging from your belt. You took it with you when your mother sent you to the store. At night you put the bag on the floor beside your bed next to your shoes. And while you practiced alone you thought about the other girls: how their faces looked in concentration, how graceful and quick and clever their hands were, how their hair shone. And you thought about them practicing at home too, thinking about you.

It was a world. Because it seemed to the rest of the world, the world outside our circle — parents, teachers, boys — that we weren't really doing anything important. We were doing something harmless, like embroidery, they thought, and generally they left us alone. Jacks was the one place we would not be interrupted, interfered with, instructed, judged, criticized, set straight. You got to school early so you could play before school. You played at recess. And if your mother would let you, you stayed after school and played some more. When you had to leave immediately after school for your piano lesson or your tap dancing lesson or lessons in voice, you were morose.

In late spring and summer we played on the sidewalk in front of the school or on the cement of the basketball court. The sun shone. The cement we sat on was warm. The sun shone, the sun warmed our shoulders and backs as we bent, leaning into the play. We played until the sides of our hands were scraped dry, until the paint was completely worn off the ball, until the rubber began to break down, until the pink and blue jacks polished back down to pure metal. We played while the weather turned cooler, while the days moved through Indian summer. We put on sweaters and played while the leaves fell, falling around us, falling into our circle.

We kept on playing while the leaves burned.

SOARING

"I've enrolled the kids in Intro to Soaring," my friend Carol says. We're having some white wine in my back yard, catching up. Carol and I came of age in the Sixties, but she had her kids late. Now Sky and Ocean are thirteen and eleven. You want me to tell you which is the girl and which is the boy? These are unisex kids, their mother is an equal opportunity employer.

"Soaring?" I say. Last year it was Zen Basketball. Before that Vision Quest. For Carol, activism and self-improvement go hand in hand. While she organized the local grape and lettuce boycott and a letter campaign against Red Dye No. 2, she was doing TM. She rallied against ROTC in the morning, ran the counseling center for draft resisters in the afternoon, and studied Chinese at night. Though she's a blonde who sunburns in the shade, she was once president of CORE. This in a community of 80,000 where there was one black family, a professor of Afro-American Studies on a one-year contract and his wife. Carol got two hundred and fifty people to parade down to City Hall and demand the city integrate its personnel. She was once chair of the local Americans for

78

Democratic Action, the ACLU, the Democratic Women's Caucus, and the PTA at the same time, and at the same time she took Assertiveness Training, Botany and Auto Mechanics.

Me, I'm all for changing the system, but I didn't think I needed to practice Tai Chi. I don't want to bare my breasts or my soul in Encounter Group. I like myself the way I am. I think I'm fine, it's The Powers That Be who need bodywork. It was Tricky Dick who needed Maracapy Dance Movement Therapy. It's Jeanne Kirkpatrick and Phyllis Schlafly, it's not me.

Carol thinks otherwise. She pickets for the disabled and for abortion rights at the same time she gets rolfed and does Primal Scream Therapy. She organizes free Financial Planning classes for single mothers, then goes off into the woods for Outward Bound Endurance Testing. Her kids have chalked up credits in Cardiopulmonary Resuscitation, Indonesian Cookery, Beginning, Intermediate and Advanced Senegalese, Western Wildflowers and Sign Language.

Now Intro to Soaring.

"Isn't trying to fly dangerous?" I say. "Shouldn't they be in the library instead?"

Carol shakes her head. "They need life skills," she says.

Life skills? These kids have them already. Their mother sat in the grass between Jerry Rubin and Timothy Leary. Sky and Ocean lay down with their mother in front of buses. Ocean's first complete sentence was "We shall overcome." These kids can sit in a circle holding hands indefinitely and not get bored. If their mother called an ice cream boycott to protest exploitation of dairy workers, Sky and Ocean would give up Chocolate Fudge Nut Ripple without a whimper. They keep a bag of gorp and plastic bottles of drinking water at hand, and they dress for arrest. At any moment their mom may decided to pile them into somebody's Volkswagen camper and head for the Capitol.

"They've got life skills," I say, "but can they read? Do they know about prime numbers?"

"Don't worry," Carol says, "they were both reading at three."

"I know they're smart cookies," I say. "I was wondering about their preparation."

"For college?"

I nod.

"They can take College Prep," Carol says. Then she changes the subject. "Did you know they've both got black belts in karate now?"

Karate. Sky and Ocean have been through Nonviolence Training six different times. Gentleness and due process have been impressed upon them. When Sky got the whole seventh grade class at the Junior High to petition the Principal until she met their demand for a vegetarian lunchroom, this kid personally wrote the Principal a thank you note. Now Karate?

"Aren't they going to be confused?" I say. "What if Sky forgets and whaps a cop next time you block the entrance to Rocky Flats? Isn't this a contradiction?"

"The human animal is a very complex organism," Carol says. "They can handle contradiction. Besides, I'm working on a plan to convert Rocky Flats from plutonium triggers to lingerie."

This woman's got optimism like it was estrogen. Startling improvements are just around the corner. The country's 586 toxic waste sites will be cleaned up within the year, she's working on this. The heads of multinationals will discover their error and turn their assets over to the Third World. She's working on that too. Meanwhile she goes door to door for Safehouse, gets asbestos out of the schools, and studies Zulu.

Me, I'm working on reading a sleazy novel. I think people can improve too much. Do I really need Right Brain Left Brain Complementarity courses? Will I fall behind if I can't do Baby Massage?

"But will they be able to pass the SATs?" I say. "Can they write the biographical essay?"

"Don't worry," Carol says. "They need expanding now." She's been reading Huxley's *Doors of Perception* again, I can tell. "Stimulation's good for them," she says.

"What about burnout?" I say.

"Not likely," Carol says. "But if they do, they can take Integrative Rebirthing with me. I'm thinking of enrolling us all in Politics of South Africa after Christmas," she adds. There's a glazed look in her eyes, she's got plans. "And Understanding Foreign Policy."

"Your kids need Physics and Spelling," I say. "It's the Senator who needs Understanding Foreign Policy."

Carol looks at me. She smiles. "Someday they'll be the Senator," she says.

Wendy Joy Kuppermann

GRANDFATHER AT THE FAIR
for my father, M. David Kuppermann, with love

Mother is swaddled in furs, napping. She leans to one side, snoring lightly, and her diamond earrings sparkle like headlights. Mellowed with wine, I prop up my feet, smoke a cigarette and daydream. Daddy looks tired and sad, oddly shrunken inside a tall, crooked frame. His hat tilts back, exposing a large black *yarmulke* and high, furrowed brow. The cherry-black Fleetwood limo glides past Flushing Meadow Park. Strange silhouette, a rusted unisphere rests there among the trees. The 1964 World's Fair. Bright Disney dolls ride an assembly line, sing *It's a small world after all* . . .

"I have a story for you, about your grandfather, *zichrono l'vracha.* Maybe it would interest you?"

"Sure, Dad. Tell me about my *Zayde.*"

"I know you think we were all a bunch of . . . how do you say it? pumpkins? . . . in the Old Country, but we weren't. Your grandfather may sound like an old Chasid to you but he was an educated man, a cultured man. He may have worn a beard and *payyes* but still he knew something of the outside world. Some of it he didn't approve of but some of it he did. He even visited Paris once."

"Dad! Your father actually went to Paris?" I picture Tevye the Milkman at the Moulin Rouge, shaking my head. Dad is beaming.

"He certainly did. He went there to see the World's Fair. It was 1937, I believe, two years before the war. I was already Bar Mitzvahed then. We were very excited about it, you can imagine. Few of us had ever seen a big city, not even Krakow, but to visit Paris yet—that was practically unheard of. But *my* father went.

"When he came home he was so excited I can't describe it. Like a little kid, he was, brimming with it. He brought back souvenirs for me and my brother, and some fancy clothing for my mother. Also a bottle of liqueur, Benedictine. There was a cross on the label but he covered it up. We drank it on holidays. At the fair, he told us, they had a special telephone . . ."

"Did you have telephones in Poland?"

"Yes, we had telephones in Poland, and indoor plumbing also. In 1937, just after the Middle Ages. Don't be so smart aleck."

"Okay, okay. So there was this special telephone?"

". . . with a screen attached to it and you could see on the screen the person you were talking to. Like television today, only black and white. My father described it over and over, it amazed him to such extent. Like looking into the future, he said. It was a strange and marvelous thing, he told us, *ach,* a wonderful world to see. I never saw him so excited like that, with such joy. And the smile on his face, I remember it all my life."

My father's eyes are moist but he doesn't cry.

"Tell her, Moniek, tell her." Mother adjusts her collar and turns to face us, speaking to me through my father. I am wise to this rhetorical trick of hers — the third person familiar. "So she shouldn't think the life back home was only *tzores* for the Jews. Just murder and suffering, she thinks. We had our happiness too, before the war, all of us did. Better even than America. Who knew what would come? No one. So go figure, *nu,* make plans. But we were happy before. Tell her, she should understand. We had good times too."

"Mother, I know you had a happy childhood. I don't mean to deny it . . ."

"Listen, your mother just gets upset that people think all we knew was persecution and no happiness. She wants you to understand that we had happy times and real good memories."

"I heard what she wants. I've been sitting right here the whole time."

"Then listen instead of always getting angry."

It's hard for me to listen. Hard especially when they speak of Poland and their longing to return. Hard for me to hear it when Dad says, "People expect us to hate Poland because of what happened. But we can't hate it, not all of it. Our childhood memories live there, beautiful ones. If Hitler changed everything, and he did, still he didn't change the good memories into bad ones. They're all we have left of home. Just to remember." It hurts me to listen. The words cut deep to sorrow, open as a wound. I want to hurt the hurt sometimes.

"Dad, do you remember anything else your father told you about the fair in Paris?"

"Not about the World's Fair exactly, but there was something else. Probably you'll get a kick out of it. While he was still in Paris my father met up with a business acquaintance of his and this fellow, he was a *goy* — what did he know from Chasidic Jews? — he took it into his head to take out my father and show off the famous nightlife in Paris. So where do you think they went? To the follies. To a burlesque show, no less, with women shaking around half-naked or worse on the stage. He blushed when he told me about it and whispered I shouldn't tell my younger brother. I think he was in shock. There were women dancing there in feathers and in beads, he said, wearing very little else. One in particular danced like a wild animal, but graceful. She was totally exposed and her skin was black — I don't know which shocked him more. Her name was Josephine Baker."

I shriek. "Are you telling me that my own grandfather actually saw *the* Josephine Baker dance naked on stage in Paris?"

"Yes."

"My own grandfather, your father?"

Dad nods his head.

"Josephine Baker?"

Dad nods again, smiling.

"You wouldn't lie to me now, would you, Daddy? Not about something so important?"

"Important! This information she thinks is important," Dad chuckles. "Why would I make up such a story that anyone else in the family would be ashamed of but you? Believe me, it happened. You have something to be proud of."

I grab his shoulders, laughing out loud, shaking him.

"Why," breathlessly, *"didn't you ever tell me this before?"*

"I didn't think it mattered that much. What difference could it make?"

"Oh *Tatte,* it makes all the difference in the world."

And it does, somehow. In my father's study, nestled among volumes of Talmud, there is a picture of my grandfather, a worn brown and white photograph salvaged miraculously after the war. I take it down and see a middle-aged Chasidic gentleman, elegant trimmed beard, *payyes* curled neatly behind his ears. Familiar features, my father's face, an early draft.

Andrea Freud Loewenstein

THE SAME OLD STORY

It's the same old story. I loved her. She didn't love me back.

Or maybe she did love me back at first, a little, but not enough to get in her car and come over that time we were talking on the phone and she said you keep saying you have to talk, well go on I'm listening, and I said I can't not with you sounding like that, and she said I feel like this is about nothing it's just air and I don't want to do it and so I'm getting off the phone now, and I didn't say anything because I was crying and she said in a begrudging sort of voice I'm sorry if I hurt you, and we hung up.

And I sat at the window grading my exams and crying and waiting a little hopefully for her to drive up in her small blue very clean car, because she kept her car as clean as the day she bought it, and get out of her car and come up my steps and into the room and take me in her arms. She could have left after that, dayenu as they say, it would have been enough, I had abandoned other kinds of hopes a long time ago. I didn't need her to say anything. Not I won't go to bed with you but I still love you. Not here I am and I'll stay as long as you want me, it won't kill me to get to bed late for once in my life. Nothing. Every night she was in bed by nine and up at five, to run, this woman. Even in the dead of winter, on the ice.

So what was I doing you might ask, what was I doing loving someone like that, a woman who kept her car as clean as the day she bought it, always went to bed at nine o'clock and got up at some ungodly hour to go running but wouldn't come over to hold her friend in her arms when her friend's heart was cracking because of what she'd said?

Probably I'm being unfair. Probably she would have come over at midnight, in her nightgown, with a deadline to meet, in a snowstorm, probably she would have come right over for someone she loved.

I would have, I was saying to myself as I sat there, It's not fair, if she wanted me and I was anywhere at all a nine hours drive away and it was four in the morning, if she wanted me I would get in my car and I would come, but the truth is I wouldn't have of course, not for just anyone, not even for very good friends, to them I would have said wait, I'll call you in the morning. Only for her, and that's what it's about, isn't it. That and needing to say her name out loud to anyone who would listen. That, yes and the way I found the ugly parts of her the most beautiful of all, the extra weight the double chin the way she hid her face with bangs and that helmet of black hair, the way she hid her beauty so that when I blurted out her name to someone some friend who had seen her, that friend said *her,* she's the one, her? and I felt triumphant knowing that anyone could see her beauty when she smiled, when she read her poetry aloud and called people dear and listened to them so well, but I was the only one to see her those other times, the armored times. That, yes, and her voice, brusque and flat on the phone, that and the stories she told me, only little scraps of stories, but still stories, about when she was a child.

The stories were when she was still being nice to me of course, when she wanted me around when she loved me maybe a little.

Maybe a little but not enough. Not enough to think about me at night not enough to wonder *what if I said yes what if I let her* because that's how it would have had to be, her letting me, even in my fantasies of her fantasies I couldn't go any further than that, she was such a femme, a straight woman and a femme so it had to be that way, her letting me kiss her and then letting me reach down under her clothes feeling her skin pulling off her shirt my mouth on her small collapsed breasts that I never got to see never not once.

She took her whole poetry group swimming in the bay last summer, it was night time, they all took off their clothes, they swam around naked in the water under the stars together but not me. Not even that and I know her fantasies were not about me. Maybe about that man in the group the one who looks like he's carved out of stone maybe him or I don't know how should I know which goddamn man she thought about, doing it to herself at night, who she imagined opening her up or if she did after all imagine being the one to do, the one to lean over and take what she wanted but from some man not from me never from me.

That, yes, and the way I thought about her every night before going to sleep and the way I came thinking about her when I slept alone, and the smell of her and the smell of the clothes she had on.

One time she left her sweater at my house and I thought, stop you fool this is stupid this is adolescent this is inane you have a perfectly good lover anyway what the fuck are you doing but I did it anyway. I took her sweater in my arms and I smelled it, inhaled it deeply as any drug. I did it quite a few times, it was not something I could stop myself from doing. It smelled of sweat and of old smoke and a little like a wet dog, it wasn't a good smell but that made it better, you know, like the double chin. If it had smelled like sweet perfume it wouldn't have been as good somehow, and that's it, that's what it's like.

I didn't sleep with her sweater though. Don't assume too much. You're reading this, not knowing me and you're probably picturing me as eighteen or if not eighteen then twenty-two but I'm forty-three years old and like I said I have a perfectly good lover of my own and this is a straight woman I'm talking about. No I didn't take her sweater to bed with me. There are limits, after all.

It's better being 43. It's a lot better. I didn't take the sweater to bed with me and when she didn't get in her car and come to me I didn't go to her house and get her out of bed and say Fuck it woman so what if it's past your bedtime I need you. I didn't do that and I didn't break up with my perfectly good lover and I never gave her flowers never not once only food, only food a very few times no books either not to keep anyway, and yes it's better being 43. That, yes, and also I knew I'd get over it, I never once thought of getting run over by a truck in front of her house and having her find me there the next morning and be sorry, I never thought she's the one I've been waiting for all my life all the others were mistakes, never once after the first month anyway. It can strike you at 43, that's what I think, even at a happily coupled 43 it can strike you, but you can cope with it better, it's not so lethal.

But it can strike you alright, and it's the same old story, just like I told you. I could stop now or I could go on writing all night, looking for her car out the window which will not come because she goes to bed at nine and because, anyway, she doesn't love me back.

Lee Lynch

JACKY AND HER MOTHER

"Get out of my closet, Ma!" yelled Jacky in exasperation. Then she heard herself: she was scared to death her mother would find *her* in her closet.

"I'm just looking to see what new clothes you've bought with the money Gramma gave you, Jacqueline," said her mother, fresh from the beauty parlor, in a salmon-colored velour jogging suit. "You know how she hates to see you wearing these ratty jeans and baggy flannel shirts. What if somebody *saw* you, for God's sake?"

"You know I'm not going to waste money on new clothes when I can get used ones all broken in."

"My daughter the bus driver. My daughter the abortion marcher. Now my daughter the rag picker. Is this why we worked so hard to give you the best? Stop pulling at me. I'm your mother, I can look in your closet."

"Come sit. I made you coffee."

"Maxwell House instant? Why don't you use the Mr. Coffee we gave you? Now let go, I need to visit your little girls' room."

"Ma, there *are* no girls here. I'm a woman. Full-grown."

"Your full-grown woman's room, then."

Jacky sweated on the couch. She could hear her mother in there, rustling around, examining everything. She should have moved to Minneapolis. Every month she had to take down all the Gay Pride posters, bury her button collection, strip the refrigerator of announcements, not to mention hiding Camille's pillow and kimono.

Her mother finally came to the table.

"I spent Gramma's money on my Self-Defense for Women class."

"She'll be overjoyed," said her mother sarcastically.

Jacky loved women, loved her quirky mother, and was out to everyone in the world but her family. They had finally made it past poverty, moved from Chicago to Elgin where Jacky trekked loyally every holiday.

They'd be damned if anything, but anything, stuck out about them. She believed in telling her mother, but not just yet, not till — she wasn't sure what, but she'd know when the moment was right.

Mrs. Pepitone rose and checked the coffee water. She picked something up from the soapdish on the sink. "Earrings?" she exclaimed slowly, a pleased surprise in her voice.

Jacky felt her insides turn to liquid. So that's where the entwined women symbol earrings Camille had lost a month ago had gone to. She'd taken them off, along with Camille's clothes, at the kitchen sink, when they hadn't been able to wait —

Her mother rushed to her and held the earrings against her face. "But Jacqueline, your ears aren't pierced! Whose are these?"

Was this the moment? How could she hold her head up in the community if she let this chance go by? How could she face herself in the mirror? She looked into her mother's eyes. What could be easier right now than to say the words, *They belong to Camille, my lover.*

Just then the pan boiled over. Both she and her mother jumped and rushed to the stove. Her mother lay the earrings back in the soapdish. Jacky rattled on about the merits of self-defense for women, and it wasn't until she was alone that she realized it. Her mother had dropped the subject of the earrings.

JACKY AND THE DRAG QUEENS

Jacky was a parade monitor the year she had it out with the drag queens.

Her partner had kissed her hard, excited, that morning when she'd finished dressing in her usual garb: long-sleeved jersey and neckerchief-headband, running shoes, 501's and a wide lavender armband. All day she'd felt the admiring eyes of women on her fierce-looking revolutionary's body.

When the drag queen contingent sashayed along Halstead decked out in every feather and bead known to civilization, Jacky felt a wave of disgust. These creatures were a perversity in a march which proclaimed gay normalcy, weak links in a display of strength. She looked daggers at them.

"*That* one's on the rag!" called a tiny laughing black queen in a ruffled red taffeta dress. "I'm Sister Modesty! Pleased to meet you, Ms. Butch!"

Jacky waved her by with a jerk of her arm.

But the queen was obviously looking for fun. Within seconds, she and her retinue had encircled Jacky, teasing her with some show tune.

"Lighten up," Modesty razzed. "You think bulldagger drag makes you stronger than fag rags?" She lifted her skirt and flashed hot pink garters at Jacky.

Bulldagger drag? Butch?

"I'm a real woman! I don't play roles!" Jacky shouted. "My clothes are about strength. You make a mockery of every feminist principle with your lipstick and high heels. Those are the things that kept women in bondage for centuries."

"And what exactly makes Ms. Politically Correct think these clothes make me weak?"

Jacky was about to respond, but a crowd had formed. She started to whistle for help when she felt the blow she'd dreaded ever since her first protest march. A heavy can grazed the side of her head. She went down.

"FAGGOTS! LEZZIES! KILL THEM!"

She heard the crowd scurry back except for those silly queens who screamed and screamed until she thought she'd go mad. Her hand came away from her head covered with red. She cried.

When Jacky looked up, Sister Modesty led the pack. Their skirts askew, the queens hauled three white men from a stoop. Some pushed and pulled at Jacky's attackers, others kicked can after open can of industrial-sized tomato sauce down the steps until it looked as if blood ran in the gutters.

Sister Modesty was ferocious, scratching and biting and screeching like a banshee.

Jacky sat up, looking at the open cans of sauce. She tasted the red stuff running down her face. By the time she stood, the police were already handcuffing Sister Modesty.

The fury of dozens of well-controlled protests rose in Jacky then. She wiped sauce from her butchy clothing, watching the police through a red haze. Then she saw Sister Modesty's defiant eyes and the real blood that ran from her nose.

She roared, and threw herself at the cops, pummeling and punching, trying to free Modesty.

The police tossed them both into the paddy wagon, the butch and the drag queen.

JACKY AND THE WEDDING

Jacky cried all through her baby sister's wedding.

It wasn't from the sense of loss she felt. Her sister was a good friend, and the guy she was marrying seemed to treat her well. But here was Jacky's own lover Camille beside her, her honored, chosen soul mate. Why weren't they up there getting the blessings of their families?

The bride and groom glowed in sunlight at the other end of the arched wooden bridge. The pond made lapping sounds as a hot breeze rippled it. The minister laughed noiselessly at some joke the couple made. It was all so sweet, so lovely for her sister. Jacky took Camille's hand.

With the ceremony over, they moved into the old Lords Park Community House. Waitresses flew from table to table.

"Jacqueline, how are you, darling?" asked Cousin Flora, her tone syrupy. "It's been ages, hasn't it?"

It had been ages on purpose as far as Jacky was concerned. Flora was a few years older, with chronically pursed lips and frosted hair.

Flora's laugh sounded about as real as the couple atop the wedding cake. "Doesn't Jacky look more like she's at a funeral than a wedding?" Flora had included everyone at the table in her joke and they obliged with laughter.

"Jacky —" warned Camille.

"This is what's fucking wrong, Flora," Jacky blurted with sudden fury. She pulled Camille's hand from underneath the table and displayed their matching rings. "We had to give these to each other in the shadows, so none of you would see. We had to act like we were ashamed of our love so we wouldn't offend you."

Flora's lips pursed even more tightly.

Cousin Annette played furiously with her place setting; Cousin Maria looked like she was trying not to cry.

Camille pulled her hand back under the table. Flora's husband told a complex honeymoon joke. Jacky cried into her fruit salad, her entree, her compote.

Then the dancing began. It seemed as if everyone but she, Camille and the grandmother in a wheelchair moved to the floor. She rose from her seat like an explosion, and stalked out past the small plastic bags of rice ready on the veranda. She kicked at one.

"I'm sorry," said Jacky when Camille joined her outside.

Camille pulled Jacky's head to her shoulder. "I understand, Squirrel."

They got into the van.

"Look at all these petals," said Jacky. They were pinkish white, and transluscent on the windshield. More fell; she felt her mood lift.

"Like confetti," said Camille with a delighted laughed.

As they began to drive away Jacky watched through the rearview mirror. The petals swirled off the van's roof. Her anger was gone.

She stopped the van and leapt out, collecting handfuls.

Camille opened her door; Jacky flung petals until they littered her hair like wedding rice.

"My bride," she whispered.

Harriet Malinowitz

CLARA'S SOLILOQUY

I remember once, sometime in the late '70s, Holly and I traveled cross-country together. I was afraid of a lot of things. Up in northern Montana I was scared of the grizzly bears. I was scared for anyone to know we were Jewish. Once we camped in the bottom of a canyon during a thunderstorm, and all night long I was scared a tree above us would get hit by lightning and crash down on our tent. In Arizona we camped in the desert, and I was scared of the rattlesnakes. You could see them slinking behind boulders, lurking in the shade. I bought a snakebite kit in a tourist shop and a pamphlet on snake safety. It said you shouldn't step on rocks, because the snakes slept under them and they could attack you. But sometimes we couldn't help stepping on rocks. I said to Holly, "What if you step on a rock by accident?" She said, "Well, there might not be a snake under it." So I said, "But what if there is?" She said, "It might just keep on sleeping." I said, "But what if it doesn't?" She said, "A snake leaps straight out at you. So if it looks like it's going to strike, jump to the side, you can fool it." So I said, "But what if it manages to get you anyway?" Holly said, "Use your snakebite kit and get to a hospital right away." I said, "What if you're not near a hospital?" She said, "Just try to get to whichever is closest." I said, "What if you're hiking and you're five hours from your car and ten hours from the nearest hospital?" She looked at me and she said, "Then, you die."

---

from the full-length play *Minus One*

Carolina Mancuso

WHAT TO DO IF THEY COME

Andrea squeezed her eyelids tight to keep the tears from falling. Her head hurt where she had whacked it on the desk as she tried to get down under. She crammed herself into the smallest possible space, her muscles already cramped and aching. There, she could turn her head just enough to catch a glimpse of Jerome, the biggest boy in the class. If Andrea had trouble fitting under here, what was Jerome Nassar going to do?

Her stomach clutched as she thought of the consequences. Jerome could be found right away, Jerome could be caught, Jerome could be . . . a tiny squeak of horror escaped Andrea's lips, and at once, Virginia shushed her from across the aisle. But Andrea made no effort to hide the tear that rolled down her cheek. All she could see was Jerome being caught. He was the only boy she had ever really cared about — even if he was too tall for her ever to have a chance with him.

A gravelly voice boomed from the doorway, slicing through her thoughts, and she cringed lower, smacking her head once again.

"Who's in there? Show yourselves, now! You can save yourselves if you do." Not one person in the room uttered a word, not even a whisper. You could hear a pin drop until, from the back of the room came a long, low resonating burp, then a round of titters.

"Tsk!" Virginia and Andrea clucked in unison. Of course, you could depend on Roger Depew making fun even at a time like this.

But suddenly the door burst open, and a blast of gunshot echoed through the air. Andrea gasped, burying her face in her hands. Heavy footsteps slapped across the floor, shooting ice up her spine. For the first time she was glad that her average had dropped that term. It meant that her seat, though still in the first row, was in the middle of the room, more protected than it might have been. She imagined Janice Burton, sitting up front, practically wetting her pants.

The footsteps fell like a guillotine, one after another, until they neared Andrea, crouched as far down as she could go. She pressed her cheek against the wooden slats that supported the desk, and held her breath until she thought she would burst. Her half-open eyes watched as the shiny black shoes passed within inches, but the shade of relief was overcome by another grip of terror. The figure stopped at the back of the room, shook at one of the desks, and grabbed for the person underneath.

"You! On your feet!"

Andrea strained to see without moving herself. It was not Jerome.

It was not even Robert. Of course. It was Anthony. Anthony Marietti. The second tallest boy in the class, but so different from Jerome. Anthony had been kept back two years in a row, so he was not only taller but older, not only older but noisier, not only noisier but fatter. And he was the only other Italian in the room besides Andrea, and that was the worst of all. Anthony caused Andrea untold misery. Her father bought bread from his father's bakery, but Anthony's behavior in class left her torn between shame and the obligations of comraderie. Still, the thought of even Anthony in this predicament brought tears up once again.

Anthony was pulled to his feet by the collar. He stood slouching, sullen, smirking. Andrea sighed.

"Do you believe in Jesus Christ?" the voice roared

Anthony folded his arms across his chest and leaned into one hip, pumping his head up and down. The gun was poked into his ribs, and he jolted, shouting, "Yes!"

"Will you renounce your faith?"

"No!" he snapped back, "I'll never renounce my church or my God!" Anthony stared at the interrogator, for one split second torn between fear and bravado. Then he snatched at his chance. In a swoop, he grabbed the barrel of the gun and twisted it toward the windows. Before it went half-circle, an elbow jabbed him in the gut, and he landed breathless in the chair. A chorus of gasps rose from beneath the desks.

The figure whirled around, triumphant, shouting, "All right, all of you, I know you're down there. Stand up, now!"

Andrea crawled out as fast as she could, scraping her knee on the way. Desks were being knocked and pushed and jarred every which way.

"Are you also believers in the church of Christ?"

"Yes!" they all cried out in unison.

"And will you renounce your God?"

"No! Never! We will never renounce our God!"

Every word was in perfect harmony, just like in choir, just like they had practiced it, better even than the Pledge of Allegiance. That would make Sister happy. In the moment of silence that followed their testimony of faith, the figure walked to the front of the room, and Sister Marian Peter's normal voice returned.

"All right, boys and girls, that was much better than last time. Except for one thing. As you can see from what happened to Mr. Marietti," her eyes narrowed on Anthony, "if you're going to try anything wild, you have to know what you're doing — and I'm telling you, you don't. We're looking for martyrs, not heroes. Remember, you have no chance against the communists. Their guns will be real and loaded, not like the toy I just used." Her voice softened as she gazed around the room, and her face took on a glow. "I just want to say that I was proud of you for not denying Christ.

Now, sit down quietly and take out your arithmetic books."

Andrea rubbed her head with one hand and her knee with the other. She pulled out her book and started turning pages. Then, all of a sudden, without any warning and all over the page on common fractions, she threw up. Sister Marian Peter told her to get paper towels from the girls' lavatory and clean it up. The class went on with math; the kids around Andrea's desk made faces and held their noses. Andrea wished she had died in the invasion.

Tara Masih

CORNUCOPIA

Thanksgiving, dad came home drunk for dessert. He left after Uncle Bob kept braggin' about the new toilet seat he'd put in for Aunt Betty, who kept snap-snapping the celery and sniffing Mom's food. And I could see Mom was in such a bad mood — she had to say grace for the first time in five years 'cause it was her turn — and she sat there thinking of things to thank God for. And she sat there, and she finally thanked Him for the family being all together, after Dad cleared his throat. When Mom said that, Aunt Betty smiled and winked and Little Bob dropped his spoon in the mashed potatoes and they flew all over her purple silk blouse like white snow, and Mom tried not to smile. And then Grammy asked what time it was and Dad said time to eat and Little Joey laughed and shot a pea bullet at Little Bob with his fork, and no one saw so he shot another and it hit the wall and went splat and Mom glared at Aunt Betty who slapped Little Joey's shaved head. And Uncle Bob said how his son'd be a good recruit and Dad said what was so great about that? Here goes, I thought, and I stabbed at my peas, trying to get four on my fork all at once. And I stabbed and got three, then squished them around in the gravy. Here goes, just like at Easter when Aunt Betty had said that she was a reborn-again Christian Scientist, and Dad had said Figures. I looked up at the expression on Mom's face, and told myself to go look at my own face in the bathroom mirror after dinner. And Uncle Bob said Dad was just jealous because he'd gone to work instead of the army, Wasn't that right, Mom? And Grammy made sucking baby noises with the yams and asked what time it was. And Dad poured more wine and Mom made a stopping face and Dad banged the bottle down so that an apple in the centerpiece, a horn of plenty, rolled towards the crystal salt-shaker and knocked it over. And Aunt Betty grabbed a pinch between purple nails and threw it over her right shoulder on the carpet, and Mom picked up the shaker and bumped it down. And Little Joey dropped the turkey drumstick on the floor and he crawled under the table and Dad said, Why would I be jealous about training to shoot men? And Uncle Bob said, It was a hell of a lot more than that! And Mom turned to Aunt Betty and asked how her cantaloupe diet was working, and then Uncle Bob was calling Dad a faggot and Dad was calling him a bastard, and Grammy choked on her yams when she heard bastard, and Mom pounded her on the back and glared at Dad, and then Little Joey started sticking his hand up my skirt under the table and Grammy asked What time is it! after a glass of wine and Dad said, Time for me to leave.

That was the night Dad came home drunk for dessert.

Janet Mason

Between Friends

"Friendship requires give and take, not one person dominating the conversation!"

Lately, Susan and I had been having our worst arguments in the finest restaurants we ate in. This place was no different: charming, well dressed male waiters — but not too effusive or swishy, at least not enough to offend the establishment's family reputation — white linen table cloths, and undernourishing but overpriced menu selections.

Not that a restaurant such as this was the finest that Susan patronized. Not the ever so discerning Susan Barringer from a long line of overfed and underworked restaurant connoisseurs.

Her eyes slowly widened behind her thick-lensed but stylishly framed glasses. Weeks before she had told me they were "very expensive but quite attractive, and didn't I agree?" She began to squirm in her seat. Several well-groomed heads had turned to the increased volume of my hissing voice.

By now her hands were gripping the edges of the table. In her best, low key, scholarly voice she tried to placate me. I could see the gears turning in her forehead. "I was not trying to monopolize the conversation."

Yes that is a better word than dominate, I thought, but at least I hadn't had to spend 15 years in graduate school figuring that one out.

"You told your story and then I told my story. That's all. You talked and then I talked. You told your . . ."

"You were not simply telling your story," I said, interrupting her in mid sentence. "You were haranguing me about the same thing you've been grinding your wheels about for the past four months. Another unrequited love. For Christ's sake Susan, why don't you ask any of these women out on a date. Go to dinner, to a movie, have a drink, talk to them. You don't have to have sex with all of them. It's like you've created a form of intellectual obsessive monogamy!"

Her jaw dropped and her eyes widened further as she slowly nodded. Then she glanced furtively around her to see if anyone overheard.

My impassioned monologue was a long time in coming. Too long, judging from my anger. Susan was used to people listening to her — nodding their glazed eyes while thinking of an excuse to leave.

She shovelled a piece of basted chicken into her mouth. I pushed some white rice around on my plate. Finally, after wiping her mouth and folding the cloth napkin before dropping it in her lap, she spoke. "Aren't the paintings in this restaurant nice. I always feel so good about myself when I come here."

Deena Metzger

WALKING WITH NERUDA
(excerpts)

II

I had imagined conversation. Surely, he was one of the great talkers. I thought I needed that talk. After all, I came to him so frightened, a dumb, teenage girl with shaking hands, essentially insecure about language. Moses, who is in my lineage, put coals in his mouth and stuttered afterwards, while I imagined that doves flew out of Pablo's mouth whenever he spoke. *Palomas. Palomas blancas con* quivering wings. Words like startled feathers. *Un nido* of burning sentences.

I imagined long literary evenings, odes intoned to the beat of the *charanga,* gossip long as gallows, speeches pregnant with clouds and grammatic shadows. *La noche escondida, la mascara* of painted *palabras,* lucid *pajaros de la anochecida....*

      Imaginé . . . I imagined. . . .

      He gave me a blank piece of paper. "Dare," he laughed.

      When I entered his day room, whirring white doves, their eyes *brillantes entre dos luces de cobre,* settled into their golden cages. I called to them, "Coo, coo," and my breath smudged the night with coal dust, *negra y pesada.*

      If I write this, if I dare to imagine the moment — as I have imagined others — where a man or a woman who had no prior existence suddenly grow ruddy with the breath of life on the page — if I dare to imagine this: myself, this poet named Pablo Neruda, the two of us together in a room — *vivendonos* — he hasn't died yet — poetry is still possible — it is raining in the south of Chile.... I know the landscape. *La lluvia* of hope. If I dare this . . .

      A woman who writes a word down is not the same as one who does not.

      When I was not yet twenty-four, I followed Pablo Neruda, the world's greatest poet into his house.

      He said, "A woman has rarely been a poet because the fathers tell her to keep her body closed and the fearful mothers agree. If you want to write, you will have to dare, to be as open as the sea. *Apertura lluviosa.*" He said, "Live in my house for a month and don't speak. *Mi casa es tu casa miento incommunicado.*"

VIII

      I saw your funeral on American TV. It was a double death. The media took away what was already gone. After a few minutes, the picture shifted to Viet Nam and you were erased.

      I collect artifacts of the dead. The wing of an owl, the thigh bone of an elk, the heel of a buffalo, an abandoned nest, all sit on my altar. I would like to have the three fingers which held your pen to keep as a talisman.

      The last time we were together is eclipsed, like the smoke of a burning city eclipses the sun, by your death. Some deaths even outrage death. Better that cancer had really taken you — the unnatural ravishing of the body — its peculiar and unfathomable decay as one cell after another turns against itself — then that you died of heartbreak in the middle of your own death bed.

      The last time we were together, I hoped the press of your fingers would imprint poetry upon me while I wondered how much terror I had to take on to write a poem. I felt a peculiar and unwelcome feminine reluctance to invite the world into my body.

96

I wanted to be one of your heirs. I wanted you to put your hand on my head the way Jacob blessed his sons and would have gladly cheated you the way Jacob cheated Isaac into blessing him. I did not want an exclusive, but a portion of a birthright. I wanted to know if you could imagine a woman continuing your line. Did it ever occur to you that a woman could carry galaxies within her womb? Is the heart of a woman large enough, in your mind, to carry a planet, or even a country, and still small enough to embrace a man and a child?

I love you, Pablo Neruda, not the way a woman loves a man, but the way your feet loved soil, the way the moon loves death, the way you walked about Isla Negra in the rags of fog, the way the sun hankers for the green rush in all living things, and the way the mouth hungers for a word. And I still love you, Pablo Neruda, and want to snatch the white bird song from your beak as you streak across the white sky, in your white plummage cawing at the bird of death.

Nina Miller

THE SMELL OF LEMONS

No matter how hard I scour I can't rub the spots off the walls, those bits of grey and red against the shiny yellow paint. The day it happened Frank wouldn't let me go into the kitchen until after Doc Simpson and the police were all through and they took Tommy away. Even then he told me to stay out while he went in with a bucket full of hot water and my disinfectant. He came into the living room to ask where I keep the plastic garbage bags, and his face looked like a blue hubbard squash. He didn't say anything else, just went back into the kitchen until he'd done all he could do.

I scrubbed the cupboard doors so hard that if the wood were still on trees I'd have drawn sap. But the maple soaked in some of the stains, and now when I open the cupboards I keep my hands away from the spots as if they might singe my fingertips. Frank promised me he'd repaint the kitchen and refinish the cabinets after he brings the alfalfa in. I think about doing it myself, but since Tommy's death I can just about drag myself through the chores we need to live.

The nights are even worse. Frank can't talk about it. He's shut down like a field gone fallow. I lie in the bed where we made Tommy and keep saying the questions as if I was in church: why did he do it, what really happened to him in St. Paul that drove him to it, what could we have done to keep it from happening. And the worst question of all, the one that keeps spinning around in the awful quiet night, is whether he was trying to tell us something, the way he did it right there in my kitchen with Frank's shotgun. When the minister was still coming by he used to say we had to learn how to live without answers, even to love the questions. After three visits he got the message and stopped coming.

The neighbors didn't come by the way they did when my father died. Back then they showed up with hot casseroles and jars of sweet pickles from last year's canning, and fresh-baked bread and pound cake so buttery it left wet yellow spots on the plate. They sat around and the women talked about their own parents, and how good I'd been to my papa, and the men talked about government subsidies and wheat prices, and there were pots of coffee and people came every night for almost the whole week.

When Tommy died it was different. Not too many even came back after the funeral, and those that did talked about the weather and the crops and who'd had to sell out, anything but Tommy and the way he died. They didn't even talk about the fact that he was dead. But I could feel them eyeing everything in the house as if the walls or the furniture could answer their questions. Sally Willets brought over a rhubarb pie, but she said George couldn't come because he had a cold. I knew better. I could tell people were looking at us differently, Frank and me, trying to figure out what we did wrong that made it happen. I started to feel like I had the disease that poor people in faraway places get, where bits of them fall off and no one wants to touch them.

Bonnie Morris

SHIPS AND COMPASSES

Later. What are you smiling at? she asks. I have to look away. I examine the solitary droplets of water on my yogurt spoon with feigned interest. After a length of time I blush. I glance up to find her still gazing at me, smiling the smile I'd smiled just then.

We leave the restaurant and walk to my car, gliding through the dense night as though underwater, very secretly watching each other's bare shoulders flex. We head for the car like two women expecting the ultimate long-distance phone call. We head for the car. And drive to Maryland.

Because we are trying to be very quiet, every sound grows arms and legs. There is the brass click of the doorknob as we enter my parents' house. There is the jangle of car keys being slung on their hook over the spice rack. Then the opening of wine. Two red gurgles. Drinking out of Dixie cups, we are.

My lips and tongue taste wine. Over the rim of my paper cup my eyes connect with hers like silver to sauter. Oh. Guidance. Help me, Rhonda. Handbags slip off shoulders sans protest. Cups travel their way to the floor. We steal downstairs. Take off our clothes.

The hot summer darkness presses its face against my little window. It is too hot, too dark, too late, too quiet to play a record.

I suddenly feel absurdly ugly. I yearn to race up the faded carpeted stairs to the bathroom, to stare at my sophomore's face. At my hair now growing in the wrong direction. My body awkward, mesomorphic. I wish to be a ghost. You know, I think you're really beautiful, she says.

So. We are finally in bed. I have discovered that I am not two-dimensional: I cannot hide, like a paper doll, between the limp sheets. I take up space. I try to adapt my nakedness to the places between the sheets. I stare straight up at the ceiling. A passing car makes planet shapes of shadow on the wall. She has raised herself up on one elbow and is saying, Tell me what you want.

I don't know, I don't know, I don't know, must I tell you, this is my first time. But I feel myself smile into the warm dark night.

She brings her lips to mine. I feel the soft energy lapping about our faces. I have for so long wanted to be cradled in a strength without tension. This is what she gives to me at last.

We sail the bittersweet sea of the unknown. There are pirates here, and desert islands. If one of us loses course the other must help steer her back into the stronger journey. I am my own compass, my own ship. And I want to sail, sail, sail, and never drop anchor.

WATER GEOGRAPHIES

I. The Drought

During the water shortage emergency the town was an iguana—dry, tense, cold. All the stores sold out of bottled water. We listened to the radio, unwashed, drank wine, made love, and didn't do our dishes. The plates accumulated, little pyres; I spent the night with Sherry, laughing deeply, brushed my teeth with milk, and helped melt ice cubes. The dirty river leered from its burst pipelines; mayors called for patience — we were safe and like old folks we sat around recalling the sweet taste of the water we once drank. Some peoples live less glibly, and the drought in our own consciousness is chronic: barren lands, throats tight with thirst are distant bells, stilled clappers. When our water flowed back in, I too broke forth: my period began and richly so, my body feeding pipelines like the river, saying: life is random, your blood runs damp, be glad you have been spared.

II. The Flood

I wrote to you and said that the waters of the river were so swollen soon we should be drowned. I worked to clear vines from the flooded driveway and put my dissertation on the roof. There are other kinds of water: this water tastes like the middle of the night: disturbing dreams, sending me to kitchens, reaching for the water jar, drinking in my sleep.

III. The Good Water

I feel safe, living near waters, as some women draw perimeters with pet cats, gardens, small collections of clay figures. Water's live, keeps moving, even as one sleeps, moving even in the dark; things grow there — cobwebs, wood chips, smells. I feel safe every time I move to towns or islands blessed with waters. Listen to the names I drew in dripping buckets: Susquehanna. Eno. Merced. Potomac. Pacific. Chesapeake. Cayuga. Kerr. Kinneret. Yarkon. Pisgah. Bania. Yosemite, Vernal, Bridalveil. Surely there are nymphs among us glistening beneath these pools, waiting for my restless paddle guarding me as guardians — Surely I am safer living near the water, living where a flood is still a dance of clans and movement, rich, my history.

Nicky Morris

SCRATCHING

We had the flowered wallpaper in the kitchen then: red and orange roses stuffed in pots. He chose it. I was pouring milk over his porridge. He always likes me to sprinkle sugar on first, and then pour the milk.

100

"Doris," he said, "what would you think if we made an arrangement?" He took out his wallet and slipped a ten dollar bill down the front of my housedress.

"Come off it, Fred. What do you think you're doing?"

"Now don't go getting all upset." The bill was scratching me, caught on my bra, but I didn't like to pull it out.

"Doris, I've been thinking."

"Don't strain yourself," I said.

"Shut up and listen a minute will you? I've been thinking, like I said, about us and being married. I thought maybe we could liven things up a bit." With that his face started to get a little pink, just like it does at night sometimes, after we've both got ready for bed and he's in the mood for it.

"I could give you ten dollars, in the morning, if I wanted it that night. And if you didn't want to, when I come home you just give me the ten back and five more. Now you think that over." And then he grabbed his lunch box.

We'd been married ten years then. I took out the bill and put it on the counter while I did the dishes. Then I sat it on the bedside table while I made the beds.

When he came home I just said "Okay, I'll keep the ten."

Something my mother said to me once: Scratch any marriage and you'll find something underneath. I didn't know what she meant.

I have a bank account. Sometimes I buy a little perfume, some lace undies maybe, to make him want more. But mostly I just put the money in the bank. I've been thinking of buying a place, starting a small business of some kind. West, I think I'd head west.

IN THE DINER

You order scrambled and I order poached. In the booth across the aisle a man speaks harshly to his daughter. I call the woman I've just left, who wants to know where I am and who I'm with, and where I will be. You watch the man's wife. She sits next to him and you find you can count the bruises under her clothes. She is pregnant with the next child and the man tells the daughter to shut up. I return to the table and you tell me you're sure he's a wife beater. You can pick them out, you say.

The day before I found two pieces of the delicate pink shell that I keep small things in: paperclips and poker die, a pair of nail clippers. I found the pieces of shell by my bookcase, and I saw the dent in the wall above the fireplace where the shell had hit it. She must have thrown it again and again. The shell must have been very large and thick.

The man puts a piece of toast in front of the child and says, here, eat. The woman on the other side eats her breakfast, as we do. The child refuses, wanting the bowl of cereal that the man had taken from her minutes before. The man and his wife get up to leave, with a second man, a grandfather perhaps. The girl reaches out her arms to them.

I tell you of first wondering what the poker die were doing in my clothes chest, then of noticing the dents in the wall, then of seeing a fragment of the pink shell, paler than I imagine the inside of your body to be, with the same smoothness. I tell of the shell thrown against the wall hard, thrown over and over until it smashed. The child raises her arms again and again but the three adults ignore her. When finally they leave you say, good luck kid.

I eat pieces of English muffin. I know her outstretched arms, the blank wall she meets each time they ignore her. The wall that eventually will move into her own body until she too, unless she is lucky, will eat in this diner, pregnant with the next one while a woman across the aisle counts the bruises under her blouse.

But then too I remember how it is possible to love someone. How she does not have to live in a house picking up pieces that she finds in corners, one by the bookcase, another hurridly shoved under the rug. If she can hold out her arms in the face of such indifference then anything is possible. She could be the woman across the aisle, with her new friend, as they eat their breakfast full of each other and not even really hungry.

Patricia A. Murphy

NINETEEN-FIFTY-FOUR

There is a porcelain bathroom with no door. White porcelain surfaces scrubbed to a gleaming perfection with Ajax. There is the smell of cleanliness but no reflection of the self. Instead, a glare and no relief. Sound bounces off the walls, the surfaces of the tub, the toilet bowl, the white teeth under the mindless smile — (more cleaners, Pepsodent and Listerine).

I am fourteen, and I want to scream. I probably have been

screaming but it is impossible to tell if I have been deafened by the reverberations of my own horror, or if I have simply become numbed as I stand in the center of this white room, smiling.

I am careful not to touch anything, and I would get my feet off the tiled floor if I could. If I touch anything, I would leave evidence of my body. Menstrual blood on the immaculate floor, pale scarlet drops leading to the toilet bowl where other unspeakable human functions take place, and are swished away in a blue chemical swirl. My fingerprints are on the chrome towel bar. The arches and whorls of my identity are glistening on the metal. I wipe it down quickly with a square of toilet paper, and dispose of myself into the pristine hole with the blue water.

I wear a dress with a peter pan collar and a girdle as white and as hard as the bathtub. The garters press into my flesh leaving red marks on the softness of my thighs. I am a good Catholic girl, and so I offer up this suffering for the Poor Souls in Purgatory.

It's no use though because I have bled through it all. The impervious plastic ironweave girdle, the lace-edged polyester slip, my yellow summer frock. I have cramps.

And I am ashamed. I am ashamed because this is not my house, not my bathroom, but the bathroom of my employer. A bathroom my family aspires to along with an automatic washer and dryer and wall-to-wall carpeting.

And I don't know how to behave. It's because my father didn't go to World War II because of his migraine headaches. My employer went to the War and so did his wife's first husband. He died in the War, and it was the ten thousand dollars she got for his death that built the house and this bathroom.

And got me — the small town girl attending St. Francis School for Girls — while babysitting and housecleaning for board and room. The ignorant small town girl who was not asked to come back for the next school year because she had hoarded slightly used Kotex pads.

I had hoarded them because I knew they were expensive, and I was afraid to throw them away. (Sometimes there wasn't enough to eat at home.) I was ashamed I couldn't bleed right. Bleed enough to soak them through, so I could throw them away. What would I do if I didn't have the money to buy new ones?

My employer's wife found this evidence of my ignorance, my body in the closet of my basement room. White Kotex pads with tiny brown stains. They didn't even stink. My fourteen-year-old menstrual cycles were as irregular and as innocent as tears.

I would never be a blond bombshell even though I was blond. I encased myself in girdles and padded bras but when the blood came, it leaked through everything.

So when I think of the fifties, I think shame. I think denial. I think screaming silently. I think white. White and blond. I think bomb. I think the War is over but something went wrong. I think I don't belong, and worst of all, I think I don't want one of these bathrooms.

Then, I think, there must be something wrong with me.

Linda Nelson

Sylvia and Durango

Really, by the time I get to the top of the stairs, I am pretty proud of myself.

> Oh, I have been waiting for you, Sylvia. Just last night, as the moon rose full and blue, flagrantly astride New York's skyline, I realized you were near.

This is the second time I've found her, and I flew right up those stairs, steep and narrow as they were. Legs still in damn good shape, good enough to kick with. Thought I might need to when I saw the door swinging into the stuffy hall.

> For so long I've waited. Waiting: when I tell you I am a lesbian, I mean to say that I choose women, pursue them. Every day. Sylvia was the first woman I ever seduced.

I ain't come all these years, looking for this tow-headed girlchild, to find her lying stiff. That door better not move an inch. I ain't come all these years. Dead, maimed, raped. Beat. I seen it. The bastard better not still be here.

> I am standing at the window, arms held gingerly across the front of my laundered shirt. The street no longer interests me. One seduces, one pursues. I want her to see my back first. After all, she is one of my mothers. To give her this, my back utterly exposed to her gaze. What will we find?

Just the tip of my boot, that's all I slide through the door. You just don't know what the fuck goes on. And if I scuff up my leather some man is gonna be in deep shit. Had to wear my best, it's been so long since I give her up.

> With my back to her, I close my eyes, suck the stars out of many nights of dreamless sleep. Feeling her approach, my past spins away from my shoulders; the walls crackle around me, white

104

becomes yellow. The air is picking up momentum, sweeping in
through the loose glass, passing quickly through my bones.
Shit if I'm not too late again. Always looking, that's the truth. She was so
tiny when I found her, only days older when I placed her for adoption.
Mother. No, no mother-fucker better've hurt my girl. Can't see nothing in
this hell-hole but too much yellow.

I am so impatient, yet still. I am that man, the conqueror, the
statue, victorious astride a mighty beast. Crossing the waters. I
am discovered. I am the woman, thick fingers shielding her gaze
as she searches across the continent, feet as firm upon this hill as
the sun gripping my hair. Holding my head up. Loved. Listening.
I stand as still as all we would make of our history.

I can't help it: I suck my breath in through my teeth and the place is filled
with the hiss. That back. She's the same sandy color as the beach I found
her on. Pale, hard reds and yellows. Maybe she only looks that sharp
because the window is so dirty and blurred behind her. Can't help
wondering where she came from. Damn girl. And didn't she ever learn to
keep a nice place for herself? Who she brought up to think gonna do it
for her?

Lesléa Newman

MY FATHER'S LAP

I am 16 years old and I am sitting on my father's lap. I am 16 years old and
I am sitting on my father's lap. I am wearing an orange sweater dress with
a white stripe around the collar and a white stripe around each sleeve. My
father says this dress makes me look sexy. I hate this dress. I am sitting on
his lap and we are in the livingroom with Uncle Seymour, Uncle Harvey
and Uncle Alex. I hate this dress and their voices drift past my ears heavy
and slow like the smoke from my father's cigar. I am 16 years old and I am
sitting on my father's lap. 16 years old sitting on my father's lap. I keep my
back stiff and my feet on the floor. My father pets my hair from the crown
of my head down my shoulders down my back down my waist down to his
lap. My hair is thick and curly and black. I will set it tonight on rollers the
size of orange juice cans when everyone leaves. When everyone leaves.
My father's hand is heavy at the back of my neck where it rests for a minute,

heavy as my uncles' voices heavy as the smoke from his cigar. I am 16 years old and I am sitting on my father's lap. 16 years old on my father's lap. He kisses the top of my head and plays with my fingers as he holds my hand. He plays with my fingers as he holds my hand and his big college ring rubs against my pinky. It hurts. It hurts but I do not move. I do not move because I am a ghost. I am a ghost and my father is a ghost and my uncles all are ghosts. The TV is not a ghost. The TV is on and it is not a ghost and I hear a football game. Every now and then a loud cheer bellows out from the screen and every now and then a loud burst of laughter erupts from the kitchen. From the kitchen where my mother and Aunt Rose, Aunt Ethel and Aunt Miriam are making lunch. I am 16 years old and I am sitting on my father's lap. 16 years on my father's lap. My mother and my aunts are taking little cookies filled with chocolate and jam out of a white cardboard box and putting them onto a plate and laughing. Little cookies filled with chocolate and jam and laughing. My mother won't let me eat any because I am getting too fat. I am getting too fat but later when everyone leaves I will eat them all. When everyone leaves I will eat them all until nothing is left. Until nothing is left and nothing remains. I am 16 years old and I am sitting on my father's lap. I am sitting on his lap and he is petting me like a dog and my dog is sitting at my feet waiting to be petted but I cannot pet him because my father is petting me. My dog's back is stiff my back is stiff the back of the chair is stiff I am drowning in all this stiffness and my father's hand is heavy at the back of my neck where it rests for a minute, pulling me down. I am drowning and my father can't hear me and my mother can't hear me and the ghosts can't hear me. No one can hear me because I say nothing. Nothing is said nothing is heard nothing is left and nothing remains. I am 16 years old and I am sitting on my father's lap. I am 16 years old and I am sitting on my father's lap. I am 16 years old and I am not sitting on my father's lap. I am not sitting on his lap because everyone has left and nothing is left and it is time for bed. It is time for bed and my mother and my father are in their bed and I am in bed and my dog is in my bed curled behind my knees and the nightlight is on. I am 16 years old and the nightlight is on because I am afraid. I am afraid of the dark I am afraid of the ghosts I am afraid of the shape of my clothes piled high on the chair. I am afraid to fall asleep because I am afraid I will never wake up. I will never wake up and then I will be a ghost I don't want to be a ghost I am afraid of the ghosts I am afraid to fall asleep. I am 16 years old and I am afraid to fall asleep so I pet my dog. I pet my dog from the top of his head to the tip of his tail. I pet my dog the way my father pets me. Sometimes my dog whimpers in his sleep and sometimes I wish I was a dog but I am not a dog I am 16 years old and I am afraid to fall asleep. I am afraid to fall asleep until I think about my father. I think about my father dying and that makes me cry and then I feel better and then I fall asleep. I think about my father dying and that makes me feel better and then I feel better and then I fall asleep.

MUGGED

for Marilyn Silberglied

It wasn't enough with the pogroms, the poverty, the cold, the hunger, with everything in my life I've ever been through, you'd think in my old age I could enjoy a little peace and quiet, but no, that would be too good for me. Somewhere it must be written that Esther Silberglied hasn't suffered enough.

Once a month I take the D train from the Bronx into Manhattan to get my hair done, at Clairol's they do a nice job for nothing. Senior Citizen's Day, they call it. Alright, I don't mind, after all I am 85, I ain't no spring chicken.

So on the platform I'm standing, and who should come screeching in on the train but some young fella who's had it too easy, he ain't got enough troubles of his own, he decides to make trouble for somebody else; after all why should they have it better than him? So just for fun, for kicks maybe, he decides he should steal the old Jewish lady's purse.

So what do I know? All of a sudden, one-two-three, the *meshugeneh* grabs my bag, the train starts moving, and I start moving with it — what, you think I'm gonna let him get away with that? This pocketbook he'll steal over my dead body.

My daughter when she hears the story, she says to me, Ma why didn't you just let go? She ain't a fighter, my daughter with the fancy college education. She don't know that in this rotten world you gotta fight for what's yours or they'll take every single thing they can get.

Besides who had time to think? One minute I'm standing on the platform minding my own business, the next minute this *momser* has me by the strap, the train is dragging me along, my head is knocking against the window, and before I could say *gevalt* I'm out cold like last year's *latkes*.

The next thing I know I wake up in Bellevue, and I ask you, is that a place to take a nice Jewish lady like me? Alright, today I don't look so nice with a broken head, my eye swelled up like a baseball and my wrist snapped like a piece of dry spaghetti, but still.

Oy and Jack was waiting with supper, pot roast he was warming up on a small light like I told him, and some string beans from the can. He's sitting in the kitchen and he's sitting, and he's sitting and he don't know what to do, should he eat, should he not eat, where can I be, he can't imagine, and then he gets the call: *Mr. Silberglied, your wife's been hit by a train.*

So up he jumps into a cab with no hat, no scarf, no gloves. He races into the room like he's on fire and I says to him, Jack, what are you *meshugeh,* running around half naked in the 25 degrees, pneumonia you want to catch? We ain't got enough troubles with me looking like a prize fighter three weeks before our 65th wedding anniversary? Some glamour girl I'm gonna be at the party — on top of everything else you wanna be sick too? I was in a hurry, he says. What hurry, I ask him. I look like I'm going somewhere?

I give Jack my supper, you think I can eat with such aggravation, and then 9:00 he goes home, but as soon as he goes down with the elevator up he comes again. Esther, he whispers, I was so *farshimmeled* from the call I left the house without my wallet. You got any money? I tell him to look in my bag. So he looks and what does he find? Five dollars and eighty-seven cents. And for that, this is where I am.

The nurse hears the commotion, they all got ears like elephants in here. She goes out into the hall, she passes the hat, and she comes back in with enough money to take Jack home. Alright, it ain't the first time we had to take up a collection. You see, as rotten as the world is, you can always find one or two nice people wherever you go.

I didn't want Jack should call the children, why should they worry? They got enough troubles of their own, everybody's got troubles, it's a rotten world after all, but thank God I'm alive. It could be worse; at least it didn't happen on the way there before I got my hair done, I could be lying here with my roots showing on top of everything else. Alright, tomorrow I'll go home, the pot roast will keep, I'll sit with Jack in the kitchen and watch the 6:00 news. It'll be just like nothing ever happened. Like nothing ever happened at all.

Camille Norton

THEY DO NOT TOUCH

The summer we were sick together, the summer I read clouds with my brother, she carried us pitchers of lemon water and mint, we were still animals then, we had no fear. Sex had not yet climbed through our bodies, we were generic, my brother's face was featureless as a newt, I loved to comb his hair with my fingers, babble the air for him, stroke his tender legs like a familiar. The kin sickness persisted, it was a way of being together, neither of us were willing to become healthy children, to go out again into the dirt and broil of our peers, ordinary hoodlums who never dreamed. We were good, we developed lesions, we were allowing the virus to run its course. After she soaked us in calomine, we lay mummified in our cots, faking death until we were bored by the silence. Then we called out to each other, threatening to come back from the grave, disguised as regular people. More than anything we wanted to be aliens, to appear and disappear through the body, to defend the country against Communists and Nazis. At night I listened to the rasp in his chest and pretended it was me in there, knocking against his ribs like a bird. One night, he began to cry like a baby and she came and took him away. Pneumonia. A dangerous game, this pretending. He stayed in a real hospital for seven days and when he came back he was a boy, she gave him a room of his own, I wasn't allowed to touch him. The last time I really touched him he was so drunk he had passed out in his own vomit. I lifted his barrel chest from the floor and pulled off the shirt he had fouled, I passed a soapy cloth over his cold skin, I force-fed him water and aspirin. At his wedding reception, I smoked dope with him in the parking lot after the parent generation had gone home. I must have hugged him. He's grown fat. He loves his wife but they don't touch in front of other people. His wife sends me birthday and Christmas cards and signs his name at the bottom of the engraved greeting. She told me she consulted a psychic who said her first husband would die young, but that she would have children with her second husband. He laughs when she tells this story, I scan his face for some sign of fear, it's my own chest knocking, I don't know him really but he's blood, and blood is what our story has come to mean, it's the only love we do not choose.

THAT COFFEE

When I say that I stole for her, I want you to understand that I did so without a moral context, I wasn't a citizen then in the sense that I define myself now, there was no house to speak of, there was only her body. There was my body, of course, why do you assume I'm such a fool, there was my body — that was the point of it all, wasn't it — I mean the pleasure, the desire, the scorching, everything. But this is the kind of knowledge that comes later, after civilization takes the place of instinct. Spurious, hearty rationalizations, your specialty. Alright, my specialty.

I met her through a man I slept with now and then, it was at his house probably, one of those brick walk-ups in the South End that has since become a condo. He liked artists, which is how I came in. I suppose he thought I was interesting, I don't know. He had put up a show of his other lover's work, photographs, very political smut shots of the poor, and there we were in our clean shirts drinking white wine out of these awful plastic glasses with the disposable stems, Michael was there, Julia was already drunk, somebody from the *Real Paper* had agreed to show up and we were all putting on our best face and then she walked in. She was alone. Her eyes were cut like halved stones. She was bone-thin, beautiful. I suppose I stared at her for a very long time because I don't remember anything else about that party. Well, yes, there was David's long arm sliding around my waist, his upstaging, faggy whisper, "Don't touch, darling. She doesn't like girls." And of course, she heard him, just as he meant her to hear him, and that's how we met — over a warning issued by a lover I had just about discarded. He was right, you know. She didn't like girls. That's what she said anyway, after the first time together. She said, "This isn't my thing. I'll never do this again with another woman." I told her I didn't care what she didn't do with other women. Afterwards, we always drank coffee out of demitasse cups, English china, her mother's set, part of the inheritance. We drank it in the bed, always, and I held her between my legs from behind as if my body existed for no other reason than to hold her like that, there was the anise smell of her skin, the heat from the coffee, the salt tang of sex lifting from her small head, the feel of the whole length of her between my breasts, my legs. She drank that coffee straight off, like a Frenchwoman, sharp, scalding sips. She never wanted more. I never imagined she loved me. She didn't love me. Did I ever say that she loved me? What I said was that I love her.

ANIMAL INSTINCT

She's more or less the blonde version of the French cousin, sparrow small, bronzed, all muscle and heart. There are, you say, two versions of the French cousin. You are the dark, lean kind, the sort that is mistaken for a boy, the sort that wears striped pullovers and sunglasses while running along wharves in Truffaut films. You're the type who's always stealing something, she's the type who's always stolen or stolen upon. This is because she bleaches the crown of her hair, the animal sign for femininity. Where I come from, feminine animals wear ankle bracelets and talk fast.

110

She refers to women she knows as masculine or feminine presences, she says things like, "Michelle brought a masculine energy into our relationship." You say she speaks this way because she's been living in California for ten years. I say she speaks this way because she believes in animal instinct, in womb ache, the drive towards fertilization, fructification in the dark.

I listen to the rich, accented huskiness of her voice, the petulance lifting the end of her sentences into questions that ask for nothing but admiration. "I have been trying to have a bab-ee, you know, to get pregnant, but so far the inseminations have not worked." She is drinking my coffee. She is sitting in my kitchen. She will be staying with us for a week. She's on her way to the Cape, where one of her admirers has lent her a beach house for the month of August. When she is not talking about pregnancy, she talks about California, its spiritual quality, its dry heat, its pure, sweet Napa Valley air. I'm an East Coast person, I say. New York, Boston, Philadelphia, are there really any other cities worth knowing? Well, London, of course. I admire the British. They never tell you anything you don't want to know.

I already know more than I'd like to know about her. She's been involved in love triangles with other women for ten years. Since she left you, in fact. The last couple wanted her to move in with them. They said they would help raise the baby. You yourself met her through your roommate, a nice guy as far as that went, but a bit of a wimp, a heroin addict who liked having a lesbian around for protection. She was his girlfriend. She began leaving his bed for yours in the middle of the night. At first she merely wept in your arms, he was so indifferent, he didn't know she was a woman, it had been so long since she'd really been made love to, and so on. What could you do? You both left the junkie, you slept together for two years, you moved to Paris with her, you were young, it was so long ago, what does it matter now? She wears little sleeping shirts that come down just below the panty line. You confess to me that when you saw her this time at the airport, after so many years, you felt nothing more than the minor gladness one feels for a cousin one vacationed with during an unfortunate late adolescence. After you put her to bed in your studio, you ask me whether I still love you. You look sheepish and odd, which is exactly how you should look in this situation. After a few minutes, your face falls apart the way it always does when you are asleep, and I'm left with your innocence and her breath in the other room. I begin to think that you are breathing together the deep suspiration of the unconscious after it has performed another brilliant act of repression. I allow myself to dislike you intensely.

In the morning, after you leave for your job, we're left alone together. I drink coffee with her. In graduate school, I learned that it is a simple thing to take coffee with people one neither likes nor trusts. She sits at the kitchen table looking mussed, early Simone Signoret, she crosses her delicate legs, she arranges her bottles and bottles of vitamins. "For the bab-ee I hope to be having," she explains. I chainsmoke with a gusto I haven't felt for years, filling the room with tars, I ask in an offhand way whether she's allergic to cigarettes, when she says yes I nod sympathetically. I light a fresh cigarette from the one already burning in the ashtray. I am kind to her, I make small, attentive listening noises that elicit all of her best stories, I notice that her mouth is very full, plum-colored, as if it has just been bitten, she talks and talks, I smoke and smoke, I tell her that I admire the way the French go on smoking and drinking, in spite of all the warnings, I draw her out, she's mesmerized, she has no secrets anymore, she's an open book, I steal her, I soothe her when her fantastic talk begins making her feel nervous, I help her pack, I lend her my subway map, I walk her to the door. There is absolutely nothing I can do to make her stay.

Patricia O'Donnell

RETRIBUTION

Perhaps if she stared at him long enough she could turn him into a hamster. Then all their troubles would be settled. She'd be more than glad to clean his cage, oil his wheel and bring him chopped lettuce for as long as he lived. (How long DID hamsters live, anyway?)

Meanwhile, she stared. Fur — was that fur? Hard to tell, he's so hairy, and the eyes wouldn't give it away, his were brown and dark. She stared. A whisker. She wasn't mistaken, it was. One long tremulous whisker, about six inches and still growing. She stared harder, encouraged. His undershirt had hitched up over his belly as he slumped on the couch; in the gap between belt and shirt a thickening down of greyish-white appeared. He was engrossed in the game and didn't notice as the fingers holding his beer pinkened and grew shorter. She stared, fascinated. It was happening fast now. More whiskers, dainty and white, appeared next to his nose which had turned a soft pink and twitched violently as the Bears earned another penalty. His forehead had flattened and was now on the same plane as his nose and his hairline had disappeared. He couldn't cross his legs anymore, though he hadn't noticed, they were too short. He sat in a kind of a crouch. One sock had fallen off, the other was hooked by the cuff to a pink toe.

My God. I've done it, she thought. Turned the little jerk into a hamster. LITTLE! Oh God! Little he wasn't. She stared. A man-sized hamster.

Oh god.

Mira-Lani Oglesby

BRONSTEIN'S CONTACT FROM THE REVOLUTIONARY WORKERS BRIGADE

Bronstein's contact from the Revolutionary Workers Brigade calls Bronstein on the telephone to tell him that he is going to bring over a coded message and leave it on the fire escape. He tells Bronstein that when the coded message is decoded, it will disclose the new location of RWB Headquarters. Bronstein's contact from the Revolutionary Workers Brigade will not tell Bronstein the new location of RWB Headquarters over the telephone because he suspects that Bronstein's telephone is being tapped. Every time that Bronstein's contact from the Revolutionary Workers Brigade calls Bronstein on the telephone, he uses a different name. Last time it was Jack. The time before that it was Arlene. This time it is Baby May. Bronstein recognizes him by his voice. Sometimes when Bronstein's contact from the Revolutionary Workers Brigade calls Bronstein on the telephone, he acts like a regular person instead of like a Revolutionary Worker. Sometimes he mentions having a headache or being tired. Sometimes he chews food while he talks.

ANOTHER DAY, ANOTHER QUESTION BY ATHENA LOUISE, FOR STEVE OGLESBY

Another day. So far today, I've figured out that poetry is dumb and that lighting is important.

Bronstein once told me that I put people in boxes.

And he was right.

But I've always rested assured in the knowledge that the boxes were cardboard boxes, picked up at the grocery store, the liquor mart, the bookstore.

And cardboard boxes disintegrate with time.

This alcoholic writer guy I knew in Iowa City, Rudy, Rudy once said on the subject of debt: I owe thirty thousand dollars this year and next year I'll owe fifty thousand — eventually I'll die.

Rudy had a Missouri accent and he believed in reincarnation. I liked him even though he was extremely draining.

Now, did I just put Rudy into a box? And, if I did just put Rudy into a box, is it a cardboard box? What is a cardboard box?

A cardboard box is a box made out of cardboard.

The American Heritage Dictionary of the English Language Paperback Edition defines cardboard as

Cardboard. Noun. A stiff pasteboard made of paper pulp.

and it defines box as

Box. One. Noun. One. A rectangular container, often with a lid. Two. The amount such a container can hold. Three. A separated compartment for a small group, as in a theater. Four. A booth. Five. An awkward situation. Verb. To place in or as if in a box. Box. Two. Noun. A blow or cuff. Verb. To hit with the hand. Two. To engage in a boxing match with. Box. Three. Noun. One. A shrub with small evergreen leaves and hard, yellowish wood. Two. Also boxwood. The wood of this shrub.

Another question. How important is the difference between a cardboard box and a boxwood box?

Linda Peavy

A COMMON LANGUAGE

"Oh, my God!"

"What is it?"

She didn't answer. He wouldn't believe it, even if she told him.

He bent low to read the small card at the base of the tangled wood. "'The Rose-Wet Cave.' How do you figure that one?"

The same way Adrienne Rich figured it. But how to tell him that?

"Who knows," she lied, biding her time.

"It's not thorny, so there's no rose image there." He set himself to the task of disproving the title. "But I guess the sticks are reddish enough to suggest 'rose.'" He backed away and studied the sculpture from a different angle, oblivious to the suggestive yawn of the elliptical opening in the intricately woven branches. "Wonder what it's made out of?" he asked aloud. "Never saw branches like these."

"Red dogwood," she answered, reading the sculptor's comments from the gallery sheet in her hand. "'Red dogwood is supple and responsive in my hands and holds its color long after it has been taken.'" She felt her own color rise, but he did not turn to see and seemed not to have heard.

"Wonder what it will look like when it gets really old? If I were investing in a piece like this, I'd want to be sure it would hold up over the years."

She smiled. If he only knew. But he didn't. And now he was peering intently at the delicate fronds of lichen that clung to the outer edges of the piece. "This mossy stuff won't hold up for sure. Going grey already," he fussed. Coming back to the front, he leaned far into the tangle, his head disappearing into the opening. "You could get lost in there," he said. "Weird."

The word was a dismissal. He moved to the right and began to study a wall of collages. She followed, but kept watch over the rose-wet cave behind her. Out of the corner of her eye she could see two women studying the tangled wood. She thought she saw them exchange significant glances. She thought she saw them nod as they read the title. She thought she knew why they did not need to speak.

THE KILL FLOOR

"It's only because she works on the kill floor they let her juggle her shifts that way. Don't have enough inspectors as it is. Long as she gets the work done, they can't afford to be too tough."

I nod my understanding. Working on the kill floor ought to carry some privilege. I try to imagine this woman I have never seen standing in swirling water, her tennis shoes spattered with the blood of the hogs whose hanging bodies she pokes and prods and stamps with her approval.

"If it hadn't been for her job, she'd have come right home when he first started in on her. But she's put in five years and the minute she leaves, there goes all her insurance."

Again I nod. She'll need insurance. I pour another cup of coffee and try to get the story straight. She's already filed for divorce, but he's changed his mind and says he'll kill her before he lets her go. Last week he broke into the house after she came home from the graveyard shift. And now the sheriff says don't go back home again. She's borrowed a friend's camper and set it up in a campground 10 miles from the packing plant. He knows she's going to work every day, and the neighbors say he spends all his time looking for her.

"Isn't she afraid he'll follow her out of the plant? If he sees her getting into her car . . ."

"What car? He's had the car from the first. Left her the pick-up, but the starter's out, so it's parked out at the plant. She's been riding with different ones that live beyond the campground."

"Why doesn't he just follow her when she leaves?"

"That's what I meant about changing shifts. She keeps him guessing as best she can. Oh, she's a sly one. Sometimes she works double shifts, sometimes single. With the truck parked there all the time like it is, he'd have to live in that parking lot to be sure when she's working."

I refrain from telling her that it's just a matter of time before he figures things out. It's obvious that's something she already knows.

"If he ever finds her, she's ready for him." The lines in her face tighten. I do not want to ask what she means by that.

I do not need to. "She's got a couple of guns and a dog. Just let him try to get into that camper."

Again I try to imagine this young woman I have never seen, strong, even in her fear. Maybe because of her fear. Waiting out her days inside an Apache camper, two guns and a dog to keep her company. "So what happens if she does shoot him? If she kills him, even?" I have to ask. Have to make her mother see where all of this is leading.

"Then she's done with him."

"With him, maybe. But what happens when the sheriff comes out to see about . . ."

"Self defense. Everybody knows Ron's nuts. His old man was certifiably crazy. Been in Warm Springs for years. And Ron would have been there, too, if it hadn't been for Carla. Time and again I told her to go on and let him go. Manic-depressive, that's what the doctor called it. Sick's all I know. Beating her up like he did last February, dropping out of sight for days, then showing up on Valentine's Day with five dozen long-stemmed roses. Five dozen! It took half her check to pay off Master-charge."

And the other half to cover the doctor bills. I think it but do not say it. Saying does not seem fair, when we both already know. I look at the woman across from me. She looks sixty, but is probably fifty at most. Once every six months, when the house gets so dirty even I can't stand it, I call

Rita to spend a long day helping me clean. A day ahead of her coming, I straighten all the surface debris, shoving things into drawers and over-crowded closets, getting far enough ahead of her so that the assigned task looks possible by the time she arrives.

This morning while she did bathrooms and kitchen floors, I washed windows. This afternoon we'll tackle dusting and vacuuming and maybe shampooing the living room carpet. If we ever get past now.

I did not ask for this. Well, I asked the question I have always asked: How is your daughter? But she has never before really told me. I have never before wanted to know. Nor do I want to know now. I no more want to hear about Carla's being beaten and raped by her estranged husband than I want to hear how people are reallying feeling when I ask: How are you?

I do not want to know that this happens to women. I do not want to have this knowledge juxtaposed against my restless chafing in a marriage that has always been viewed as perfect by those who don't live in it. I do not want to have one more reason to see how lucky I am to have such a wonderful husband.

And I do not want to know about something I have to do something about. It is clear that Rita is right. Carla can take care of herself — if that means a shoot-out. But it is equally clear that Carla has no idea how to keep her need to defend herself from this man from turning into a murder rap.

"Look," I say at last. "We can't do anything about this ourselves, but there are people who can. It's the end of October. We've already had snow. She can't stay in that camper all winter."

"She's got a catalytic heater and a down bag. She won't freeze."

I do not bother to talk about what kind of life this woman will have, there in her camper, snug in her bag, her guns lying close by her side, fear weighing down on her, keeping her warm through the night. All of that oozes out of the silence and arranges itself in front of us on the table. A proper hostess, I cover the ooze with words.

"But when she's the last camper left, when she's the only one out there, what's to keep him from driving by and getting suspicious?"

"She'll be ready for him."

"But there are other ways." I grope for what they are, for whatever solutions there must be to problems so foreign to my own. "She can go to the Battered Women's Center. They'd have to take her in."

"She's never talked about the place."

"Maybe she doesn't know about it."

"Maybe there's not one down there."

I go to the phone and dial the local center. Surely there are state-wide referrals for such services. The woman on the line is most interested.

Too interested. She snatches eagerly at every detail I am willing to give up, right down to how many times he raped her. What if this were my own story I were telling? I would never have gotten beyond describing the way he used the crowbar to break the window on the back door so he could open the deadbolt. I would never have gotten far enough to explain about how he didn't put the crowbar down, once he got inside.

Only when I have gone through the litany of abuse, the chronicle of tears and regrets does the woman from the answering service explain that the staff is out. Too spent to be angry for what this woman has done to me and to the woman who waits at my table, I hang up, armed with another number. All those expensive details have bought me but seven digits to share with the woman who waits.

Her face does not change as I explain that the number is for the county welfare office. There is no center in the place where the young woman waits in her camper for a visit from the man with the crowbar and roses, the man who has no intention of letting her go. There is no home in which she can live without two guns and a dog and the fear.

There is nothing to tell me the woman before me has heard what it is that I have so carefully told her. She knew there was nothing that could be done before she sat down at this table. She will know it when she stands up and moves beyond this small, small moment in which we have sat and talked as if what we said might actually matter.

I rinse out the cups, toss the half-eaten sandwiches into the sink, and flip on the disposal. The water gushing out of the tap cushions the blades that slash at the unfinished bits and pieces.

Natalie L.M. Petesch

WEDDING NIGHT

You ask yourself how this particular life rather than any other became yours. It all seems so simple. . . . You grow up, you think about hair, about a cold sore on your lip, about whether you should shave your legs, whether you should wear lipstick, rouge, powder base, tweeze your eyebrows, study music, trying to think of ways to be both soft and hard, coaxing and passive, alluring and decorous: an obedient child, yet resistant to suitors with bad breath.

118

And now suddenly it's all irrelevant whether you have a pimple on your forehead on this wedding night, or whether your nails have lovely half-moons so that your hands will look elegant, slender, and graceful in the wedding photographs. You discover quickly what was important: what was important lies on the sheets, scandalously revealing that all the satins, bows, bridesmaids, the smiling groom, the crushing of glass, the chupah overhead, the dances, the stamping of feet, the wine and the huzzahs, the tweaking of cheeks, the winking of eyes, the blessing of hands and the tears of your mother, are all about *this:* that this act was what the ceremony sanctified; that the glossy gown, the crystal goblets, the sanctimonious prayer, the falsetto voice of the band leader, his musicians playing, "Goodnight, sweetheart, Goodnight" — were all mere diversionary ploys meant to distract you from this reality: that the man who had declared that he adored you — tenderly, worshipfully, barely touching your fingertips to his lips could, if he so desired, use you between midnight and morning as if you were a mulatto slave.

RAPED

It struck her now that she had lost the freedom ever to open a door again without first giving it serious thought: never again would she answer the ring of the telephone without a quickening pulse . . . never again cross a deserted parking lot. No, never again would she sleep alone on the beach, gorgeously free. . . . Never again go backpacking alone in the hills nor slip out to a restaurant at midnight; never drive five thousand, ten thousand miles alone on the Pan American highway in her van; never ask strange men for directions, nor for desperately needed help on the highway; never wear shorts on the boardwalk unless "escorted"; never go to dinners, movies, dances, alone. . . . Never again speak-to-strangers except with careful diffidence, nor look a man straight in the eye as she passed him in the park, on the city street or a country lane; never go jogging at night, and only in certain public places during the day; never work in disreputable bars, off-beat moviehouses, walk home alone from off-Broadway plays. Never walk through the curtained Pullman section in the pre-dawn hours; never work in a building on the night shift; never speak too loudly in a public place, attracting the "wrong" kind of attention. Never to answer the phone at one a.m. without terror in your voice. Never to enter your own house by way of a poorly lighted back door or a garage without fear; never to fly to Acapulco, Istanbul, Veracruz or Hawaii alone because "you-never-know" what's going on in their heads when they see you alone.

And that — she told herself in the full wake of her horror — is the real reason you are trembling with fear: because you have been robbed of your future. *That* is the real problem. Because, who are you, if you must always have an escort, always have a bodyguard, always have someone prepared to rescue you from unpredictable violence? Are you Yourself, or are you merely a part-person, an unfinished person, in need of a secondary survival system? Or is the person you must eternally take with you to protect your person the *real* person in this *ménage à deux* — your poltergeist, your *alter ego,* your doppleganger — is he/she/it the real person and not you? Because isn't it true — you ask yourself — that never again to go anywhere alone means not to be Anyone at all, not even when you are appearing in public: doesn't it mean you have become a shadow of your identity?

Pat Pomerleau

SHE HAD A WAY

She had a way of greeting her friends by putting her hand on their crotch. The first time it happened to me I was a bit disconcerted but I soon grew used to it and in time looked forward to seeing her if only for the charm of her greeting.

She was always nonchalant and calm and had many interesting things to say about détente and the latest plane crash and any other items in the news.

After she had taken her hand away, I hardly noticed its absence because she had so beautifully established contact with her eyes and her voice.

She was a little bit Spanish; it was her way of saying ¡HOLA!

Louise Rafkin

WHY I'M SO SCREWED UP TODAY

Here is a summary of why I'm so screwed up right now.

First I was supposed to like Chris (God, how I *hate* the word supposed) and as I was informed by many, he liked me. . . . So, I went to the football game which we won. It was a really good game and I even cheered a little. I thought that he would not be at the game because I was also informed they (meaning him and Steve) were working. But as I arrived at the party at John Dik's they were there. Must have got off early. Anyhow, David Linder gave me some beer. Like three bottles. What a bro. I talked to Chris for a second, but I was too busy looking at Steve. Fuck, did he look nice! Gina was talking to Steve and I decided that I wanted him. So as the night wore on, I got talking to Chris and he (Steve!) walked up. So I said to Steve: You're the one who doesn't give people any beer. And he said: Come out and get some. So I did. And we were just going to come back in and I asked him if he was even going to be my friend. So he said yeah and then he just put his arms around me. So I proceeded to say some things I shouldn't of such as: The only reason I liked Chris was because I was horny. And some other good ones like, I really like you and missed you so much when I was at camp. To that he replied, I heard about you at camp. But he wouldn't tell me what he heard. Then we walked back into the house. And I saw Chris and this is the only word I can describe what I felt: Fucked. So Steve walked me home and I just left him sitting on my front porch. I told him I was going to kiss him and he said: Who said you could? But I did anyways. Then I told him he must have been practicing. So I left him sitting on my porch. Then he went back to the party and he told Gina that it was a big mistake that he was with me. Also Chris couldn't understand why I was with Steve if I really liked *him*. I feel so fucked. Chris is such a neat guy. They also said I was all hanging over him at the beach that day. But I wasn't even doing anything at all! I can't believe how everything gets fucked up when things start getting around. The fucking grapevine in Rancho Del Mar has got to be worse than any. . . . Tomorrow at school is going to be very touchy. All I'm going to say to Steve is: I'm sorry for how I acted the other night, and if you want you can just forget it. . . . To Chris I'm going to say: I'm sorry I was so screwed up at the party, I really didn't know what I was doing and what I was saying. I knew you knew I liked you and I do. (I'm only going to say this part if I know Steve doesn't like me. . . .)

Talking to Steve is going to be easy compared to talking to Chris. Anyways, that's why I'm so screwed up right now.

121

Shelly Rafferty

The Skyline Expedition

Cautiously, Buck and I checked our footwear before leaving home base. We knew it would have to be sturdy to carry us over the untested terrain across the black water.

"You got everything, Buck?" I inquired.

Buck patted her waist pack, then quickly pulled up the flap to double check. The silver synthetic material made a popping, ripping sound.

"I hope so," she muttered. "Looks like I've got it covered."

"You bringing a weapon?"

Buck shrugged nonchalantly, as if already defeated. "Anyone who attacks us is bound to be bigger and/or smarter." She slapped her hip smartly. "I left my six-shooter at home."

"I guess you're right," I admitted. "I wish we knew what was out there."

"If we knew, we wouldn't be explorers, now, would we?"

I checked my own supply bag: water and food, a large area plan folded over about a hundred times, gloves, headgear, and for good measure, my rabbit's foot. I was nervous. It couldn't hurt.

"Let's go," I said. Buck was smiling, all confidence and cheek. "Lead on, MacDuff," she said.

I triple-locked the heavy door behind us. We stepped off onto the concrete walkway and started the strenuous trek to the transport point, about a half mile away. Residential units, mostly concrete and steel, lined the distance with an ugly uniformity. There was one larger structure too, the health-care unit, which we passed up quickly.

Word was, lots went in, fewer came out.

Then I remembered our cards: the plastic keys, encoded with personal identification information, would be essential for our survival on the other side. I reached inside my uniform jacket. No cards.

"Buck, I can't find the cards," I said, stopping.

"I've got them, remember?"

"You do?"

"Relax. There's no way we could travel without them. Come on." She patted me encouragingly on the shoulder.

Good old Buck. She was turning out to be a reliable companion. Our only previous experience together had been some low-risk exploring in the southern sector earlier in the year; I'd liked her then too. But this next

122

assignation was different: I knew others who'd been in the island world. Sometimes they came back changed. Once we'd set out, turning back would be much less negotiable. I needed someone I could count on.

Buck and I had spent hours talking about it. We both knew the risks. Periodically too, we'd had the good sense to remind each other that talk is cheap.

We'd heard both remarkable and frightening things about our destination. It was a small world, but densely peopled by multi-colored beings who day and night traveled underground. It was often difficult to distinguish natives from explorers; in some places bands of marauders were known to indiscriminately attack the unsuspecting, often leaving their victims for dead. Still, we'd also heard tales of incredible treasures; our maps indicated several reputed locations. Our sojourn would last three days; we hoped by then to have seen enough, and survived.

Up ahead, I noted several other explorers at the transport point. Many carried photographic or recording equipment. I didn't see any weapons, but I was sure that at least some of our fellow travellers were armed. We queued up with the others.

Buck turned to me. "Ready for an adventure?" she asked. Her eyes were shining.

"It's now or never," I responded, nodding. I reached for Buck's hand and squeezed it reassuringly, more for myself than for her, I'm sure. "I've got a good feeling about this —"

"So do I," answered Buck quickly, stepping forward. An MPV, hissing hydraulic gas, drew up in front of us. The people in front of us started to load. "This must be it."

I leaned to my right, still hanging onto Buck, not wanting to let go, so that I could see the destination tag on the front of the bus.

"New York City, that's us."

I grinned, and glanced casually over my shoulder, and wished Jersey a silent good-bye. "All aboard, Buckaroo," I added.

Jocelyn Riley

FILE 13

I should have slugged Oscar. I know that now. The first time it happened, I should have ground the heel of my shoe into his instep, slapped his lardy cheek, punched his bulbous nose. I should have shoved my fist into his paunch, elbowed his eyeballs, thrown a pen or pencil or stapler at him.

I should have screamed. I should have picked up the telephone, right in front of him, and called Personnel. I should have told his wife, his mother, his daughters. I should have told him again and again and again, until he got it, that I wasn't going to allow him to frighten me, to push me back, make my body feel offensive because it was too near him when he approached too close.

I should have written letters, postcards, telegrams, interoffice computer memos telling the world what a perverse little bastard he was. I should have said something, done something, screamed, thrown things, run him over with my car. I should have brought in a manual typewriter and returned the carriage into his eye when he was leaning close, closer, too close, his garlic breath and fake yellow teeth nearly touching my ear, pretending to instruct me when all he wanted was a cheap feel.

I should have rammed his stubby fingers into the electric pencil sharpener. I should have wheeled my chair back into his crotch when he was bent over me as I sat at my desk, each of his hairy fat arms covering each of mine as I sat trying to work alone at my desk. I should have oiled the wheels of my desk chair and taken off for a ride, a wild spree around the enclosing office I called mine for far too many months.

The only thing I did do, when I realized I was going to have to leave, was put a message into the computer system I'd been hired to set up. It is timed to appear on all the screens of everyone in the office on the first anniversary of the day I left the company. A little anniversary reminder that I really was there; I really existed; I still exist. Less than a year from now, a message will come up on Oscar's screen first, and then on everyone else's screens, that will say "Leslie was here." The dates of my employment will be right there below my name, like the dates on a tombstone.

Inside the box will be a drawing of a man, his arms draped around a computer monitor, his head resting on its top. He'll look down at the computer, not as though it were alive but as though he were afraid of it. "Duh," he will say in a little cartoon balloon. "I wonder why I can't make her do what I want." The computer blows off smoke.

Elisavietta Ritchie

CATFISHING

When I slash the catfish you look terribly shocked. I'm told you are hung like an elephant: did castration flash into your head?

The children hauled the oyster basket up to the dock dripping seaweed and two huge catfish, whiskered giants who haunt the nightmares of tadpoles and grace dreams of those fishermen who can nail the broad head to a board, slit quickly around, peel the skin away like a sock or a condom. You refuse to clean any fish.

No hammer or nails. My knife is silver and small, but it cuts. I grasp that live head with a flowered towel, avoiding the spines, rows of teeth, gash, and wish for pliers, cleavers, your help.

You stand there, aghast at the guts. But the children admire life rebelling, persisting, fetch the pail to rinse the filets off.

You like my catfish stew, make a proposition but I turn you down.

ECONOMIC MEASURES

You'd be proud how I'm thrifty with liquor now: only one drop stains the brandy glass. When guests look surprised, I explain: I killed the bishop.

Or at least, after I poured his snifter brimful with the best — Armagnac, Drambuie, some flask studded with stars, my instincts generous, innocent, but you were aghast at the waste — the next year the bishop died, alcoholic. Far off, yet you blamed me for the crime.

Later, in Malaysia, the antique lute you had just given me, your final anniversary gift — as if to play out the forthcoming dance of divorce — fell from the couch cushion cradling it and broke on the tile floor, I was also at fault although when it crashed I was three towns away to the north.

That same day you discovered the tiny black kitten I'd rescued from the road, in our driveway squashed in the ruts of a car. You accused me of that murder too. Even when our neighbor in tears proved it was her Peugeot, I remained under suspicion.

Now you've gone. Like the brandy, the cat. I repaired the lute.

Even without you, now I've learned to ration each drop of my life. I barely sprinkle kirsch over the fruit. I keep kittens in, neighbors out, lutes wired to the wall. All is sober, stingy and silent now.

I, too, avoid any risks, except those of love. Here, I am profligate, and it floods.

Laura Robert

LEAVING

When it came time to leave Elma I cleaned the house as I did the Saturday before. I shook the twenty-two throw rugs. And vacuumed the living room. Elma vacuumed the kitchen as she always did. With the small round vacuum. Like a pot vacuum. I used the long hot-dog vacuum.

I took down all of Bobbie's hats in the front hall. Bobbie had nailed up a two-by-four and dug double headed nails, the kind used for foundations, double headed so's they could be pulled out and used again; dug the double headed nails in the long two-by-four, and it was on those nails she hung her hats. Every kind of hat. Not just the same hat saying something different. But a straw brim hat, and a green army ear flap hat, and a goofy rabbit ears hat. About ten or twelve hats in all. I took them all down and dusted the walls clear up to the ceiling which I think is twelve feet.

The rooms always seem like a box, so twelve feet seems about right. I have a little hesitation because I know most ceilings aren't twelve feet but this is an old house in the country. And the floor you could see through to the ground if you knew what you were looking at.

I took the purple floor mop, the dust mop with the green handle and wiped up and down the walls catching the corners for spider webs. And then I put all of the hats back on their nails, which had to be done with a stick because the two-by-four was that high off of the floor. And Bobbie a short person. No one ever used those hats. I shook them good first. And tried some on. But Bobbie and her grandmother both were small people and I am not.

I know I didn't pack in the last week. Only cleaned. I didn't pack because there was nothing to the packing, and I didn't want to pack a week before I left and then be living out of my trunk or my suitcase whichever, or my backpack until the end of the week. That would be too unbearable. I did not have much. And what would take care to pack, my papers, were in order as they always were in the square wooden box I had made for their travel. And in order. I had made catalog sheets during the winter of their order, and they were still in order.

Consequently on the last day I was to be there, a Saturday, I cleaned, and then as I cleaned I brought my things to the front porch. When I was finished with a room I took out what belonged to me and put it on the green front porch. And after noon dinner I pulled the blue stationwagon which I was to return to the city to Robert and Judy up to the front porch

126

and loaded the car from the front to the back. I had a bike and a backpack, and a trunk. And enough stuff to fill that car. I packed from two until four, and then I was done. And it was time to go.

I told Elma I was going. Elma said okay. I kissed her and gave her a hug and went out to the car. And started it. She was always a hard starter even in the warm weather. So I sat waiting for her to warm up. And Elma was not on the porch. Elma was not on the porch to wave goodbye. So I let the car run and I went into the house, down the front hall through the study outside the bathroom between the kitchen, through her yellow carpeted room to the laundry outside my old room, and caught her standing at the dryer cleaning out the lint.

Don't you want to come say good-bye I asked. She said okay, and came to the front porch. I gave her another hug and a kiss and got in my car and drove down the red dust road.

I called her on Sunday and she said she wasn't feeling well. On Tuesday I talked to Judy and she said Elma had gone to the hospital.

RIGHT BESIDE

Terri who works down the hall told me that she brought her pictures in from Christmas vacation. She and her brother and his kids went to Guatemala. She lives with her brother and I guess raises his kids. At any rate they were nice pictures. I saw them at break. I took ten minutes longer at break than I was supposed to. My feet didn't want to get up, and Terri had brought the pictures for a second time to show me. I wasn't there the first time she brought the pictures in. Maybe it was my day off. She said when I saw her first thing in the morning that she wanted to show me the pictures. I said maybe I can see them at break. She said actually I had an idea I could show you them at my desk.

But when I went to the bathroom just before my break she recognized my socks, and took the stall to my right. The only one besides the handicapped one. And started right in talking. I can't recall what about because I was listening to her plop plop, in a somewhat regular slow rate. I remember she was telling me about her party, the bingo party she and her brother had. She said she had a sign on her door, the church of the immaculate oven, and she said everybody that came in wanted to see her oven. I said was it immaculate. I was holding my breath. I wasn't ready to plop plop that conversation going there.

She said of course not. It was filthy. She said her brother dressed as a priest. She had given me a handout. It was a bingo card and where the tiles would be for the numbers called was all the information. Bring your own chair. Bring your own snack, adults only. Things like that. She said a lot of her friends had children and she didn't want them bringing the kids. I didn't ask what about her brother's kids.

She said when everybody got there they were slow in starting, like they weren't quite sure what to do, but then she said, I had to kick them out. I didn't ask what time. She said she had a bingo party before and it was real fun.

She told Jimmy all this same story when we had break which was right after the bathroom. Terri left the bathroom first, I guess she heard I wasn't doing anything. And then when she flushed I had a plop, and then when she opened the door and it squeaked as it always does, I plopped.

When I got to the break room my favorite chair was open. It's one of the old ones. Only one left as far as I know. Story I heard was that when the movers came to take it away the woman that was in it wouldn't get up, I wouldn't either if it was me. And so the chair got left. And all the new indoor outdoor wear furniture got put in around it. The new furniture is purple and the old chair is red. I don't mind. So I sat down in that chair and started to eat my burrito which is what I always do at break, eat my lunch. And Terri came and sat down on that purple indoor outdoor purple couch exactly on my right. And I had to take two looks because I could not get out of my mind that picture of the two of us sitting there in our stalls and her talking about her bingo party dressed as a nun and plopping all along. I had to look twice and listen to her telling that bingo party story to Jimmy who got a flyer also.

Then she showed me the pictures. Which were very pretty because she was there in Guatemala when it was festival time and the dresses were very pretty, lots of reds.

CHRISTMAS DINNER

For Christmas dinner I opened a can of Progresso New England style clam chowder. That's the white chowder, not the red like Manhattan. The clam chowder was the only part of the meal that wasn't planned. We had said soup, but we hadn't said what kind.

When we talked about Christmas dinner the week before we said everything we wanted. I didn't want turkey and I couldn't think of anything else. So we agreed, brie, French bread, boiled shrimp, apple pie, yams and white wine. Which is what we wanted for Christmas dinner.

I found artichokes when I went to the grocery on Christmas Eve and bought four. I made a cocktail sauce of ketchup, horseradish and tabasco. I took out the cheese ball from work, the one rolled in walnuts, and sliced the French bread. The bottle was with a screw top and we washed two wine glasses. We didn't bake the yams or the apple pie but I opened the can of soup and we started our meal with soup.

We ate at three. It was a very nice meal. This is the first time we have had Christmas this nice by ourselves. We said Merry Christmas when we clinked glasses even though Ulaz is Jewish.

LEARNING TO WRITE

I had a dream about learning to write, and I would like to tell you about it because actually I thought it was a pretty good idea. And if I were to try it out I think it might actually work.

There were three people in my dream. Aunt Ann, my grandmother who we call Marilee and a doctoral physics student. What was also interesting was that I was each of these people at any particular time. Like there were three people's stories going on at the same time.

In my dream, Aunt Ann and Marilee were college professors and in their eighties. Two grande dames. They were responsible for seeing that this doctoral physics student, who was a man, maybe in his twenties, with a beard, and dark curly hair where you couldn't tell where the hair ended and the beard began, with dark-rimmed glasses, passed.

Just before their final approval they decided that he really didn't know how to write, and so they devised a short curriculum that would, they believed, insure that he knew how to write. Once he went through the curriculum. The curriculum was this: they would give a short oral statement, more like a little story. Which they would just say. Not read, but they may have something on a paper in front of them. Then the doctoral student was to write what they said, not word for word, but giving the information. And if he left out anything, or added something that wasn't there, or didn't have complete sentences, or didn't follow any of the rules, then he would have to do it over again. It wasn't like he would flunk, but he would have to do it again until he got it right. And always the information would be the same.

And it would count for thirty-five percent of his grade. So the professors hoped that he would do this. Because they knew that he really couldn't write. And he knew he really couldn't write. Not really write. Like the way that they were talking about. Writing about what he heard. What he was hearing. And put it down so that it was understood what was heard was what was being written.

But he also knew, and the teachers did too, that he wouldn't have to do it if he really didn't want to. And the reason was because it was such a crazy idea that he could appeal.

And he didn't do it. He wouldn't do it.

The teachers told him it would take maybe six times. That was how many times they thought they would have to repeat the information. So six weeks. But he said no. He said they were crazy.

And so he left. And they were sad, the teachers, because they knew he was a very bright student, but that he couldn't write. And he was sad because these teachers were his friends, and now he had to go get someone else to help get him graduated. And he was sad too because he knew they were right. But this really was too much that they were asking.

Lou Robinson

SEX DYSLEXIA

Riding behind him when I was five, I pretend to be French. His shoulders block the sun. My mother teaches French. It is a special female domain, intuitively decipherable, like a language of known affections. I spare myself the meanings to keep the mystery, the purr, and to have words of my own that my father can't explain. And there is more, French is sex. A sly connection to the motorcycle magazines I discover in the rack at the candy store. Finding the one where they put their hands down the women's blouses. They handcuff a woman to a motorcycle and drag her. My father's wide black leather saddlebags say Eddy in rhinestones. Intense rise and guilt, reading these things. Riding behind him all the way to Indiana, bugs smash on my teeth, I say le, la.

Was vanilla female, was chocolate male? Why was a chair a woman? A kind of sex dyslexia set in. I still say wedding when I mean funeral, and vice versa.

Riding behind them in the back seat of the van, through all the snow to Maine, I compose his obituary; it will be stern but forgiving, glossing over the obvious wounds. At Lynnie's funeral that afternoon I hear him telling my aunt that he has noticed a new trend in obituaries: they say "survived by her companion," or "by her friend and partner . . ." Father and daughter, writing each other's obituaries, anxious to find a form that will be acceptable to the dead, slumbering at last in forgiveness and vindication.

HITCHHIKER IN PILLBOX HAT WITH NET

"I was wondering if anyone would pick me up or if someone would pick me up and kill me, but I think my vibes are too good for that since I stopped being depressed. I was really depressed last week, I used to think about killing myself a lot, like from a doorknob or something, but all the ways you can kill yourself are too painful, know what I mean. I guess if you're too depressed to do anything, killing yourself is just too much work. Anyway I decided to stop being depressed because it was so boring talking about myself all the time. I mean when I was depressed I would have gotten into this car and started telling you all about how I lost $500 my rent and I don't have a place to live and everything. I was hoping to get in the car and hear a lot of interesting things from you that I could think about for a change. Drop me off at the bus station I'm going to Toronto to be an actress. When I was depressed I used to look terrible but since I stopped I've been dressing up. I've been looking good for about two weeks now. I don't know if I can keep it up. Gloves, hat, colors — I make sure I wear some color, salmon or lime or lemon — food colors, you know. You should wear some color yourself, you wouldn't just eat black things would you? I dropped out of school but I'm in college. My own college, I call it the College of Trial. I study whatever I want, but at the same time each day, history, same time, current events, music. I'm adding an anti-sexist class that will go on all day. This way I can study anywhere, in Ireland when I go to find Stiff Little Fingers. Drop me off at planned parenthood. Did you ever feel like death is just 20 feet behind you? I'm just ahead of mine, that's why I'm going to Ireland. Look at my tongue. I painted it green. In Ireland they paint their tongues green so their words have the power to make things real."

IT IS MUCH HARDER TO TAKE BACK THE BODY THAN TO LEAVE IT

D. has been intrigued by methods for leaving the body all her life. Seeking out the old women who live on Skippy and Roman Meal, who rely on spirits to keep them safe in traffic when hearing fails. Or the family of Polish women spanning four generations who leave a list of necessities (an avocado dish-strainer, cinnamon stockings size eight...) out for the spirits on Friday night, and then go collect the items at rummage sales on Saturday. The older ones have never used birth control, never had an unplanned child. They were taught how to will their menses to flow each month, and it worked. D. knew of an Anabaptist woman who flew down unknown country roads every night while her husband slept, and everyday while he worked, drove all over the back roads verifying the sign posts she'd seen in her midnight float. The woman's hands would shake so violently right before she 'went out' that she was finally forced to give it up for fear of waking her husband, who would certainly have been convinced her vision came from satan.

In 1980, one local medium, surrounded by chalk-white religious figurines blinking blue under the light from the Busy Bee Diner sign, said to D: "You work in a museum? There is something bad there. Silvery. Something very bad in the air."

It is much harder to take back the body than to leave it. D. remembered the warning several years later when the women museum workers began to get sick. Ovarian cysts, bartholin gland infections, bleeding from the rectum, hemorrhaging, chronic herpes, cancer, hysterectomies.

A gummy deposit on the paintings is discovered to come from a chemical in the humidifier. The women call in OSHA. The man from OSHA says "No known chemical causes reproductive problems." The woman from OSHA, forced to remove the gynecological evidence from her report, quits. They destroy her records.

A gland in D.'s vagina swells with the poison. Surgery. The doctor puts something cold between her legs against the throbbing stitches — his white rubber glove, all five fingers bloated full of water and frozen hard. She keeps it in the freezer.

ADULT CHILDREN OF BABOONS

I go out to gather solace from strange women in the service occupations. "Isn't her hair beautiful? Can we keep a swatch, this red is really hot now, and hard to match. You just can't dye natural red, it's every color."

"Coffee honey? Bide your time. Just holler. I'm back here reading too. *City of Glass,* though I hardly ever read men, but somebody left it in a booth. Do you mind if I ask you who cut your hair? I want mine like that, kind of wanton. Would you care?" (A good day, I'll gather four honeys and maybe one babe.) "Hey, you know who you look like? What *is* her name, the one — you know, was on drugs, had a TV show, father was a Mama and a Papa?"

She should see my sister. A dead ringer for MacKenzie Phillips. People ask for her autograph in grocery stores. Our father was also a mama and a papa. I don't like to be reminded at a time like this. It's a terrible thing to have a father for a mother. He rushed to phone me about the baby baboon at the Columbus Zoo. Its mother died and now its father is doing everything, making a nest, cradling it, feeding it a bottle. Feeding it a dark thick liquid of mourning, pity, and possessiveness. Perpetually wounded and grieving, insatiable, cornering his hapless cub in the garage, making it sand the grainy primed shoulder of a car, hours on the same infinitesimal circle, pouring out his baboon concern in the form of warnings about molesters or judgements against certain movie stars.

Sitting in the Rosebud Cafe, trying not to think about motherless cubs, hoping to overhear a good conversation, I realize the only other two people in the cafe are therapists and they are telling each other their clients' funniest dreams. I had hoped to avoid therapists by staying away from the nicer restaurants, but now I realize that those who smoke have to come here.

I think of all the dumb things therapists have ever said to me. "Where was your mother during all this?" "Have you always thought of yourself as a strong person?" "What did you expect? Some people are in therapy for years." "Kahlil Gibran says (so dumb I can't remember, even though she repeated the same quote three times)." I think of what they said to Jean Seberg, "Can you be sure your baby was white, if you only saw it once?" To Joan of Arc, "Well what made you think you could save France?"

The therapists leave (two dimes, eleven butts) and three dykes sit down.

"Get out, fly. Come on, we're gonna burn you. Don't you understand? Oh. He's got a broken wing. Sorry dude. OK, we're gonna save you."

"This new housecleaning job is shit. After I do her house, you know, make sure all thirteen ketchup bottles are lined up labels *out,* then I have to go do her husband's office. He's a shrink over on Buffalo, tenth floor. Jesus Christ, I open the door, and I feel like a big hand is pushing me straight over to the plate glass window and a deep voice is saying 'Jump.' And I'm *sane*. I mean it's like the walls are saturated with tears. Closet is full of boxes of kleenex. Refrigerator is full of pills, syringes, and Diet Dr. Pepper. I shove the vacuum around a little, change the paper doily on the leather couch, and beat it out of there before I catch something."

"Could we get some, you know, service?"

"What do you think this is babe, a restaurant? This is a therapy group. See, here's your water. I always give her that water."

"This water is hot."

"You said you wanted water. You didn't say you wanted ice."

"This water is hot like spit."

"Take a bath in it, honey."

"Jesus. I'm gonna go home and write my personal narrative."

FORKLIFT

I dream she says forklift. This is something a snake can do with its tongue. It also means put four fingers in her. And I do, but instead I'm putting inside her words, pieces of words, some syllables italic some roman. Named écriturisme by a French pastry cook who invented two parallel alphabets in icing sugar, who said "all is words" and, drawing with both hands at once, binah and hokmah, was able to describe the meaning of the universe. But here I am sending a jagged zigzag line of syllables slanting in different directions into her, pushing, pulling her, sending her off through all the levels of the realms.

Leslie Aileen Ross

RISK

I used to wake up, alone. Even as a child, I woke up from nightmares, alone, and handled them myself. I was convinced the nightmares came from sleeping on the wrong side of the pillow. So, I'd turn the pillow over, and try the other side. Now I know better.

Now, I wake both of us up with the screaming. You must wish it would stop — that I would stop screaming. That you could get a good night's sleep.

I used to write fantasies about having someone with me; and now, you're here, making both my fantasies and my nightmares more real.

I woke up screaming, again. You ask, "What did you say?"

You're still half asleep yourself.

I don't believe I want to tell you. I don't believe I should say. I don't believe what's in my subconscious. I'm not sure I want you to know where it has taken me. I am shaking. Although I'm usually warm, I feel cold. I feel the heaviness of silence in the air. The silence encourages my mind to spin. I argue with myself. I've always wanted someone to be here when I get this scared. And now, I'm torn between telling and not telling. And, I know that the silence is growing — that if I wait too long, the moment will be gone and telling will be covered by sleep. After an entirely too long pause, I say, "I said, 'Get away or I'm calling the cops,'" as, almost a question. As if I don't trust myself, my perceptions. As if I don't trust my subconscious.

"Your father, again?"

"No, my mother this time."

You ask me more questions as gently as a spring rain. The rain primes my pump and tears rush from my eyes as if I were a lost child crying for her mother. And, I am. I shiver and shake. Fear is shaky for me. You put your arm around me to quiet the fear. I take your arm and wrap you around me like a blanket.

THE IMPOTENCE OF LANGUAGE

"Don't misconscrew what I said," she ordered. "You know I wouldn't stoop to such heights. I'm not a coheart in some misaligned polop to overstep the government. I mean, I know how to coach things carefully so as not to offend some extinguished dignitary."

"That's just my point," I said. "Words just aren't important to you."

"Oh, I peg to differ with you," she responded. "The impotence of words are hugh on my list of aprioities. After all, I granulated from one of the most prodigal schools around. A most illustrative instincatude of higher education."

"I'll bet. But what language did you study?" I persisted.

"Are you casting a slenderous remark agin my person?"

"I wouldn't dream of doing such a horrific deed but surely you know how much the government contract means to our company."

"If we get this contract, we'll come up smelling like bandits. A rose by any other name wood smell as sweat. But now we've thrown the fire in their chair. So, we have to run it up the flag pool and see who saludes.

"Did you here about our contact, Jeff Dickoff?"

135

"No. Is something wrong?"

"Yeah, we'll have to wait until he gets out of immensive care to . . ."

"Dickoff is in intensive care?"

"Yeah, cerebral hemorrhoids. From reading too many oo-ee magazines."

"Oo-ee magazines?"

"Yeah. You know. Those girlie magazines."

"Oh, you mean 'Oui' Magazine."

"That's what I said."

Pat Schneider

IRMA

It was the smell of his shoes in the closet that kept Irma from opening it for twenty-two years after John died. Even though she sometimes could imagine, lying awake at night, that the smell had changed in all those years — that his sweat had been replaced entirely by the smell of aging leather, she still believed in her heart of hearts that John's sweat was more powerful than the skin of any cow, and that the accumulated odor of all those years would be a reincarnation so powerful she would again feel herself married, and the very thought of it would give her a spasm of anxiety about the things that had bothered John — his eggs cooked not quite to perfection, his underwear imperfectly ironed, a kleenex lost on the backseat floor of the car.

Over the years, the closed closet in their bedroom loomed larger and larger, until exhausted by insomnia, Irma moved her things to the bedroom across the upstairs hall. It was smaller, but cheery, she told herself. And besides, she didn't need a double bed anymore. She never used the old bedroom for guests, because it would be too embarrassing to try to explain why they shouldn't open the closet on John's side of the bed. That was in the years before she put a combination padlock on the door; after that it was too embarrassing to explain the lock.

Since she never used that bedroom any more, it came to never be opened, either, and in time, it, too, was padlocked. Then it was embarrassing to have guests go upstairs — she felt obliged to explain a locked

136

bedroom door, and who would understand if she told them the only problem was the smell of the shoes of her husband, dead now for 10, 15, 20 years?

And so it came about that Irma decided to move her things to the downstairs bedroom. It was not so cheery, but it was handy, she told herself, and besides, who would know if she fell on the stairs some day?

By the twenty-second year, Irma had moved bed and baggage into the kitchen and the rest of the house was all boarded up, locked with combination locks. She had hired a young neighbor to come in and do the carpentry, but she herself chose the locks and she had all the combinations memorized because she planned, sitting by the woodstove in the kitchen, in the very small place left free for her rocking chair, she planned the day when she would go lock by lock out into the downstairs hall, up the stairs, into the master bedroom, open the closet and clean it out. In the meantime, the kitchen wasn't so handy with everything in it, but it was a great saving on heat in the winter, she told herself, and the smell of woodsmoke was so full, and rich, and clean.

Lore Segal

LUCINELLA APOLOGIZES TO THE WORLD FOR USING IT

"What's the matter, Maurie?"

Maurie says a week ago he slept with a poet who kept her sharpened pencil underneath the pillow. At breakfast she stuck it behind her ear. Today she sent him the poem.

(He can't mean me, I know. I've never slept with Maurie and keep my pencil in my pocket at all times.)

"Isn't that a shabby thing to do by a friend?" he asks.

"But, Maurie, what's a poor poet to do with her excitements? Take them back to bed? Paste them in her album? Eat them? When all she wants is to be writing!"

"About the literary scene again!" says Maurie.

I ask him if he recognized himself.

"No," he says. "The man in the poem must be three other lovers."

"Did you recognize her?"

"Only the left rib out of which she'd fashioned a whole new woman."

"Will you publish it in *The Magazine*?"

"Yes," he says. "It's a good poem. But why won't the girl invent?"

"And don't you think she would, if she knew how? Pity her, Maurie. She'd prefer to write about sorcerers, ghosts, gods, heroes, but all she knows is you."

In the middle of the night I wake and know: Maurie meant me. I call him on the telephone and say, "I use you too, and I know that it is indefensible in friendship and as art."

Maurie waits for me to say, "And I'll never do it again," but I am silent a night and a day. For one month I cannot write a word. The following Monday I sit down, sharpen my pencil, and invent a story about Maurie and me having this conversation, which has taken root in a corner of my mind where it will henceforward sprout a small but perennial despair.

I put the story in an envelope and send it to Maurie.

Ruth Knafo Setton

THE EDGE

I have cheated in my life. I have straightened and whitened my teeth, remodeled sagging breasts, tucked in a puckered cheek, shortened and uptilted a ponderous bulbous nose. Far worse I have suppressed my rage, smiled when I wanted to run free and run away when I should have stood. I cannot come too close to my father. I tremble with nausea. And my mother's smell is too strong, too female and overwhelming. I recoil from all that is me. I have forgotten so much. I no longer remember who I am or who I was or what brought me here. All I know is I am here and I have climbed out a window at night to be here. And I must talk. And I have been cheating myself.

EMBROIDERED HANDS

In Debdou, a village in the heart of the Atlas Mountains, festivities, celebrations. Everyone rejoices. Thirteen-year-old Mazal is about to wed sixty-five-year-old Joseph Afriat. The loveliest girl in the village to marry the richest man. Joseph has already survived two wives and is ripe for a third. Grizzled and hardy, he sees no reason why he shouldn't outlive the third one as well. His fourteen children roam over the hills. They are all older than Mazal. Joseph has been betrothed to Mazal ever since he first noticed her at age seven, playing with one of his daughters near the well. He has been biding his time until her blood arrived. Now she is a woman and he can hardly contain his impatience.

The women are plucking and painting her in the back room. Shaving her pubic hair, staining her hands and feet orange with henna until they look embroidered, criss-crossed with tiny delicate lines, painting her face with bold colors until she looks like a barbaric idol, her head weighed down by a heavy jeweled headdress, her body encased in a green velvet jeweled gown. The gown is the pride of Mazal's mother, Sarah. Her own grandmother wore it. It is said to be a relic of a distant aristocratic Spanish past. They are the only family in Debdou to lay claim to such noble origins, a fact which makes the others resent them. But Joseph does not mind. Mazal, painted, jeweled, perfumed, motionless in the chair in front of him, fills him with passion. Staring at her, he senses that he will love this wife more than any of the others. This one is still ripe, unformed. The first two were already over fifteen when he wed them, stubborn and sullen, set in their ways. This one he will teach to obey him, to satisfy him before she learns prudishness and slyness. Amused, he watches her small foot in the pointed gold slipper tapping impatiently. She is a child. What delight he will have in teaching her the ways of love and how to run his household. This one will keep him eternally youthful.

After the wedding celebration is over, late at night, he retires to their room and is surprised to find it empty. He calls her name and gets no answer. He walks outside in his babouches in the twilight, searching for her among the rocks with his penetrating eyes. He does not make a sound, ashamed to have the villagers witness his predicament. Cursed girl! Where did she go? A child, a child. Her mother would beat her senseless if she knew. Or perhaps it was her mother who led her to this. Sarah always did give herself airs as if — wait! What was this? Someone crying from behind the rocks, near the cave. Joseph sits on a rock. "Mazal." He hears her heaving sobs. "Come out."

She comes out from behind the rocks.

"Come here."

She stands in front of him in the moonlight. Gone is the painted icon of this afternoon, her eyes elongated and blackened with kohl, her lips and cheeks reddened and sultry. Standing in front of him is a tearful little girl. It could be one of his daughters. He has never been soft with them, never holding or cuddling them, feeling it beneath him. He has never wasted what he terms "unnecessary" caresses on his wives either. But this child moves him. On the other hand, it could be his advanced age. He sits up straighter. He refuses to get old. He will *not* get old. "What is it, Mazal?"

She sighs and wipes her eyes.

He draws her to him and sits her on his lap. How small and light she is. A feather. He could break her in half if he so wished. "You can trust me."

"I — I — I don't want to be married."

"Ah." He smiles. This is normal at her age. "And what would you like to do instead?" he asks indulgently.

"Play. Learn."

"Learn?" He raises his eyebrows. "But that's not for you, my child. That's for boys. You'll have enough to think about soon with children and the house."

"I don't care!" she cries. "You're an old man, I don't care what they say, you smell old, I hate you and I'll never be happy married to you! I wish I was dead!"

She struggles to leave his arms, but he tightens his grip until she grows limp and bursts into tears once more. He pats her hair absently. A bit of spice in this one. But nothing he cannot tame. He will have to lull her fear and disgust first. Here is the advantage of an older man. His experience. He will not jump blindly on her. No. He has time. After all, she is his now. He rocks her in his arms and sings her a lullaby about the blue dream that enchants children until he hears her jagged, harsh breathing grow regular and soft. With a sigh, he gets up slowly, his bones creaking, and carries her back to their bed.

-

Dani Shapiro

HIGH HOLY DAYS

Rosh Hashona. 1968. I am old enough to go to temple with my father, and I am excited. I wear a matching maroon skirt and jacket, and swing my very first pocketbook alongside me. I sit on his lap in the sanctuary, busying myself with the tassles on his ceremonial robe. His lap is so big, and I am so small.

Rosh Hashona. 1975 through 1979. Eddie Fishbein is so cute. He sits with his family within eye-shot of me, and we make faces at each other, even though he is twenty and I am twelve. Later, Eddie Fishbein will get me pregnant, and we will never speak again.

Yom Kippur. 1982. I never go to temple. I don't believe in atoning for my sins. I don't believe I have any sins to speak of. I walk down to the Hudson River with my golden retriever, and smoke a joint. My father doesn't understand. His mouth sets in one straight line, and he avoids my eyes. A few years later, my golden retriever will be stolen, and I will stop smoking pot.

Yom Kippur. 1985. Before the customary fast, I have dinner with my parents. It is a huge meal, which I try not to eat, because it is not my intention to fast. They have moved to Manhattan, and we are now neighbors. We eat off paper plates, because the china is not unpacked. I tell them I will meet them after temple; they are used to this by now. Walking down eighty-sixth street, a sea of older couples in hats and overcoats walk towards me. I cannot distinguish their faces, and think: I have lost my parents. My father will die less than six months later.

Yom Kippur. 1986. It is not a happy time. I go to temple with my mother. I am a woman now. Suddenly, my mother has become old, and I help her down the aisle to the first row. She holds my arm, and I hold her walker. The men sit in the center of the sanctuary, their backs turned and swaying. I pray. The unfamiliar words come to my lips as if I had spoken them in my sleep all these years. I atone for my sins, and for the sins of the world around me. A year later I will be happy. But I have no way of knowing this, here and now.

Deborah Shea

THE BABY STORY

We had been on the highway twenty-five minutes when the baby flew out of the convertible. It went out and up, a renegade kite, flying high into the air. Looking up, we saw it there, riding the air currents, gliding. Mary pulled the car off the road. "How do we get it down?" she asked.

"For sure that baby will hit a draft and fall," I said.

A sudden gust of wind blew the napkins off the dash. We looked up. The baby took off across the sky — mobile weathervane, arms outstretched, hands pointing east and west. Mary stepped on the gas. "Keep your eye on that baby," she said, "and guide me down this road."

The baby was heading west. "Turn there," I said. "Take 9 to Highway 12." I looked up — blue crocheted jacket and hat, tiny white mittens, arms still splayed in a crucified position. "I'm losing it," I said. "It's blending in."

At the junction of 12 and 116, the baby started falling, fast. It came straight down, like a rock tossed into a well. "That baby is history," I said. "Sure thing."

Mary parked the car. "Nothing is fixed but the stars," she said. "Let's go."

We started off across the field. As we walked, I told the story of Tony Garcia, a construction worker who fell down an elevator shaft, landed flat on his back, stood up and walked away. "It happens," I told Mary. "It's not real common, but it's not a miracle either."

We came up on the flat grey ledge where the baby was lying flat on its back. The arms and legs were rigid, still pointing east and west. But something had happened to the baby while it rode the air currents up in the sky. Now the baby was covered with fur. The fur parted down the center of the baby like a path through tall grass.

"The belly is soft," I said, stroking the fur. "Touch it."

But Mary wouldn't touch the baby. "What do we do now?" she asked. "A baby covered with fur."

"We could make a pair of mittens."

"It's ninety degrees in the shade."

"We could leave it in a cave to be raised by wolves."

"It's not a wolf. It looks more like a marsupial. Without the tail."

"We could bury it."

"It's still alive."

"We could kill it."

Mary shook her head.

We sat down on the rocks to make a plan. If the baby stayed out all night it would die, sure thing.

It was impossible to know what the baby wanted because the baby couldn't talk.

Finally, I had an idea. I picked up a stick and held it over the baby. "If it reaches for this stick," I said, "it wants to live. If it doesn't, it wants to die. Now we'll let this baby decide."

I waved the stick over the baby like a magic wand. The baby

followed it with its eyes, but the baby didn't move.

I jimmied the stick up under the baby and flipped it like a pancake. "Let's see if it can crawl," I said.

The baby didn't move.

Mary poked the baby's foot with the toe of her cowboy boot. She took the stick and prodded the ribs. She pulled a gold lipstick tube out of her purse and passed it back and forth in front of the baby's face. The baby stared up at her and blinked.

"For sure you've got to pick it up," I said.

Mary took a piece of Zwieback from her purse. Then Mary did something I had never seen before. She got down on her knees in front of that baby, got right down there and lined her eye up against that baby's eye as if she were shooting craps. "Come on," she said, "come here to me. What you harvest with your hands is yours to keep."

The baby started to move, first the back legs, then the front, like a lizard it slid forward toward the food in Mary's hand.

"This baby will survive," I said. "Sure thing."

Mary put the Zwieback in the baby's mouth. It struggled to sit up, pushing hard against the ledge. Mary watched it for awhile. Then Mary leaned forward, uncoiled the furry fingers from the soggy crust. Mary got up off her knees. Mary picked the baby up. Mary looked up at the sky. Then Mary said this, "Let's put this baby back where it belongs."

Martha Shelley

WALKING THE RIM

You know you must go it alone. rising at midnight you leave your pack in the hut, canteen and flashlight are all you'll need to climb the cobblestone path. it's steep and you're panting, sweating in the equatorial night. guides and horsemen pass you but you decline the offer of a ride and rush ahead when they pick up tourists at the rim.

then down into the caldera, the dessicated plain that once was liquid stone, under the last rays of the gibbous moon you traverse the black plateau, boulders and jagged crevasses painted in the palette of the night, anthracite charcoal obsidian ash. the lifeless land silent but for a distant breeze. looking back you see the riders on the rim, a string of winking lanterns starting to descend. you press on. the moon's gone.

the peaks rise before you, one a cinder cone and one the true volcano but which? you left the map behind. what seemed a breeze is now the earth's heart roaring beneath your feet and you turn right to the breast-shaped rise, approach like it was your first lover, like a god.

you've lost the path. you scramble over broken rock, detour round a chasm; your flashlight flickers and dies. well, you wanted to go alone. now what. looking up won't help, you can't decipher the southern stars.

a guide steps out of the darkness. you ask the way and he quotes a fee. you'll pay him to show you the path, you just want to walk it yourself but you don't speak the language, can't tell your desire and he turns away in disgust.

over there it's getting lighter, that must be east and oh god it's Orion about to set, the stars of home, this must be where they summer. there, the glimmering lanterns, the riders turning towards the other peak. backtrack, hurry after them, you won't be first but you'll make the top before sunup, up, up, so steep they've built stairs to the lip of the crater.

an observation platform swathed in sulfurous clouds, fart smell, bad egg smell, the roaring engulfs you as you stare down a hole a half mile wide, the bottom a field of burning brimstone, the crimson dragon's eye. staring transfixed till dawn outshines the glowing coals, till all you see is greyish-yellow rock and a tongue of flame. the heart? the eye? or is it the asshole of the earth, spewing its rich volcanic soil all over the Pacific Rim.

you must abandon the platform, circle the abyss. the path is barely wider than your foot, knife-edged rock and treacherous sand. fall outwards and shatter against the boulders below, tumble in and burn.

now a divine wind arises, a terrible yearning pushing you in-wards. now you know what you're here for: you want to fly into the heart of the god, you want to swallow that fire and live.

when you finish the others are gone. you look out over the caldera, over the rust-colored moonscape, a cloud of dust and horses vanishing over the ridge. the sun is already too high. shake your canteen, take a drink. you'll be walking back alone.

Susan Stinson

MARTHA MOODY

Martha Moody was a religious woman who liked a good apple pie with thick cream, but didn't have the grass to feed a cow. She always had dried milk, but never cream, and she suffered from grasshoppers and the sparseness of joy.

Martha herself was not sparse. She was a fat woman with thick red hair and a past that had acquainted her with the Bible, but also with the pleasures of an Italian ice, of a good tart from the baker in town. She had eaten turtle soup. She had dressed in white to shoot a bow and arrow, and had hit the mark. Her prowess in the fashionable sport of archery pleased her father, who was a lapsed Methodist with a gold watch fob and social ambitions. But Martha had met Wilbur Moody in a dry goods store, and he had come around the counter to hand her a bolt of cornflower blue cloth. She was married to him in a dress of that material in the spring. She didn't miss the grey city she left with Wilbur, toting dry goods, but she did miss cream. She liked the West, though. She nodded at the big sky. She asked nothing of the mountains, except that they keep her pointed straight away from the city, and let her survive the pass. She came a good distance, then said that it was enough. She was walking beside the wagon, singing to herself in a dry voice that had carried her across a lot of country. Wilbur was up on the seat, driving the oxen. They reached a creek. Water was news and a reason to stop. There was a small twisted kind of rare prairie tree, maybe from a seed dropped by some other traveler. Martha looked at the sharp limbs and grey bark, and decided that this was enough to satisfy her need for company. She would winter here. Wilbur was gold hungry, land bored. He'd seen water enough in the East, although he filled every container he could find with the stuff. The rest of the party put their wagons in a circle, built fires (the tree branches suffered), and spoke against leaving Martha for dead. But she had provisions, time to dig a sod house before the ground froze, and she had gone as far as she was willing to go. Wilbur knew better than to speak of love, but he did mention family honor. Martha laughed. The sound of the water bordered the night. He told her it might dry up in the summer, and then there'd be no one to watch her parch.

She took some bolts of material, and the panes of glass she had packed with good quilts for padding, because she thought windows were worth the trouble and cold they leaked. She took a barrel of beans and a barrel of meal, and the dried milk. Wilbur poured half of each packet of seed into its own tin cup and lined them up in front of her on the ground.

"Martha," he said, "you can't live on seeds and water, so I hope you can live on your fat."

"I'll need Shakespeare and the Bible," she said, and he gave her a hand digging a hole for a shelter, shoring it up with posts that came off the siding of the wagon. He still had plenty to travel with, though. The party was already a morning ahead, so he looked into her brown eyes wishing they were cornflower blue, gave her a kiss and rode off, rattling.

Martha picked up her shovel, thinking of barrel tables and barrel chairs, without a thought about who she might be cheating in claiming this land as hers, or who she might be seeding in her dry good store by the stream. She didn't bother with naming, either, but the people passing, and those staying, said Moody to tell where they were.

FRUIT

One day a fat woman came down the street. She wore burning apples in her ears. People stopped. They pointed. They laughed, raucous. They were terrified. She decided to stop being so obvious. She reached up and unhooked the apples. She dropped them both into her mouth at once. Smoke poured out as they sizzled in her spit. The people coughed and dropped to the sidewalk, except three women coming out of the Stop-N-Shop, who inhaled deeply. One, the fattest, swung her plastic shopping bag up onto her shoulder, then walked on with her hand on her hip to balance the weight of all the fruit she had bought.

Amber Coverdale Sumrall

SIESTA

Grandma's house has a green gate that opens on a courtyard with brick-red tiles from Mexico. Bright blue and yellow pots, filled with cactus, sit on the adobe ledges. Birds of Paradise border the patio. Grandpa's hand-carved gourds, painted with Indian symbols for rain, hold mounds of walnuts, figs and peaches from the backyard trees.

We sit in wicker chairs, in the summer sun, drinking Postum from tall orange mugs with wooden holders. I pretend it is coffee. I always feel like I'm on vacation when I visit, even though we live in the same city.

Grandpa leaves to work in his garden. When we're alone Grandma tells me stories about her family. She's proud to be Indian. She's descended from three different tribes, one's called Mohawk. Whenever she says Mohawk, I think tomahawk. I know what a tomahawk is; I've seen them for sale in souvenir stores in Yellowstone National Park. Indians used to scalp white men with them. Grandma says tomahawks were the first axes. She says that if white men had minded their own business instead of poisoning Indians with alcohol, shooting them and stealing their land, the Indians wouldn't have had to scalp them.

She sighs, "You'll never find the truth in your school books, honeygirl. It's all been turned to lies. Same with religion. Got to look real hard for the truth nowadays."

Grandma calls me honeygirl. So does Grandpa. Every morning he gets up before dawn to grind wheat in the basement for his breakfast. Grandpa cooks all his own meals. That's because he likes to eat his supper when most people have breakfast, and have milk and fruit in the evening. He even washes his dishes and puts them away.

Grandma and Grandpa love each other more than anybody I know. He brings her flowers from his garden and they hug and kiss a lot. I mean real hugs and kisses, not the quick dabs my father gives my mother before he goes off to work. Grandma scratches Grandpa's back too. Lucky Grandpa. Having my back scratched is just about my most favorite thing. Grandma says love is the most important thing in the world.

"That's why we're born, honeygirl," she says. "To learn how to love each other. And it takes all the time we've got. Some folks never get the hang of it."

We finish our Postum and Grandma says it's "siesta" time. She and Grandpa nap together every afternoon. Today she has promised to nap with me.

The house is cool and dark. I follow her into the spare bedroom and climb on the four-poster bed. Grandma looks like a gypsy. Her dresses all feel like silk; she wears scarves and bracelets, earrings and glittery brooches. I think my Grandma is beautiful. Her dark braided hair is rolled in circles on the back of her head and held by two silver clips.

Grandma pulls back the white chenille bedspread, then the blankets. I take off my shoes and socks, jeans and shirt. She lets me sleep naked, says it's too hot for covers. I crawl across the bed until I touch the cool plaster wall, then lift the sheet over me. The cracked yellow window-shade flaps in the afternoon breeze.

"Santa Ana's are blowing again," she says. "Wind's full of evil spirits. They make folks crazy." She chuckles. "Even spirits got to create some mischief now and then."

She slides her flowered dress over her head and lets her slip fall to the floor.

Grandma's huge breasts rest on her belly. Blue veins run through them like tiny rivers. I've never seen real breasts before. Mother hides hers. She says women are cursed because of Eve's sin with the devil, and I'll find that out for myself someday. She says I'll have breasts someday too, but I don't believe her. I hate dresses and perfume and patent leather shoes. Daddy says I'm a tomboy. How can a tomboy grow breasts?

Grandma rolls into bed with me. She is naked too. I thought grown-ups had to wear nightgowns or pajamas to bed. That they could get arrested for being naked.

"Someone's been filling your head with foolish notions," Grandma says. "I won't mention any names. Come close, honeygirl."

I snuggle next to Grandma, nestle against her warm breasts, her soft round belly. She holds me, kisses my neck, then moves slightly away and begins to scratch my back with her long fingernails. I feel goosebumps all over my body. Her nipples graze my back. I want to touch her breasts, suck on the hard nipples.

She traces circles round and round with her fingers until I can barely keep my eyes open.

When I wake, Grandma is gone. I have to pee and pass by Grandma and Grandpa's bedroom. Their door is shut and it sounds like they are bouncing on the bed. I want to peek but I'm scared. They are making strange noises that I've never heard before. I know what they are doing has something to do with Grandma's breasts. I just know it!

I go back to bed and pretend I am napping with Grandma and Grandpa. My hands find the safe, tingly place between my legs.

It is almost dark when I wake up again. The smell of stewed rabbit gets me up real quick. I put my clothes on and go out to the kitchen. Grandma and Grandpa are sitting in their bathrobes, smiling at each other. They are smiling and rocking in their rocking chairs, looking like they've got a secret.

"Supper's almost ready, honeygirl. I fixed your favorite: stewed rabbit and dumplings. And Grandpa made fruit salad for dessert. Are you hungry?"

"I'm starving!"

"Well, we all seem to have worked up powerful appetites," Grandma says. She winks at Grandpa, then at me.

"Powerful indeed," Grandpa says.

Julie Szende

LOVE SONG

Sit next to him on the couch. So close we're actually touching. My right arm rests against his elbow; my knee touches his bony knee. He's engrossed in his book and temporarily oblivious to my presence. I steal furtive sideways glances at him, gloating hungrily at the gems of his body available to my eyes at this close range: the big square right hand, knuckles adorned with four dark brown freckles; the slender arm with its smooth, honey-gold sunburned skin. My glance travels up to his profile, which is something Botticelli might have concocted: high round forehead, long curving dark lashes, straight nose, sharp clean chin and the most beautifully cut mouth, the full upper lip, edged with a tracery of feathery dark hair, swelling ever so slightly over the lower. Ah. It's wonderful to be so near him. I close my eyes for an instant, savoring the exquisite peace of the moment. I can hear his quiet, regular breathing, with its characteristic snuffle at the beginning of every inhalation. And I can smell him. This part isn't so good; he smells awful. Several rank odors emanate from him simultaneously: the dark sweaty aroma of unwashed hair; the sharp vinegary reek of unbathed armpits; the fusty stench of clothing permeated with dirt, foodstains, sweat. Worst of all is a horribly pungent stink that is immediately recognizable as human excrement. I know where this stink comes from — his filthy underpants, which he wears for days on end. He has no use for toilet paper, merely ambles out of the bathroom after defecating; stray bits of shit cling to his ass and find their way to his cotton shorts, where they slowly dry and harden into a dark-brown lumpy smear. The smell coming from this dark brown smear is unspeakable, but I know better than to remonstrate with him about it.

I shift my surreptitious glance a bit more to the right and find myself staring directly into his ear. It's nice, this ear, covered with almost imperceptible blond down, beautifully shaped and hued in several shades of pink: bright, almost shocking fuchsia at its outer rim, fading to a pale rose near the lobe. Around the ear are tiny glistening brown curls, whorls of hair that lie charmingly in clusters, like little brown grapes. The urge to touch these curls is very strong. Just let me feel them for a moment, I think longingly. Quickly I reach up my hand and grasp one of the crisp brown circles between my thumb and forefinger and twirl it lightly, savoring its silky crispness. . . .

Oh Jesus, now I've done it. He lowers the book and turns his head, stares down at me accusingly. His dark blue eyes have a stern, implacable expression; so might the young angel Gabriel look when he comes to judge mankind at the last trump. I brace myself, for I know violence is coming. And sure enough, even as I stiffen my body, he seizes my left arm with both hands and shoves me unceremoniously to the other end of the couch.

"Keep your fucking hands to yourself, Mom," he says severely. And returns to his book.

Lee Talley

Gossamer Thread

My mother told me about menstruation shortly before my girl scout troop watched a similarly opaque film strip on the subject. A true southern lady, she found this discussion difficult; but at the end of our mother-daughter talk, I realized that getting one's period was a sign of becoming a woman and that "poor Ann" had started hers already and couldn't swim when she came over to play the next day. However, I did not understand how menstruation related to swimming or to the funny black spots underneath my mother's arms.

The girl scout film strip illuminated some of the finer points of puberty, but still left be baffled. It had pictures of girls sprouting hair between their legs and under their arms at a rate that appeared to excel the rapid growth of the bean sprouts we were watching in science class. Sometime during the film strip I did have a small revelation though: girls get hair under their arms too, so the black spots underneath my mother's arms must be razor stubble.

Karen, who was asked to spy for another friend whose mother forbade her to attend, was very puzzled by the film strip. After the meeting Karen went to Amy's and explained that "once a month the uterus sloughs off the layer that would protect the baby if you got pregnant." However, Karen couldn't figure out what this protective layer was.

Felt sprung to mind immediately since we had just finished making felt-covered pin cushions in girl scouts, but Karen realized that humans can't make felt. Fur was also carefully considered since it would keep the baby warm and dry during the rainy season, but animals have fur — humans don't. For weeks she wondered what this elusive "protective layer" could be. After a great deal of deliberation Karen concluded that women must menstruate gossamer thread. Several yards of soft gossamer thread would surely keep a baby safely lodged inside its mother's womb. She was thrilled to have finally discovered what this substance was, and wondered what her mother and sister did with theirs. Karen guessed that her sister dyed hers brilliant colors to use for embroidery thread, and that her mother probably used hers more practically to tie the tomato plants to their stakes. She made plans to save hers carefully until she had enough to make fishing nets for tadpoles.

When we discussed it and confirmed that in fact one menstruated blood not thread, Karen was disappointed. However, we all vowed to share every detail of what it was like to get one's period, and we placed bets on who would get theirs first. At nine, we were convinced that menstruation would start imminently, even though we had only seven pubic hairs and one breast among the five of us. Rachel was the proud owner of the single breast of the group, which gave her a peculiar position. We viewed the lone breast with awe and revulsion, as did she. Eventually, Rachel began to worry that the boys would notice too, so she wore a bathing suit under her school uniform until things "evened out." Sadly, I had to move after my third underarm hair grew in and long before I ever got my period.

At thirteen, my best friend and I devised a discreet code for sharing the news when the big day finally occurred: "Snoopy's wearing *red* pajamas today!" Then I wanted my period almost as badly as a bra and hairless legs and arm pits. I consoled myself by dressing Snoopy in his menstrual pajamas complete with a matching red hat, patiently waiting for the day when I could proudly tell my friend what he was wearing. By the time I announced that "Snoopy's wearing *red* pajamas," his real menstrual ensemble had long been lost.

At fifteen I was shocked to learn that my period was going to last a whole week and that it *really* was blood. As I practiced walking up and down stairs with what felt like a canoe between my legs, I calculated that I had thirty-five more years, 455 more periods, and approximately 3,185 days of bleeding until I hit menopause — a notion almost as elusive as Karen's gossamer thread theory.

Celeste Tibbets

COMBING

When we were young and still going together, did I ever tell you how Frederick used to comb my hair for me, just like he was another girl, a girlfriend instead of the boy I was going to marry? He seemed to know just how to do it, like he'd been combing his own hair and braiding it up all his life. First he'd sit me down on the footstool in the living room. This was at night, you see, after Mama and the children were asleep. And then he'd draw the curtains down tight because men, of course, weren't supposed to know of such things. He'd get up behind me, pull me up close and take down my knot. Then he'd start to separate the hairs one by one until they were already smooth, and only then did he start to stroke.

And you know, the funniest thing is that when he touched my hair that way that he had, you'd never have known he was a boy or a man. But I always imagined he was a girl, another girl like you or Judith Ann. Like we used to do for each other at those sleep over parties at your house. You remember how we'd comb each other's hair for hours, pulling and smoothing with long, long strokes a hundred times till we'd pulled out all the sparks and silk. Well, if I hadn't a known better, I'd of thought it was one of you all pulling on my hair in the night and not Frederick. When he had it all silk and shine, his fingers seemed to know how to part and twist it just so til they made the sweetest braid and tied it up just right. And that's how I went to sleep every night that summer we were going together before we were married.

DEMONS FALLEN FROM HEAVEN

Ardelle, in Snellville, go ahead please.

Yessir, is this the host, am I on the air?

Yes, go ahead.

Well, good. Say, listen. I've got to talk to you about this here thing that's been on my mind. I would like to make a comment about this New Age Cult that's going around. Have you heard of it?

You mean "Meditation"?

No, New Age Cult.

You mean vitamins and health foods?

152

No, that ain't it.

You mean channelers and crystals and Shirley MacLaine?

Yeah, yeah that's it, the New Age Cult.

I take it you don't subscribe to it.

No, I don't and I'll tell you why. It's nothing but demons fallen from Heaven.

Ah, well, I think it's really just a bunch of folks trying to make a fast buck.

No, no that's not it at all. Cause it's demons and the Bible talks about it and I heard this here Christian preacher the other day on the radio speaking about it and he told about a book that's been written about it by some lady and they say in there what the Bible says. And this here fellow says they say that before the 2nd Coming there will be false prophets and demons fallen from Heaven. And that's what they are, and I just thought your listeners ought to know that.

Thank you, Ardelle.

Somebody needs to speak up about this and expose it and put it in all the papers instead of all this other mess they're always putting in there such as murders, and taxes, cause that's in the Bible too. And like it says, "Them who hasn't stopped worshipping demons will be killed, nor did they repent of their murders, their magic arts, their sexual immoralities."

Because see here, it talks about the seven bowls of god's wrath on the earth, and the first angel has already gone and poured out the first bowl with its ugly and painful sores and that's this here AIDS thing we've got. And the second angel poured out his bowl onto the sea and every living thing died and that there's the petrified forest out there in Arizona. And then the third angel poured his bowl on the rivers and they became blood and that's this Chattahoochee River thing, are you following me?

Well, not totally, but go ahead.

And the fourth poured his bowl on the sun and was given power to scorch people with fire and that's why there's such a high incidence of skin cancers among young people today. And the fifth one poured his onto the throne of the beast and there was darkness in the kingdom and you know that's all these power shortages and blackouts or brownouts or what have you. And the sixth poured his on the Euphrates and its water was dried up and there were three evil spirits that looked like frogs and that there I believe is these here New Age people because they are spirits of demons performing miraculous signs. Are you still listening?

Yes, ma'am, this is all very interesting. Thank you for your call. We're going to have to be moving along to our next caller. . . .

But I'm not finished with the bowls yet, there's one more. . . . And the seventh angel poured his bowl out and there was lightning and thunder and earthquakes and you know this has happened.

Excuse me, Ardelle. . . .

And you see, if you read it right, the Bible I mean, it tells you that it's this New Age cult, and it's demons fallen . . .

Thank you, Ardelle, for your call —

. . . from heaven.

Jessica Treat

WEEKDAYS

Sunday, Monday, Tuesday, Wednesday, Thursday and Friday she forgot about the plant. It sat on its stand in the corner of the room with its healthy green leaves, its commendable height. The curtain drooped from its rod. The bookcase tilted to one side. The plant sat there, firm in its soil.

Saturday he rose from bed (she watched him), lifted the plant from its stand, placed it in the sink with water to spray over it. He spent the morning in the bathroom while she lay in bed, finding patterns in the cracks in the ceiling. When at last she rose, she found it in the kitchen, filling the sink with its leafiness. She felt the need to do the dishes, to rinse out the milk bottle. She wanted to fill the kettle with water. It was in the way. She didn't want to touch it, wanted him to lift it out. She waited. Waited until he emerged from the bathroom, dressed, moved about the kitchen, telephoned (she watched him), picked up crusts of bread and ate them. She felt she must remind him, "Could you take the plant out of the sink?" Yes, he said he would.

At night he took it to her corner of the room, its soil dark and moist. She faced the tilting bookcase, the drooping curtain. For a week she didn't see it. Saturday it was in the sink again. It seemed to have grown. Its leaves reached the cupboard's base, then bent and splayed. When she walked past the sink, its leaves brushed her skin.

She lay on the bed, seeing the cracks in the ceiling like the plant's splayed leaves. Another week and it had grown too large for the sink. He placed it in the bathtub with water to spray over it. She sensed it growing in the tub, basking behind the shower curtain.

The bookcase toppled over. The curtains slid from their rods. Cracks in the ceiling split deeper. When it rained, water dripped through. The house was growing, tilting, cracking.

She felt the plant all around her. Its branches reached out like fans. Its topmost leaves formed a canopy. He no longer moved it. It was watered by the rain.

WATCH

If he knew he would not love her. If he knew. He would not love her if he knew. Like now: how she is lying in bed, naked, a candle by the bedside. She studies her underarm hair. She pulls out a strand, places it near the flame and watches it curl up into itself. An acrid smell. If he knew this about her. She plucks out another one, listens to it sizzle. The last time she saw him they talked over pizza in a restaurant. He cut his with a knife and fork. In between bites he used his napkin. She noticed his watch then: a thick gold band, a square clock face. Not so large as to be ostentatious, but it looked expensive. She remembered his voice on the phone, "Why? What time is it?" He had called her at 3:00. She'd waited all day for his call; she'd given up thinking he would. "Why? What time is it?" when all along he knew. He had a watch that would always be accurate. Her own watch had two faces, one set above the other one. Two small faces set vertically. He had asked her the meaning of it. She shrugged. "It was a gift. Fashion, I guess." He stared at it. "It's eerie," he said. Eerie? She hadn't seen it that way. Humorous, maybe. "It's really very eerie," he said, finally looking away from it. She watches the flame of her candle. At any moment the phone might ring.

SESSION

He waits until I've finished speaking. "So," he says, "other people's opinions are very important to you." I nod. My therapist hardly ever says anything; I listen carefully when he does. We have one of our awkward silences then. "Well," he says at last. "That makes you very vulnerable, doesn't it?" I nod before it catches up to me; I haven't really understood what he said. "Why?" I ask. "What do you mean?" He crosses his legs the other way. "Why?" he says, "because it impacts you." I stare at him. But that's not a word. "Don't you know that's not a word?" I want to ask him. Why is he making it into a verb when it isn't one? "Do you see that?" he says, "do you see how it affects you?" and I nod very slowly at him.

SISTER

"Where's Sophie?" he asks his father. "How come she didn't come?"
"Your sister was a bad girl. God changed her into a goldfish," his father
says. "A goldfish?" Timothy stares at his father. His father starts to smile
but Timothy has already dropped his father's hand and is backing down the
sidewalk in slow steps, before he turns and starts to run. "Timothy!" his
father calls after him, but he's too far away to hear. He runs past his mother
and her questions, through the kitchen and living room, into the room with
the aquarium. There's a new fish, bigger than the others, with long
speckled fins that flap as it swims. "Sophie," he says, placing his hands on
the glass, "Sophie . . ." and his sister's large fish eyes seem to meet his
before his vision blurs.

Rosalind Warren

GOOD EVENING LADIES AND GENTLEMEN

My name is Mandy and I'm your narrator. I'd like to welcome you aboard.
You will be reading at the approximate speed of 350 words per minute.
Total reading time will be about fifteen minutes.

At this time I'd like to point out several of the safety features of
this story. Exits are located at the end of every line, and also at the
beginning and in the middle of every line. In fact, you can stop reading
whenever you want to.

Although it is unlikely you'll ever have to use one, a dictionary
is located at your local public library. Should you come to a word you don't
understand please continue to breathe norm*ally*. Extinguish all smoking
materials. Look the word up.

This is your writer speaking. Welcome to my story. I apologize
for our delay in getting started. We were in a holding pattern with a number
of other stories trying to get into this book. We'll try to make up the time
by cutting corners — terse sentences, keeping plot developments to a
minimum, and so on.

Well folks, the introduction is over. If you look below, you'll see
the plot and a few major characters.

Mandy again. I'm happily married to Joel, a crackerjack taxidermist and a wonderful guy who loves me like crazy. But last week Bob, the former love of my life and Joel's ex-best friend, came back into our lives unexpectedly when he was the seventh and we were the third car in a nine-car collision on the local interstate. That's the three main characters and our conflict in a nutshell. You can mull this over while I serve you refreshments — a few descriptive paragraphs.

> Joel, although 38 years old, has superb muscle tone.
> His eyes twinkle, he loves to stuff animals and his
> family has pots of money . . .

This is the writer speaking again. Sorry to interrupt, Mandy, but we're encountering a little unexpected reader resistance. I've turned on the NO DESCRIPTIVE PARAGRAPHS sign, and I'd like to ask those readers whose minds are wandering to return to their original outlooks.

Mandy, again. Don't be alarmed — a story without descriptive paragraphs is very routine. Thousands of stories carry their readers safely to their conclusions without any descriptive paragraphs whatsoever. This superbly designed story is equipped to continue safely, relying only on ingenious plot twists and snappy dialog.

As I was saying, Bob was not only my high school sweetheart but he was allergic to cats . . .

This is the writer again. The editor has just informed me that there seems to be a problem with our story. It's probably nothing — just a misplaced modifier or two, or a loose epiphany — but to be on the safe side we'll have to cut this short by jettisoning 15 or 20 fascinating paragraphs and return as quickly as possible to the bookshelf. Please pay attention as Mandy shows you how to assume the emergency reader protection position.

Mandy here. The emergency reader protection position is as follows: firmly grip the book with both hands. Breathe deeply. *Keep your mind open.* Repeat after me: "What a fine story! What a fine story!"

If you wish, you may remove your shoes.

Wonderful! We've got everything under control. Just enough time for me to wrap up the narrative. Yes, I decided to stay with Joel. I couldn't abandon our life together. The near-fatal incident with the remarkably lifelike stuffed pachyderm in the Jacuzzi made me realize that I needed him now more than ever. It was a tough choice. But isn't tough choices what life is all about?

Thanks, Mandy. This is the writer again. Although the narrative is successfully completed, we ask that you please remain reading until the story comes to a complete stop.

Thank you for reading us. We hope that if your future plans include literature, you'll keep our author in mind.

Martha Waters

WHAT WENT WRONG?

"When did you stop loving me?" she asked.

We were saying good-bye. My car was packed full and I was leaving for a new job in another town. She leaned against the car door and reached for my hand. "I just need to know where it went wrong."

I didn't say anything. I couldn't believe she had to ask the question in the first place. Of course, I could have told her exactly when I stopped loving her — or at least the moment I knew our relationship wasn't going to survive. It was when she came home from an afternoon with her new girlfriend, gave me a big kiss on the mouth, and I tasted someone else's private juices still lingering on her lips. The least a person can do is brush her teeth between lovers.

And use a different bed. That was the second thing that killed it for me. I came home early from work one day and the door was bolted. My angry pounding finally produced an angry naked woman — how dare I alter my schedule without advising her first. Our bed never seemed quite right again — my side wasn't anything more than rented time and space. I felt the fool for having willingly agreed to an "open" relationship. It was something she had all the right theory and desperate need for because I wasn't interested in frequent sex and it was driving her crazy. But I hadn't realized the impact second-hand tastes and smells would have on me. It was all great talk about us still being the primary relationship and anyone else just being someone to have a temporary fling with. What this actually meant was that I was the one to do laundry and grocery shopping with, while the fling was the one to get dressed up for and meet at restaurants.

So maybe I should have told her all this as I was leaving, but I didn't think it mattered any more.

DEEP IN SLEEP

Deep in sleep I merge with air in a blissful suspension of elements. My body is light and effervescent, moving through walls like music and I sense I've reached a holy place. I recognize Jan in a crowd of very young and busy college students, all of whom seem to be running around at her command. She's the only one who recognizes me and beckons me into her office, closing the window shades as I enter, motioning me to close the door. "Let's take a walk, you and I," she says in a voice that rearranges my molecules to flesh and blood. She takes my hand, pulls me close enough to smell her powdered skin and leads me through a door to a giant warehouse full of odd objects — dusty desks, chairs, filing cabinets, lamps stacked in precariously high towers. She pulls me into a shadow to kiss me lightly on the neck and whisper urgent pleas in my ear. It is clear she wants to unleash a great flow of passion and I give myself over to the idea without hesitation. We want desperately to be alone so we can explore our desires with great abandon. We climb a long flight of narrow open stairs against a dark wall and go out to a lush, green garden where birds improvise songs in the soft yellow evening. We embrace and become one person in a split second of passion that is enough to change our individual chemistries forever. Then suddenly we're back inside the dark warehouse, still in each other's arms, and a group of people are glowering at us in disgust and shock. A man in a white shirt and red tie points his finger at Jan, says "You are finished here as of this minute," and marches off in a virtuous huff. Jan doesn't seem to care or be concerned by this man's harsh judgment of her, of us. I am terrified for her.

Now I'm sitting in a recital hall. Diane, my college lover, is to my left and several gay men are chatting and squealing to each other on my right. A large pipe organ rises up from the floor like a range of mountains. Suddenly the wall above the pipes turns into the New York City skyline at night, all lit up and full of promises. I lean over to Diane and say "When I see those lights out there I want to dive out of the window and fly around like a bird." She says, "I didn't know you were one of those, too!" Then Jan appears — I think she's going to give a recital — but first she comes and sits in the row in front of me, talking to the guys with great flair and affection. Someone brings me a telephone and I hear the voices of my mother, my brother and an aunt I don't know, all talking at once and wanting to know where to meet me for dinner. They are upset that I haven't been in touch with them, haven't shown them around the city. Jan is now standing at the door and a long receiving line has formed, everyone very eager to pay their respects to this famous organist. Not a note has been played on the organ and I feel like I must have missed something. Suddenly my mother, brother and mystery aunt are there, waiting to shake Jan's hand, uncomfortable standing so close to people they don't know. They talk to each other in loud southern accents.

I wake up, feeling as though I should have taken charge of the situation and done something.

Debra Riggin Waugh

SICK LEAVE

You come visit me for the weekend on the way to your brother's in Colorado, even though my house is not on the way at all. We hardly know each other (in the biblical sense), but I'm fantasizing about how it might be when you get here, if you still like me as much as you did a few weeks ago when we first met up North.

I clean my house really good before your arrival (clean sheets and everything). I don't want you to know "the real me" yet since we both still think each other's kind of perfect. I leave you a key in my mailbox just in case you get here before I do. I encourage my dog to be nice and let you in and not bite your shoes or anything.

I tell my boss I'm sick and come home early from work; you're happy to see me. We go out to lunch and end up at the gay bookstore downtown. You linger too long in the s&m section. I pretend not to notice, but, yeah, I'm a little worried.

Once back at my house, I pop Holly Near into the cassette player, expecting songs about women rocking each other in their arms and being crushed out. But damned if Holly doesn't start singing about genocide and living in terror and women disappearing in Chile. I change that tape real quick and find something instrumental, just to be safe.

By this time, we're underneath those clean sheets, and I light a candle and shut off the lamp. But no sooner have I rolled over to kiss you, then a bag of Fannie Mae dark chocolates sitting too close to the candle catches on fire. You're amused as I manage to put it out quick with a glass of white wine you hadn't finished. I wash my hands, and we get back to where we were before the fire started. Somehow, we're both still aroused.

We hug and kiss and then your lips brush my arm and one of my armpit hairs gets caught between your teeth and, well, I really couldn't help but scream.

160

After the screaming and laughing subside, we admit that we're both kind of scared of what we might say in a fit of passion. So I come up with a "rule" — anything said without clothes on doesn't count. By the end of the weekend, we're saying "I love you" even with our clothes on, and your weekend visit turns into a week. My boss thinks I have an ovarian cyst, and, fortunately, is too polite to ask for details.

Dottie Webb

WHEN SHE LEFT ME

When she left me I realized I could fall apart in two hundred words or less. That it would atomistically be considered successful experimental fiction. But, the fiction part baffles me and no one will tell me if an ellipsis is one word or two. Just the other day, I was asking if my socks matched. I kept looking at them nervously. Maybe I'd been wearing them too long. My bed, I said, practically makes itself, does yours? I heard the toaster when it rang, but the shower burns my bagel daily. Do you . . . ever have trouble with toasting? There are crumbs, at the bottom. Underneath. Where I can't get them. The weather radar tries to sweep the entire area. When I tried to turn it off, the countertop neatly folded itself into thirds, the seams just stared back. The keys to the sofa disappeared while the breakfast dishes neatly pressed my blue-pleated skirt. I slipped the successful phone into my brown paper lunchbag, pushed the top orange hard and rolled down to the normal floor. Carrying an umbrella or two. Hundred. Happy to be there.

WINKIE

When her cat "Winkie" died, she caused quite a flap in the neighborhood by taking him to the taxidermist, saying simply that she was not able to part with him. And, thus immortalized, he took his place on the ledge of the bay windows, standing nobly poised, his plastic gaze aimed at the bird bath in the front yard. She put his empty cat bowl by his side. He was framed tranquilly in the billow of the gauzy white curtains, still snagged and jagged at the edges, leftover from his lazy-stretching, claw-sharpening days.

Whenever she entertained, she always proudly parted the curtains and remarked how fresh and handsome "Winkie" looked. No one in the prayer circle wanted to sit on the couch near the windows: seven plump women fighting over a horse-hair wing-back and three folding card chairs without cushions. She still baked the best peach cobbler in the county; it kept them coming back against their better judgment.

Batya Weinbaum

I HAVE NEVER HATED

I have never hated the members of my immediate family as intensely as I did during the three days of my grandfather's funeral. I was relieved to feel this hatred, actually. Prior to the funeral I had complained to my shrink, Doris, that all I could feel was detachment. To prove it, one session I kept repeating all the things I hated about my mother.

In the short space of a 45-minute hour, I listed incident after incident unfeelingly. My recitation wore on and on about how I could never remember my mother feeding me. She never bought me the camel-hair pants I wanted, or finished the graduation dress she was making me . . . But Doris didn't respond. I began to admire the plump red lamp, the frilled white shade, and the green plants which decorated her somber office. Straight ahead of me (I was flat on my back) I could see rooftops of other houses filled with shrinks (we were in the Village). I offered an interpretation so Doris wouldn't get bored. "You know what, Doris? Underneath all this is a projection on my part that my mother was always furious."

"At you?"

"Yeah." I crossed and uncrossed my ankles nervously. "I don't know why or how. But that must have been why she refused to feed me."

My throat, suddenly dry, constricted. I got frightened. "What do you think I'm doing?" Pause. "I said, Doris. . . ." I urged, getting no response, musing how my mother was too angry to feed me.

"Why do you want to know?" Doris, swishing stockings and flicking ashes from an ivory cigarette holder, finally asked me.

"I don't know what I'm doing." Every time, I try to trick her into answering a question — against shrink principles.

"What do you think you're doing?" I never win. Doris always refuses to verbally feed me.

"I said I wished I could feel hatred for my mother. But I only feel frozen so I'm listing all the things I hate her for. My idea is, if I keep saying all the things I hate my mother for I'll scream. Do you think that will work?"

Doris reached over and put her cigarette out in a goldleaf miniature saucer. "Do I think what?"

"Well, isn't that what you had in mind when . . ."

"Why do you think I had anything in mind?" Doris tidied up for her next appointment, straightening an array of black leather account books.

"Of course you do. You're the shrink. You do your part. You're not my mother."

Now Is Not A Time To Mourn

"Now is not a time to mourn, now is a time to rejoice," said the Jewish Minister. A rabbi, really, but so reform a minister he might be. He gesticulated over the front pew at my grandfather's funeral. We were in a candle-lit memorial chapel on Avenue J. My grandfather lay behind him in a pine box, draped with a blue and white flag like an Israeli soldier. In the first pew over which the Jewish Minister ministered sat my brother the Doctor and his wife. And next to them sat my father the Doctor and his wife. On my brother's hip was perched his baby daughter. My brother's wife is German. Next to her sat my 79-year-old Orthodox aunt with her shopping bags from Macy's and Gimbell's. Before the funeral, this one had burnt all my grandfather's shoes insisting religiously, "You grew up in the Midwest. What do you know. In Jewish we call this a ritual."

"Now is not a time to mourn, now is a time to rejoice," the Jewish Minister repeated. "After all, today we place the last vestige of ghetto mentality in the grave. With this man passes an entire generation. The last travelling salesman in an otherwise professional family. The last lady's man and gambler and pauper. No Nussensweig will ever again bet on the horses. No Nussensweig will ever again come crying to a relative for money, that is if everything goes OK." Here Jewish Minister peered over his spectacles at me. "The last man to speak English in inverted Yiddish sentences," he continued. "Today we rejoice, believe me."

I cried, my head on the lap of one of my friends.

The Jewish Minister goes on. "Louie always had an intelligent question to ask of Israel, and if he didn't, he would have wanted to . . ."

"My god," I heaved, sobbing, the only one, "don't put the man down on his dying day!"

My friends and I followed the funeral procession in my beat-up car. We drove behind the limousine all the way to Mount Lebanon Cemetery, where they lowered the pine box. I felt a thud as the box hit the bottom of the grave. I pulled my dark blue shawl, purchased from the Lower East Side for the occasion, around me, tightly. Family turned and left. End of funeral. No sitting *shiva*. No tradition.

"What am I going to do?" I asked one of my friends, aghast.

"Maybe," one of them said, "you can sit your own *shiva*. Take over his apartment and write a novel."

The one who said this had a grandmother who lived in Sea Gate so I believed her.

STAR GAZING: PLANETARY COLLISION AND NARCISSISTIC COLLUSION

TWO STARS, PLUTOTARCH AND ANDROGENE, WERE SPIRALLING TOWARDS EACH OTHER IN OUTER SPACE.

He was the most revolutionary man she knew. She was saying she wanted to drive to town. That she had some important phone calls to make; these he shrugged off indifferently as her "arrangements." She felt so inadequate next to him. Everything he did demanded energy. Intense energy. And she was so trite, so mundane next to him.

He was insisting he had to do the dishes. That she had to wait.

Everything he did and said was so profound. Yet it was the boyishness in him that appealed to her.

She thought it odd that he was insisting he had to do the dishes. How many times had she withdrawn her rage into herself and done the dishes. Focusing on tiny little knicks. Wiping the counter clear of poetry books, wheat crackers and Chaucer next to Ezra Pound.

He was insisting she had to wait to drive him into town.

PLUTOTARCH WAS SPIRALLING AT A VELOCITY UNKNOWN TO ASTRONO-MERS WATCHING THE STARS THROUGH TELESCOPES, AND PLOTTING HIS PATH TOWARDS ANDROGENE FROM EARTH. THEY WERE CONCERNED ABOUT THE COLLI-SION AND THE SURVIVAL OF ANDROGENE, THE LESS CONGEALED SWIRLING AND MORE FLUID OF THE TWO COSMIC BODIES.

164

Inside, her rage was mounting. When with the others, he loved and exuded the warmth of candlelight, sitting by fire, singing songs. One of the others always had a guitar. He was too pure to own an instrument. But he wore wool, and adopted the shaggy bearded presence of the comforter.

She knew it was necessary for her to make long distance phone calls to get to her performance at least 1000 miles away. She had said as much in the morning at 7:30 when she had started to leave the house and get away.

He had insisted she wait for him, as he had to do the dishes. She had agreed, having had the dream of being in public the night before — the strain, all the phone calls. The demands upon her in many directions. The complaint that she had insulted a follower's mother. The dishes, after all, how harmless. She could wait, she said to herself.

Then, after the dishes, he was saying it was necessary to clean the cabinets. Before she could say no and resist him, all the bins of brown rice and lentils were spread out in their containers upon the filthy floor. Then it was necessary to sweep. Then to make coffe. Then . . .

She was in a rage, throwing chairs in the living room where the jam session had happened the night before.

PLUTOTARCH WAS PLUMMETING AT SUCH A VELOCITY THAT ANDRO-GENE WAS SWEPT INTO HIS CYCLE AND DRAWN OFF COURSE. THE VORTEX OF SPIRALLING ENERGY DISINTEGRATED THE LESS CONGEALED PLANET. THE AS-TRONOMERS WERE CHARTING AND PLOTTING THE VEERING AS THE YOUNGER STAR WENT OFF ITS COURSE.

He was the most revolutionary man she knew. A man of integrity. He did everything according to his lofty principles. Then she went outside and threw flower pots off the tree trunk. And the rocks and the children's toys towards the lake. He followed her, giving her attention at last, saying he did not like her behavior. She screamed at him that she needed silence, that poets often did things like rip doors off walls, historical events he had recounted to her before.

A man of integrity. A man who in this day and age still managed to live according to principles that were sound.

She lay in the field of summer daisies and berated herself for not making the phone calls early enough to get away. This meant she would have to drive 1000 miles herself, or fly, and that much she did not desire to pay. She didn't want to be taken care of, just cared for, and now he was calling from the porch that he had to sweep away the mouse shit, and that the woman with the child had said she was too intense to be around the house anyway.

Then he decided to mop the floor. Company would return that night, and he wanted to be ready.

THE PARTICLES OF THE YOUNGER PLANET HAD SEPARATED. PLUTO-
TARCH, THE ELDER, WAS SUCKING HIS PARTICLES INTO HIS VORTEX. THE YOUNGER
PLANET HAD LOST ALL FORM.

Jess Wells

DINNER TABLE

Three buckets of fear and an ally sit down to a dinner of fissures. Gulfs and fissures gulping fish. The bucket of explosive jelly is wiggling, nervous, transparent but impossible. Where is the point of danger, where is the trigger? Where is the hot-spot, mother, mother? Her progeny, her pride, her first-born boy sits to her left, alike, alight, her sainted one, a pail of seeping acid.

The brother is silent and dark, a deep pail emitting a hiss of corrosion, a burble, a gurgle, a bubble, a glop of venom, he is fluid that sings at destruction, liquid made to burn.

To the brother's left is the father, a shallow, dark-glass placid, a small, shallow bowl light and sound does not disturb, a fragile, petted feted, pampered glass with a rim of power.

The jelly is trembling, but where is the friction? The acid has slopped and is seeping across the table towards me.

The dinner table.

Three wire figures sit in a triangle, at a rectangle, connected by fishing line, electric lines not to be nudged, spy wires to slit your throat, yet glistening light and delicate in the moonlight. Wires from her to him, to him, through their eyes and ears, sewn to flesh, clear string pulling faces into distortions, an isosceles of wire. The words slither through the web, slide along the lines, a cable to the mother point: Should I, can I, may I, when should I, why should I, would it be possible please? Do I meet inspection? What are the currents tonight? The sparks fly from mother to brother. Why don't you, why can't you, why do you, must you? It is simply. Not. Necessary. The sparks and currents, cables down after a storm, are hopping on the ground alive and deadly mechanical tail of a snake.

When I am blue and distant and fourteen I tell my mother, with all the courage I can muster, the boldest thing I have ever said, "Mother, I know you love me, but sometimes I think you don't like me." Waiting. "Yes, sometimes that's right, I don't. Pass the meat to your father."

LOVE AND DECAY

I.

In greens of different shades, minds and lives and love fertile and moist are left to mellow, mold, rot, to drip a sticky over-sugared puss. It has the smell of spinach in a hot sink.

II.

Liam sits on a gas drum in the sand, watching the fat boat bobbing near the clean shore. Men in hip-high boots load all the provisions and passengers to this Irish island in the narrow, motorless curraghs, black, over-sized canoes of wooden bones and tar-paper skin. They row hard with thin paddles. Liam watches the blue and pink morning streak the sand, the dogs running and barking, the donkey carts, the two motorized lift trucks, the crates of milk, of processed food, of mail-ordered parcels and a small, frantic dog. Liam sucks in the morning and is calmed. Before him is the smooth, smooth sand and the clear blue water, the glinting jellyfish, the simple, sure, black-banana curraghs. Behind him is rock. Rock to tufts of grass to shrubs to hill with the one-room post office, to hill with the one-room school, to hill, and winding all around are fences of stone, black stones piled on, stood on end, laid on their side, no mortar but balance holding them in place, fences waist high winding around the island and cutting spaces into squares, fences that start and then end in the middle of another square with no purpose, like the beginning of a maze. Fences to contain nothing, to rid the ground of rocks. He sucks this slow morning, sees no questions here, no riddles of why to be and how to hold his head up.

III.

Joan lies in Liam's tent on the bluff, on the grassy shelf for campers at the base of the cliff. She cannot sit, she pretends the roof is further away. It is raining, the Army green canvas is damp and dank and the tent is ringed with diapers, the only thing in the local store to stop the water. The floor is covered with Pampers and sand and dirty socks, food wrappers and the heavy, sweaty sleeping bag, one for the two of them because his was soaked through. Joan lies with him wrapped around her, corseted together by the sleeping bag, bound and zipped together in the heavy air and the rain like black jell outside. He is sleeping. His breathing is regular. He is heavy against her like the air. The air is pressing with the smell and wetness of him.

IV.

The Egyptian women in their finery are locked inside the tomb with him, like his trinkets in a box. Standing around the slab with the man's body, the women are silent while the men file out and take the door with them. Are the women, in their robes and jewels, left in the pitch dark of no boundaries and still a wall at every inch of skin, left alone with the fear? Are there torches to eat the air and show their eyes burning towards the women they have lived with? Is it a tiny room where they are pressed tightly and tear and climb over one another to suck at the wall, to scratch at the stones? Or is it a big room where they run away from the inevitable pain? Do they have ceremonies for themselves? Do they speak chant and comfort their sisters or do they push away the ones who scream and howl, gulping air, preferring not to see their eyes, their twisted faces, hands clutching their caving chests? Anthropologists in the Pyramids found piles of skeletons, women's bones in grotesque positions, suffocated, contorted, sucked to death. How many tombs have they built for us? How many lethal jewelry boxes?

V.

Joan and Liam lie in the tent on Inisheer, a cold wind pouring the sand towards the grass and slicing through the stone fences. He is lying at her breast, a hollow man drinking to fill himself. Joan feels he is a plant growing in her care, breaking her down to pulp like a root breaks dead leaves into peat. Joan's breathing is shallow from the heavy head on her chest. His soft, limp hand strokes her arm at the shoulder and she shudders. It is a lifeless hand, a bit of falling meat, a carcass, this weight, smelling of decay. He is fruit to sit and grow soft.

Terry Wolverton

THE WEDDING

She is talking about furniture. She is telling me the reasons why she is unhappy in our relationship. It is Sunday morning and we have an extra hour to lie in bed because daylight savings time has "fallen back" into standard time.

This is not the first time we have talked about furniture, and about why our relationship cannot work. But I still do not understand and so I am trying to listen.

It is important for her to live with her lover, she explains. But she could never live with me because I am too messy. Our household aesthetics and decorating tastes are incompatible. She hates my furniture.

Then there is the problem of cats. She doesn't want to live with cats, doesn't want cat hair on her clothes or cat scratches in her furniture. I have two cats.

There are other reasons. As she talks I compile the list in my head and I realize there is nothing I can do about any of this. We do not even agree about what is important in a relationship.

We decide that we will have to break up. We both cry. Then we make lover ferociously. Cry some more. Stop talking about it.

Then it is time to go to the wedding.

Dolores and Tina are getting married today. We drive an hour to Claremont, to the home of Dolores' parents. The ceremony will be held in the garden. The day is bright, and the garden is decorated with hanging ribbons, angels, birds.

The trysting is simple. We sit on folding chairs in a circle, Dolores and Tina in the center. Dolores' parents are part of the circle. Tina's parents do not speak to Dolores and are always trying to fix Tina up with men, and thus are not invited.

Each of the guests is asked to speak: to recount something that we know about the relationship — some memory, some insight — and also to make a pledge to this relationship. One woman recalls knowing the two when they first met. Another woman promises to babysit when Dolores and Tina have the baby they are planning for. One woman vows: "I'll never give you advice."

Then Dolores and Tina make their pledge to one another. They commit to love and honor each other for the rest of their lives. They state their intention to have a child together. They drink wine from silver chalices, they exchange necklaces, they kiss. There is no mention of furniture.

We partake of a lovely feast, bestow gifts on the two brides. Then it is time to go. It is evening as we head back, she and I, our headlights pointed bravely toward Los Angeles. The gravel beat of old Motown on the radio, the only thing that cuts the silence.

Ruth Yarrow

MAY

After the garden party, the garden.

Irene Zahava

GOOD CANDY, BAD CANDY

Any kind of Hershey's chocolate is good, especially Hershey's kisses. Anything that comes in an individual wrapper, like butterscotch or lemon drops, is good. Life-savers are very good; best of all is a package of all cherry. Mint flavored life-savers are really medicine and should never be confused with candy. Licorice, if it's wrapped in plastic and doesn't come from the large glass container that sits on the counter in the candy store, is good, but black licorice tastes awful. Cake can sometimes be candy and is good as long as there is no chocolate: pound cake, cheese cake or cheese Danish. Vanilla wafer cookies and Graham crackers also fall into this category. For some reason, so do fig newtons.

All other candy is bad.

Any candy that is sold in a movie theater is bad and should be avoided at all costs, even if it looks exactly like candy you're allowed to eat when it's not bought in a movie theater. Any candy that comes from a machine, especially gum balls, malt balls, hot or sour balls and all-day suckers: bad. Little pastel dots that come on long strips of paper: bad. Pez, in any flavor, from any kind of dispenser: bad. Little wax bottles that you bite the tops off and suck the juice out of: bad. Ices of any kind, unless they're made from real juice, by your mother, and frozen in your own freezer at home: bad. Gum — any kind, any color, any flavor, even Chiclets: bad. Long strips of dried fruit, wrapped in a cylinder (even if it says Real Fruit on the wrapper): bad. Mars bars, Snickers, 3 Musketeers, Mr. Goodbar, Chunkies: all bad. Any kind of Easter candy, especially little chocolate eggs (not to be confused with good chocolate, which is only

170

Hershey's): bad. Christmas candy, even candy-canes that come individually wrapped: bad. Halloween candy of any sort, no matter who gives it to you: bad. Any candy that tries to pretend it's something else, by being shaped like a peanut, a kernel of corn, a banana, a slice of watermelon, etc.: bad. Anything made out of wax, especially if it's shaped like a tongue or like lips: bad. Candy cigarettes: bad, bad, bad.

General guideline to be used whenever you're in doubt: if all your friends can eat it, it's probably bad. If no one else would want to eat it, it's probably good.

SUBLIMATION

Marcia Dalton was a rich kid from a Chicago suburb. She was my college roommate for four months of my freshman year. Every night she sat at her desk and wrote a letter to her ROTC boyfriend, her hair wrapped up in empty orange-juice cans.

I had long hair, too, but I didn't wrap it around juice cans to straighten it. As far as I was concerned, the frizzier the better: I was a hippie.

Marcia and I didn't have a lot in common so we didn't talk much. She was interested in sororities (how to get into one); her boyfriend back home (they were going to get married as soon as they graduated); and her neices and nephews (what she could make them for Christmas).

One night Marcia came into our room, her hair dripping water all over the lamb's wool collar of her coat, and she plunked herself down on the edge of my bed — an uncharacteristic action on her part.

"I'm exhausted," she complained. "I just swam twenty laps at the gym."

"Why?"

"Sublimation."

"What are you trying to sublimate?"

"My sex drive."

It turned out that Marcia had a major confession to make: She and her ROTC boyfriend had had sexual intercourse — I'm using her exact words — the night before she left for college. Now that she knew what it was all about she didn't think she could live without it. The only way to stay sane, she said, was to swim twenty laps a day.

I couldn't believe it. "Why don't you just masturbate?" I asked her.

She looked at me for a few seconds, her mouth slack and her eyes hard. Then she shot off my bed and sprinted to her corner of the room.

"That's the most disgusting thing I've ever heard. I can't believe you said that to me. I just can't believe you said that to me."

She probably would have gone on a lot longer but I left the room.

After that, the strain between us was more obvious. We were not even polite to each other. I played my music loud: Laura Nyro, Joni Mitchell, James Taylor. I kept the light on until after midnight, reading Hesse.

Marcia continued to write her letters and to swim. At night she lay in her bed with her arms conspicuously placed on the top of her blanket. She started mumbling her boyfriend's name, as though deep in the throes of passion: Barry. Larry. Gary. (I forget which.)

INITIATION

Grace Burton was never a friend of mine. She was just my college roommate. I was a junior and she was a freshman and I made it clear to her from the start that she was not to tag along with me and my friends. We went to Bergman movies, we planned demonstrations against CIA recruiting on campus, we marched on Washington, we scoured Collegetown for decent pizza.

Grace was a music student from Iowa . . . or Idaho. She was a Good Girl, an A student, a member of the college orchestra. She wore peter pan collars and Bass weejuns. To me, she was beneath contempt.

Grace played the oboe. In order to keep her reeds supple, she explained, she had to suck on them all the time. That meant all the time. The suck suck suck sound drove me nuts.

One afternoon I was sitting on my bed writing a letter to the school newspaper, demanding that the administration fire a particularly fascist history professor. Grace was on her bed, huddled under her Snoopy bedspread. It took me a while to realize that she was crying. Her sobs, little bursts of air that she sucked back in, sounded a lot like the noise she made on her oboe reeds. By the time I looked up her face was red and her nose was running.

"I don't know how you can do it," she said.

I asked what the hell she was talking about and she said she didn't understand how I could live with the pain of using a tampon every month. It turned out that Grace had just tried her first tampon, but she hadn't removed the cardboard tubing. She was in agony. I walked her down the hall to the bathroom and stood outside the toilet stall, instructing her, step-by-step, in the proper method of tampon insertion.

When we got back to our room I boiled two cups of water on my illegal hot-plate, added some Tang and a few splashes of *very* illegal red wine, and Grace and I had a sort of celebration.

THE FIRST DANCE, 1975

I had recently moved from the Bronx to Brooklyn. I saw a flyer in the laundromat, advertising a dance at Barnard College, so I took the subway up to 116th and Broadway. I didn't know anyone there. I stood in the corner where the shadows were deepest but a woman sought me out and asked me to dance. I was too terrified to say no so I said OK. Her head was completely shaven — she was 100% bald without a trace of hair on her smooth and glistening scalp. I noticed this at almost the same moment I saw she wasn't wearing a shirt. I tried not to stare at her breasts. I stared at her bald head, instead. It struck me that I was dancing with a three-breasted woman. This was not a particularly comforting or amusing thought. Eventually, the band took a break and we stopped dancing. I thanked her, excused myself politely, and quickly walked away. I went back to the shadows in the corner and stayed another five minutes. Then I took a taxi back to Park Slope.

HAIR OBSESSION

I get a postcard from the woman who cuts my hair; it's signed "Your Hairstylist." She writes that in two weeks she'll be going on vacation for ten days. I panic. I wait until the next morning and call her up at 8:00. She's not in yet but I leave a message and sit by the phone until she calls me. Yes, she has an opening, she can take me in half an hour. I get there, panting, grateful. I say "Cut it real short, it has to last me until you get back from vacation." While I'm there her phone rings constantly. All the others who got a postcard and need to see her before she leaves. I am smug. I got here first and they have to wait until the end of the week, some of them have to wait until next week. She cuts my hair very short. It sticks up in a slightly uneven arc around the top of my head. I don't mind, it will last me. My ears are more exposed than usual. I only mind a little bit. It will grow all too quickly and then I'll be sorry my ears aren't even more exposed.

Now it is a week later. I examine my hair in the bathroom mirror.

Should I call her? Should I get one more cut while there's time? There really isn't anything to cut. But there will be, next week, when she'll be gone. Gone for ten days. By the time she gets back my hair will be long. But now it's still short. I hate this pressure. The anxiety is making me sick. I could always go to someone else if I really have to, just this once, in an emergency. But I know I won't have the courage to do that because when she gets back she'd know.

Gene Zeiger

BY THE WATERS OF BABYLON

One of my first memories goes like this — actually, I'm not s*ure* it goes like this. You know how it is when someone tells you a story, like your parents for example, a story about how, when you were small you wouldn't eat very much, not much appetite and who knows why, but the point is you just weren't very hungry. But your mother, you know her main occupation is to get you to eat — "eat, bubeleh, eat," — at least that's how it went in my family.

So my mother, actually quite thin herself I notice from old photos, is getting pretty frustrated by my refusals, pretty desperate. She has a neighbor up on the third floor, let's say, and this neighbor, we'll call her Mrs. Ross, has very little to keep her occupied. Her husband has died, her kids are grown — one son in Texas, another on Long Island. She mostly cleans her apartment and reads Ellery Queen. One day, my mother is telling Mrs. Ross that her baby Genie is not a good eater, "won't even open her mouth," my mother says. "Oy, what a terrible thing," sighs Mrs. Ross and the way she sighs you'd think her left eye just fell out. "Yes," continues my mother, wringing her hands, "I want only that my Genie should be a Gerber baby, some more flesh on her legs, her cheeks."

Well, the two women sit down, each with a cup of Swee*t-Touch-Nee* tea, at the kitchen table in our apartment on Willoughby Avenue in Brooklyn and they wrack their brains in the ancient tradition of Jewish brainwracking.

"We could put extra sugar in her cereal," says Mrs. Ross.

"No, it rots the teeth."

"But she doesn't have any teeth."

"She *will* have teeth." A long pause, both of them staring out the same window, my mother smoothing the yellow tablecloth with her fingertips.

"You could give her fewer feedings, then maybe she'd be more hungry and eat more at one time." My mother shakes her head languidly. The next proposal is to try another brand of baby food. "No," says my mother, "I blend it from the fresh fruits and vegetables. More vitamins." Mrs. Ross nods vigorously.

Soon I wake from my nap to the ordeal of the next feeding. I am bibbed and tucked into my highchair. The inevitable longhandled silver spoon cradling some pureed spinach comes hurtling towards my face. I screw up my mouth as usual. My mother as usual tries to force it open with the spoon, the spinach dribbles down my poor chin, she scrapes it up and tries again. Mrs. Ross sits beside her watching with an expression of horror on her face, like she was watching, perhaps, a beheading. My mother coos and mews, tries the sweet potatoes, the applesauce, all, of course, to no avail. Mrs. Ross is getting more and more upset — she wrings her hands, she even begins saying a *brocha*, a prayer. At one point, in her ardor (I am watching her face, her expressions are really interesting), she drops her mouth and her false teeth lower off her top gums onto her tongue. The rest is history — I must have been aghast at the sight of mobile teeth — although I'd seen a lot of faces and teeth, I'd never seen them falling inside a mouth.

Well, as I said, the rest is history. I opened my own mouth in astonishment and, you got it — in went the food. This practical drama was replayed over and over again. Whenever she could, Mrs. Ross came down in the elevator, knocked on the door, was enthusiastically greeted by my mother and plopped into a chair in front of my highchair; the teeth fell, my mouth fell open, and *whammo,* in went the food. And this is the method by which the Lord, blessed be His name, in His great wisdom, helped my mother in her efforts to insure the health and longevity of her firstborn.

The Crossing Press
publishes a full selection of
feminist titles.
To receive our current catalog,
please call —Toll Free—800/777-1048.